M000229641

her
silent
husband

BOOKS BY SAM VICKERY

One Last Second
My Only Child
Save My Daughter

The Promise
One More Tomorrow
Keep It Secret
The Things You Cannot See
Where There's Smoke

NOVELLAS
What You Never Knew

her
silent
husband

SAM VICKERY

bookouture

Published by Bookouture in 2021

An imprint of Storyfire Ltd.
Carmelite House
50 Victoria Embankment
London EC4Y 0DZ

www.bookouture.com

Copyright © Sam Vickery, 2021

Sam Vickery has asserted her right to be identified as the author of this work.

All rights reserved. No part of this publication may be reproduced, stored in any retrieval system, or transmitted, in any form or by any means, electronic, mechanical, photocopying, recording or otherwise, without the prior written permission of the publishers.

ISBN: 978-1-80019-855-5
eBook ISBN: 978-1-80019-854-8

This book is a work of fiction. Names, characters, businesses, organizations, places and events other than those clearly in the public domain, are either the product of the author's imagination or are used fictitiously. Any resemblance to actual persons, living or dead, events or locales is entirely coincidental.

For my dad, for whom storytelling is as vital as breathing. And for the Conger Eel.

PROLOGUE

I'd expected something different. Something far different from this. Today I turned forty-one years old and the things I'd hoped I would know by now have yet to materialise. I thought I'd understand my purpose. That I'd feel calmer, more stable. That the hurts of my past would no longer visit me at night and I'd have figured out the secret to being happy. Whole. A complete person, as opposed to these fragmented shards I continue to cling to, certain that any moment they might scatter to the ground for all to see.

But what I've learned in my forty-one years is this: I know that life isn't always fair – that pain gets dished out to hard-working, kind-hearted people, while others who are far less deserving leapfrog the hurdles with ease. I know that life is not an adventure – it's a treadmill, and every year I find myself gripping tighter to the handrails for fear of being flung off.

I know that if I don't make the effort to tell my wife how my day was, she can go sixteen days without thinking to ask, and even then, I'm not sure she listens to the answer. I know that my children don't hear when I speak, or at least not unless I raise my voice, give it an edge of impatience that makes me feel ill at ease, an imposter pretending to be someone I'm not. They don't notice me... I know that. By this point, I've faded away to the extent that I'm not sure there's much left to see.

I know that no matter how much I do, it's never enough, never an end, just a new beginning on the impossible path of life. And I'm failing at it, as a husband, a father, a brother, despite trying my hardest to pretend I'm not.

And what I know most of all, what I've tried to hide for so long now, is the simple fact that I'm not strong enough to keep going. I hate that it's come to this. That I can't be a better man – a stronger man. I hope they won't hate me, that they'll find a way to understand. To finally see me and know why I had no choice but to leave them.

But right now, I wouldn't be surprised if they didn't even notice I'd gone.

ONE

BETH

Day One

The house phone was ringing, the trilling sound sending waves of irritation through me as I piled through the front door, laden with overflowing shopping bags, watching Amelie and Cecilia run into the kitchen without bothering to take off their school shoes and Rufus drop his satchel on the floor. I had given each child their own hook, lined up on the hallway wall, when they'd begun nursery, a one-level cubed storage rack with a cubby for each of them intended for their shoes on the floor below. In my naivety, I'd hoped they would develop the habit of using them for coats and bags without my needing to remind them, but the reality was far from the picture-perfect row of neat child-sized macs I'd envisaged whilst picking out individually designed name plaques. I sighed as Rufus disappeared into the living room. Tristan tossed his muddy rugby boots on the oak floor of the hall, scattering chunks of dirt everywhere.

'Tris! For goodness' sake, the cleaners left less than two hours ago. Clear that mess up!' I snapped. 'But first answer the phone, will you? I shouldn't have to ask – you're old enough to know when to help,' I reminded him, kicking the front door shut and lowering the heavy bags to a clean spot of floor, my shoulders throbbing.

My fifteen-year-old son, already halfway up the stairs, glared over his shoulder as the ringing cut out. 'Sorry,' he said, his deep voice flippant. He didn't wait for me to reply as he turned and jogged up the rest of the way. A moment later, I heard the slam of his door, followed by the thunderous blare of his music.

I rubbed my fingers into my aching temples, counting to ten under my breath, then picked up the bags and stepped over the mud, trying not to let it bother me. A scream echoed through the room as I entered the bright kitchen, the sun streaming through the floor-to-ceiling bifold doors casting a soft light over the white tiles and marble counter on the new island. Seeing Amelie and Ceci in a tangle, I dropped the shopping on the floor, hearing the distinctive sound of breaking glass from within, hoping it was the olives not the wine that I'd damaged. I lurched forward, arms outstretched. 'Girls! Girls, no! Stop it right now!' I yelled, my voice shrill with impatience.

Ceci had her fingers entwined in Amelie's long brown hair, her round little face red and scrunched up in anger as she pulled hard, a high-pitched wail emanating from her lips. Amelie swung a hand round, slapping at Cecilia's body, trying to wriggle out of her grasp. 'Get off me!' she yelled, swiping viciously.

'Amelie, no! Don't hit her, baby – you know it's not her fault. Just hold still,' I said, covering Cecilia's chubby hand with my own, easing her fingers back one by one, the same way I'd done dozens of times before.

'So she's just allowed to hurt me then?' Amelie snapped, darting back before Cecilia could grab her again. 'Just because I had a drink in the red cup?'

I sighed, hating that my nine-year-old would think I was taking the side of her six-year-old sister. I knew it sometimes felt that way, but Amelie knew Ceci needed support. This wasn't about taking sides. 'You know it's her favourite,' I said gently, still holding Cecilia's hand so she wouldn't go for Amelie again. '*You* don't mind which cup you use, but she does,' I said over the top of Ceci's head.

My younger daughter thrashed against me, her wails growing louder.

'Calm down, sweetheart. It's okay, it's okay... You know you need to use your words and your signs. We don't hurt each other, Ceci,' I said as I eased myself onto a chair, pulling her onto my lap. 'Go and get ready for swimming,' I told Amelie, meeting her incandescent glare as I adjusted my hold, crossing my arms over Ceci's body. I could feel her anger radiating through her limbs and knew I had to nip it in the bud quickly if I was going to be able to leave her with Drew and take Amelie to her competition in twenty minutes. Drew never could cope when she was having a meltdown, and Amelie couldn't miss this competition. She'd put so much effort into her training sessions this term.

'I don't even want to go anyway,' Amelie said, her voice sulky as she stamped out. 'I hate swimming and I hate this family!'

I sighed, closing my eyes for a second, trying to find the energy to have the same old conversation with my youngest about gentle hands. I'd talk to Amelie properly later, when I had her alone – make it up to her then. So much for the chance of a coffee and a snack for me. There would barely be time to put the shopping away at this rate.

I glanced at my watch, wondering where Drew was and why he wasn't back yet. I hoped he wasn't going to turn up at the very last minute again.

Cecilia wriggled against me and I summoned all my patience.

'Sweetie,' I said, making sure to keep my voice calm and low, the way I always did when I had to remind her of something. It wasn't that she didn't understand. It was just that she didn't have the ability to regulate her emotions – not yet. I liked to think she was getting better, but even I had to admit it was slow progress. I held her tightly, the way she liked, knowing it would soothe her, and she pressed the back of her head hard into my collarbone, humming a low, repetitive tune as I felt her frustration ebb away.

Drew hadn't wanted a fourth baby – said we were drowning in responsibility as it was – but I'd been determined to have just one more and persuaded him that we would manage. I would make sure of it. I'd known the moment I saw Cecilia, still breathless from pushing her into the world, that she had Down syndrome. I'd nannied for a family in Mayfair for a few years, long before I'd met Drew, taking care of twin boys. The mother, Saskia, had gone into hospital with her husband to have her third baby and I'd stayed behind with the twins, both rambunctious and loud, never far from trouble. When Saskia and Jim brought their third son home, they told me he'd been born with an extra chromosome. I'd cared for the three boys for two years before moving on, learning about what it meant to look after a baby with Down syndrome, watching Saskia and absorbing her calm energy and determined attitude. I'd loved those children like my own and been sad to leave when the time came.

I'd recognised the distinctive features in my own daughter instantly. The paediatrician had come on to the maternity ward to look at her, and after a long silence had asked me to call my husband so we could all have a chat. I'd told him there was no need – I already knew.

'I'm so sorry,' he had said, his eyes full of sadness as I held my daughter close. I'd shaken my head, offended by his apology, his insinuation that Cecilia was less than perfect, a disappointment somehow.

'What are you sorry for?' I had asked. 'She's exactly as she should be and I wouldn't change her for the world.'

Though I'd never wavered in my love for her, I knew that being her parent would likely involve more challenges than we'd anticipated, and I'd been afraid to tell Drew about her diagnosis. He'd walked into the ward that evening, having gone home to check on things, looking stressed and harassed, complaining about the kids, the mess, the noise, the work he had to get through, an endless cycle of dissatisfaction. I'd sat quietly, waiting for him to finish his rant and relax a bit. When at last he stopped, I handed Cecilia to him wordlessly. He'd looked down at her, his body finally relaxing as he lowered himself into a chair beside my bed, then sighed. 'Sorry,' he'd said. 'I'm just so tired.'

I smiled, biting back a comment about my having just been up all night giving birth, then spent the day trying to figure out breastfeeding our newborn baby. Drew had held my hand through the labour, but I was pretty sure I'd had the harder task.

He seemed to realise his faux pas. 'How are you doing?' he asked, summoning a smile.

'I'm okay. Bit sore.'

'And the baby? She's okay?'

'She's fine...' I met his eyes. 'She has Down syndrome,' I said, keeping my voice light, determined not to adopt that same apologetic tone the doctor had used on me earlier. My daughter was not something to apologise for; I would never speak of her in that patronising way. 'The doctor confirmed it, but I wasn't surprised. I could tell as soon as I saw her. But she's fine. Feeding well. Two dirty nappies.'

'She—' He broke off, looking at Ceci as if he was seeing her for the first time. 'Beth... Oh God, how will we cope? How can we manage this?' he whispered. He stood, passing her back to me, folding his arms tightly across his chest. 'Are you certain?'

I nodded.

'We can't... I can't do this.'

'We can. I can.' I forced a smile, annoyed that as usual he was making such a fuss, building it up to be something impossible. Drew always focused on the what-ifs. He dramatised every situation long before there was any need to worry. I wished he could just go with the flow and be more present. Acknowledge that right now, he had four wonderful children, a wife who loved him, a great job and a beautiful home in a safe, pretty area. My dream home, in fact – the kind of house I used to walk past and fantasise about living in, the four-storey Notting Hill townhouse my teenaged self would have traded her soul for.

Most of the time I felt like I was living a lie, a pretence. That any minute someone would turn up and tell me to get out, the dream was over and I needed to pack up and go back to the damp, dark two-bedroom terrace I'd grown up in across town. The childhood home my parents still lived in, refusing to accept my offer of Drew paying for their heating bill, insisting they could manage, though my time there had shown me what their standards of managing meant. I hated to think of them cold or hungry, and invited them over whenever I could without making it feel like charity, something I knew they wouldn't stand for.

Our children were at the best schools I could hope for, paid for by Drew's fantastic income, derived from his position at his best friend's thriving business. We had a lovely family, expensive holidays and everything we could possibly wish for in life. We were so lucky. I didn't understand why he always had to spoil it. I didn't get what he was even fretting about. It always fell to me to take care of the children anyway. He was the career man; I was the stay-at-home wife. It was how things worked between us, and old-fashioned as it might be, I loved it. I wouldn't have changed it for the world.

As we'd sat in the maternity ward that day, I'd squashed down my frustration, wishing he could see how much I did, how I always made it work, putting him and the children first to make sure of that. 'Don't worry so much, darling,' I'd insisted. 'It will all work out in the end.'

And it had. Mostly because I'd made it work. I'd taken responsibility for getting Cecilia to her hospital appointments, her speech therapist. I'd taught her Makaton signing when her struggle to communicate caused behavioural difficulties as a toddler. I'd read up on techniques to help her thrive and develop, to support her in any way I could. Last year, when she'd needed life-saving surgery on her heart, it had been me who'd sat outside the hospital, waiting to be called to recovery, me who'd spent three sleepless weeks by her side on the children's ward, barely finding the time to shower and see my other children as I'd managed their schedules from the hospital room, my phone permanently attached to my hand. The predicted one-week stay had morphed into three after she'd aspirated fluid into her lungs during the operation, and then developed an infection in her healing wound requiring IV antibiotics just a few days later.

We'd known since she was seven months old about the hole in her heart. A condition known as atrioventricular septal defect, which I'd read about and knew to affect up to twenty-five per cent of children with Down syndrome. It meant that the blood flowed unevenly through the chambers, putting too much pressure on the right side of her heart. In the majority of cases, it would be a death sentence without surgery to repair the problem.

Our consultant, when he'd broken the news to us all those years ago, had told us to my disbelief that we were among the lucky ones. Ceci hadn't shown any signs of a struggle, her feeding was strong, her breathing unaffected, and in her case the hole was very small. If it hadn't been for the routine scan, we might never have known about it. He'd told us that in a rare handful of cases, the condition could rectify itself without surgery, and I'd grasped hold of that hope, needing it to be true for my daughter. We were given a deadline of her fifth birthday to wait for it to fix itself, with scans every six months to monitor the situation, though it seemed impossible to imagine it could be as simple as that. And as it turned out, impossible was the right word, at least in Ceci's case.

Two days before her fifth birthday, I noticed her looking paler, breathing more heavily, refusing to eat. I told Drew it was no doubt a bug, something one of the children had picked up and passed on to her, but I'd known. I'd felt in my gut that it was more serious than that. The emergency scan I'd rushed her in for while Drew was at work, unaware of the severity of the situation, showed the hole had opened further, was slowly killing her, and if we didn't act fast, she would be heading for heart failure. I hadn't allowed myself time to process what was happening, what I was agreeing to. I hadn't even cried when I realised what the doctor's words meant. I'd simply gathered my strength and agreed to the emergency surgery, knowing it was the only choice we had left.

I'd done it all without a word of complaint, because I couldn't bear the thought that my husband might resent our youngest child, regret letting me persuade him to try just one last time. I wanted him to see, to really understand, that our daughter wasn't a mistake. That we *could* cope. But sometimes it would have been nice if he'd offered to step in and help. Just because I didn't complain didn't mean I didn't sometimes feel like I was drowning.

I looked to the bifold doors now, taking in the perfectly mani-cured garden beyond, the new little fountain on the terrace where blue tits were perched enjoying a drink. Cecilia's body softened and I smiled as she pushed away from my hold and stood up, pulling open the door and heading towards the swing set on the far side of the lawn without a word. I was grateful that this time a meltdown had been avoided.

My stomach rumbled and I glanced at the clock again, wondering why Drew hadn't arrived back yet. He really was cutting it fine.

I stood up, pulling my phone from my pocket to see if there was a message from him, and realised that not only was it on silent, but there were four missed calls from Drew's office too. I hoped he wasn't intending to spring a last-minute meeting on me. It wasn't on. I was about to call him back when the house phone rang again and I strode over, picking it up.

'Drew?' I snapped.

'Beth, thank God, I've been trying to get hold of you for half an hour!'

'Sandra?' I said, frowning as I wondered why my husband's secretary was calling me. 'What's wrong?'

'I... I...' She broke off, taking a breath. 'It's Drew, he's been taken to hospital. You need to go.'

'What?' I shook my head, wondering how on earth I was going to manage everything I had to do this evening without Drew's help. 'I don't understand... What's happened, Sandra?'

'He's... well, he's had an accident.'

I sighed, squeezing the phone between my shoulder and ear so

I could refill Amelie's water bottle. I would have to take Rufus with me to the pool, and that was going to mean he'd have to make do with snacks poolside rather than a proper dinner if I was going to get him to his trombone lesson straight afterwards. I wondered if Tristan would help take care of Ceci for a few hours, then thought better of it. The hormones of a fifteen-year-old boy were something I'd been unprepared for, and I could only imagine how he'd react if I asked him to babysit, though he knew as well as I did that at this time of night, expecting Ceci to sit patiently poolside was asking for trouble.

'Look, Sandra, I've got a packed evening. Just tell Drew he'll have to get a cab home from hospital. I'm going to have to phone my mum as it is to come and look after Ceci,' I said irritably, knowing she'd argue about my paying for a taxi to get her here quickly. There was no time for the Tube though, and it wasn't as if the money was an issue. I'd have to insist.

'No, Beth... you don't understand. It's... it's serious.'

A cold fist clamped around my heart and I froze in the middle of the kitchen, Amelie's water bottle clutched in my palm. 'How serious can it be? He works in an office, for heaven's sake!' I exclaimed, my voice shrill and shaky.

There was a long silence, which seemed to answer the question for me.

'Just go,' Sandra said eventually, and I wondered how I'd missed the tremor of fear in her voice. 'Get there as quickly as you can, Beth. I have to...' I heard a muffled noise and then the line went dead.

I stared at the cordless phone, my hand shaking, my pulse echoing in my ears. I walked slowly to the kitchen counter, placing the phone down gently in its cradle, then turned, staring out the window as Ceci swung back and forth on the swing. For the first time in as long as I could remember, I had no idea what to do next.

TWO

I sat waiting for the light to change from red to green, the traffic heavy around me as I wondered if I'd taken the best route to the hospital. It had been more than an hour since Sandra's dramatic phone call, and I knew there was a part of me that wanted to delay getting to Drew. Now that I thought about it, I couldn't imagine how it could be anything too serious. Of course Sandra would make a massive fuss. She was notorious for dramatising every little thing. Drew had told me of numerous occasions when she'd made something out of nothing, and reflecting on the phone call now, I was sure it was nothing too awful – a bad cut or broken bone maybe. Still, I'd found plenty of reasons to delay my leaving, even after Mum had turned up.

I'd hated having to ask her to drag herself across town and take care of the children for me. She was seventy-two and Dad was three years older. I knew she fretted about leaving him, worrying that he'd have a fall or forget to drink, and my children were hardly a dream to take care of.

I'd tried calling a few of the school mums before I called her, but none of them had got back to me and I wasn't surprised in the least. At this time of day, they'd all be rushing around, ferrying their children to dance classes, music lessons, all the things my own evenings were usually filled with. Week nights never stopped. Every parent I knew had a jam-packed schedule, and I knew they would be too fearful of missing a club or a class to drop it all and come and help me.

Drew was always going on about doing less, delegating and cutting back. He didn't understand though. It wasn't that I wasn't good at asking for help. It was that when I did ask, I never got the answer I hoped for, so I'd learned to do it alone, take the responsibility myself, and I wasn't going to disadvantage my children by limiting their opportunities.

The light turned green up ahead, and I indicated left, despite the fact that turning right was the quicker route. I ignored the guilt in my belly, the churning anxiety as I pictured my mother at my house – where she'd never felt comfortable due to it being, in her words, a show house, not a home – having to take care of my children. I hoped Ceci was still occupied with the movie I'd put on for her. I hoped Tris was being polite and Rufus wasn't forgetting to do his homework. I chewed my lip as the car in front of me moved forward, then, with a sigh, flicked the indicator right and turned before I could change my mind.

Frustratingly, when I'd broken the news to Amelie that her grandmother was coming to babysit, and she wouldn't be able to go to her swimming competition after all, she'd acted like it was good news, giving a cheer and rushing upstairs as if she thought I might change my mind. It annoyed me that she didn't show more gratitude for the life she had. I didn't mind giving up my time to make sure she got to her practice sessions, didn't resent the 5 a.m. start on a Saturday to take her to the pool, but a little appreciation on her part would have gone a long way.

Julia would be pleased when we didn't show. The school mums I'd met and tried to befriend over the years could be more than a little catty, and there was a competitive thread that ran through every conversation we shared. I could just picture the look on Julia's face when she saw Amelie missing from the poolside and realised that her daughter, Raya, might take first place. It wasn't fair after all the work Amelie had put in.

I glanced up at the sign beside the road, following the route to the hospital, trying not to think about Drew and failing. As little as I asked him to do with the children, the simple truth was I knew I couldn't manage without him. If he had to stay in hospital for a few days, it would throw everything into chaos. Tristan had his guitar lesson tomorrow and Rufus had his karate class – he couldn't possibly miss that, as his grading for his next belt was due at the end of the month. Mum would never be able to take them to their classes, as much as she might like to help out.

I drove into the car park, looking for a space close to the entrance and frowned, wishing I'd put my foot down and insisted on getting a nanny. I always felt embarrassed when I had to admit at the school gates that I didn't have help with the children – it took me right back to my own school days, when I'd turned up wearing last year's uniform, my ankles sticking out beneath my school trousers, my shoes scuffed and too tight. I often complained to Drew about it, unable to understand why he didn't see how important it was to me. Right now, a nanny would have been able to step in and help my mother while I had to rush out and come here. We would definitely need to revisit the possibility. I was sure he'd see my point after the pandemonium of this evening.

I picked up my bag, pulling my lipstick from the inside compartment and slicking it across my mouth, then running my travel brush through my long dark hair, not wanting to have to speak to nurses looking like a slob. I spritzed some Chanel on my neck and then dropped the bottle back in the main compartment, looking longingly at the cereal bar beside it. I couldn't recall if I'd even had time to eat lunch today, and breakfast had only been a smoothie at the café after my hot yoga class. I sighed, zipping up the bag before I could give in to the snack, and with no more excuses to detain me, headed towards the doors, my heels clicking on the tarmac.

My mind was still whirring with everything I had to do, and I tried to remember whether I'd told my mum not to let Rufus go to the park across the road. He always seemed to end up in a scuffle with the other boys, part of the reason I'd chosen karate for him, to teach him to channel his energy and control his impulses. Mum wouldn't know what to do if he came back covered in blood and bruises. I tried to keep thinking about the children, the lists of tasks, anything but Drew, but as I walked through the hospital corridors, it became more and more difficult not to give in to the fear that bubbled up at the thought of what I might be about to find. I asked a cleaner for directions, then, finding the ward, threw my shoulders back and headed for the nurses' station.

'Hi, I'm Elizabeth Spencer-Rhodes,' I said, smiling warmly. 'I believe you have my husband, Andreas, here. May I speak to him?'

The nurse shook her head, rising to stand. 'Mrs, uh... Mrs Spencer-Rhodes, I'm afraid that won't be possible. Did someone explain to you what's happened?'

I looked down, realising that my hands had moved to the edge of the desk and were gripping it so tightly my knuckles had turned white. A sudden fear hit me, and I knew I had to see Drew, had to know he was okay, though the look on the nurse's face made that hard for me to convince myself of. I couldn't stand not knowing what was happening. Was something really wrong with my husband?

'What do you mean?' I asked, leaning closer, my voice shrill, shocking. 'Why can't I speak to him? I *insist* on speaking to my husband right now!' All the warmth evaporated from my voice as I finally let the panic pour through the gates of my heart. 'I need to see him!'

The nurse nodded, reaching across the desk, her hand gripping my forearm as her eyes met mine. 'You can see him. I'll take you to him now. But he won't be able to talk to you. I'm sorry, I thought someone would have explained.' She took a breath. 'I'm sorry to have to tell you this... your husband is in a coma.'

·   ·   ·

I followed the nurse along a corridor, my mouth dry as her words replayed over and over again in my mind. A coma... a coma... How could my husband be in a coma? How on earth could something have happened that could have hurt him so badly? I clasped my hands together, wringing them tightly, my acrylic nails pressing indents into the soft skin between my fingers and thumb. The nurse pushed open a door, waiting for me to summon the courage to step forward.

I wanted to run, to turn away, go back home, pretend I had never got the call to summon me here. I didn't want to see my husband, the man who'd been my partner for more than a decade, lying broken on a bed. Drew was not the kind of man who broke. He was strong, a born alpha, always driven and full of vitality. He worked hard, and even when he complained, he gave his all.

The first time I had seen him, dressed in a deep blue suit that screamed money, his dark eyes sparkling and confident as he held the room with his smooth, self-assured voice, I'd known I wanted him. It had been at a party at a swanky bar that had been hired for the occasion, full of the kind of people I aspired to be like but never could. I'd wangled the invitation from a friend of my old employer, Saskia, and spent a month's wages on a dress, determined to be noticed. And Drew had noticed. I'd felt his eyes on me from across the room as soon as I arrived, and once I had his attention, I was determined not to lose it. I played it perfectly: not too eager, just enough to show him he might have a chance.

It wasn't just his success that drew me to him. It was his warmth. He wasn't sneering and smug like so many of the men I'd encountered at events like these before. He had it all, but it didn't seem to affect who he was. He was surprisingly down to earth, and as that evening passed in a blur of champagne and music, I'd found myself wanting to talk to him more, able to be myself in a way that never seemed to come naturally to me. He was a born listener, never cutting me off to impart his own opinions or stories, and I found I didn't have to put on a pretence, or at least not as much as I usually might. I knew I'd met someone special. The strong man I'd always craved, someone to take care of me, to protect me. To provide for me and Tristan, the three-year-old son I'd had with a man I wished I'd never met.

I stepped up to the open doorway now, gasping as my eyes fell on my husband lying flat on his back, tubes and wires snaking across his chest, machines beeping and whirring all around him. 'What happened?' I whispered, moving through the door. 'Was it... a car accident?'

The nurse didn't answer as I stepped closer to the bed, afraid to touch Drew for fear of knocking one of the tubes.

'You can hold his hand. Talk to him. It might help,' she said softly.

'He'll wake up soon though, won't he?' I asked, not turning to face her. 'I mean, there's hope? A coma means he's healing. There's hope, right?' I said, finally spinning to face her.

'There's always hope,' she said, her eyes full of sympathy. Pity.

I shook my head, wanting to reject it. Her sadness frightened me, made this all the worse. 'Tell me what happened.'

'I... I'll go and find a doctor, ask for someone to come and speak to you. I... I'm so sorry,' she added, leaving in a hurry, not giving me a chance to object.

I turned back to Drew, reaching slowly towards his hand, then changing my mind for fear that it might be cold. I didn't want to feel that, to feel like I'd already lost him.

I stepped back, pulling my phone from my pocket. The last person I wanted to talk to right now was Gemma, but I knew I had to call her. It was what Drew would want, and as much as I might resent the bond he had with his younger sister, I couldn't keep this from her.

I closed my eyes, lifting the phone to my ear, and unable to look any longer, turned my back on my husband.

THREE

GEMMA

I stood over the bathroom sink, gripping the edges as I swayed unsteadily, trying to get a hold of myself. I felt like I'd been hit with a nasty bout of flu, but I knew my symptoms – the nausea, the cold sweat coating my body, the aches and chills – were entirely self-inflicted. I'd made a mistake, that much I was certain of, but though I was aware of the impact my idiotic choices could have, the dangerous path I was on the verge of going down, I still couldn't prevent myself from wanting to do it again. If there was anything else that even came close to making me feel better, taking away my pain, if only for a short while, I would have grabbed at it with both hands, but the truth was, now that I'd gone there, taken the step into a place I'd always steadfastly avoided, I knew I wouldn't find a replacement.

I turned on the cold tap, cupping my hands beneath the water and splashing it on my face, my neck, feeling it trickle in rivulets beneath the collar of my work uniform. I unbuttoned the pale blue shirt, letting it drop to the dirty tiled floor, kicking it aside as I reached for the towel on the handrail.

Eight hours I'd spent sweating through the polyester uniform, scanning item after item at the checkout, trying and failing to make polite small talk with the customers as I fought the urge to vomit. Working at the supermarket had never been thrilling, but up until now, I'd been content to do the job with a mindless, robotic attitude that got me through each shift. I didn't like the interactions with the public and would have preferred a job out the back, but I didn't have the option of turning down work, and I needed to pay my bills. I would never rely on government benefits – I refused to let myself fall into *that* trap, believing that I could relax, trust someone other than myself to provide what I needed. I'd rather do the shitty job and deal with the chatty, complaining people and come home to the tiny studio flat I rented with my own money. I usually got through the day without much trouble, but not today.

I straightened up, opening the medicine cabinet and pulling out the little brown bottle of pills. I flipped the lid, swallowing my daily Zoloft pill, though I had little hope that the antidepressant would make the slightest difference to my bleak mood. My eyes lingered on the white cardboard packet on the shelf ahead of me, the pills I really wanted to pick up, and my fist tightened around the bottle still grasped in my palm.

I'd been prescribed the codeine two years earlier after slipping on an icy pavement on my way home from work, hitting my coccyx hard on the edge of the kerb. My back had been in agony, and not wanting to miss more work than was necessary, I'd begged the GP to prescribe me something – *anything* – that might take away the pain. She'd written me up for a four-week supply of codeine, and it had helped, numbing not only the pain in my back but the constant noise in my head too. I'd been surprised to realise it was more effective than the antidepressants ever had been at ridding me of the anxious thoughts that had plagued me since childhood, and I'd been grateful to discover there might actually be a magic pill that could fix the mess I'd made of my life.

But when that four-week course was finished, I was no longer the same person. I found I couldn't cope without the codeine, the lure of the pills far more powerful than I could possibly have imagined, the escape they offered something I craved. Something I couldn't give up. My back was fully recovered, but my mind couldn't deal with the noise – not now that I knew there was something that would make it stop.

I had to find a way to keep taking them, so I went back to the doctor. Lied. Rubbed the base of my spine as I told her I wasn't ready to stop just yet. Needed more time to recover. The pain still kept me up at night. Which was the truth, in part, though it was my memories, not my back, that plagued me.

I'd been surprised at how easy it was, how quickly she'd handed me the prescription with barely a second glance. I'd been elated, but as the weeks passed, the effect of the pills seemed to lessen and I returned to the GP, asked for a stronger dose, something more powerful. She seemed willing to help, and even conceded that the antidepressants I'd been on since my teens might be having an impact on the efficacy of the pain relief – that she should have known I'd need a higher dose. But when those stopped having an impact too, the anxiety trickling back in, the panic attacks and nightmares visiting me more and more frequently, and I ran through my supply faster than I was supposed to, her support dried up.

'You need to cut back, Gemma, or you won't see the benefits. You have to be careful – you're relying on them too much, taking too many. These things can be addictive,' she had tutted, as if I should have known better.

I had stared at her, shocked at her words as I realised just how true they were. Why had she never mentioned it before? Why wait until it was too late? Until I was already so entwined in my need for them that I couldn't begin to fathom an alternative? I'd seen the judgement on her face, the stubborn refusal to give me what I so desperately needed, and instantly pulled back from her, refusing to talk, to attend appointments. She sent a referral for me to see a therapist, but what was the point in talking? I didn't want to go over my past, didn't want to remember the things that had messed up my life and caused me to be this way. I just wanted to block it out and numb the pain that haunted me.

She had known better than to cut me off cold turkey, of course, keeping my prescription ticking over, though she steadfastly refused to increase it, but it wasn't enough. I needed something else. Something more. Alcohol had never helped; besides, I hated waking up with my stomach churning and the smell of tequila seeping through my pores. I'd noticed that some of the younger guys at work smoked pot on their breaks. I'd gone out to join them, surprised at how willing they were to share, and they'd put me in touch with a guy called Jason who seemed only too happy to help. The effect of the weed wasn't as good as the codeine, but it helped a little – quieted my thoughts and smoothed down the jagged edges of the pain so I could handle it better. Jason also managed to get hold of an extra pack or two of codeine for me every now and then. I didn't ask where or how.

I had precious few options but to manage with what I had. I had never wanted it to go further than that. I knew how easy it would be to lose myself, given the opportunity. My whole life, I had felt like I was fighting not to sink into that black hole, from which I doubted I'd have the strength to claw my way back out. How easy it would be to fall if I let myself. That was what made what I'd done all the worse, because I couldn't pretend I hadn't known.

It had been a week since Jason had turned up at my place with a little extra. He'd asked to come in, and though I wouldn't normally have agreed, I'd had an awful day and hadn't had the energy to turn him away. I'd wondered if he was about to make a pass at me, and part of me hoped he would. The distraction from reality would have been welcome, though I'd never got the vibe from the younger man that he thought of me that way. Instead of trying it on though, he'd pulled a small, clear glass pipe from his jacket pocket and said, 'Gems, babe, you look rough. Have a try of this – it'll help.'

I'd been reluctant, unsure what it was I was being offered, but as I watched him put a pinch of sandy brown powder in the bulbous end of the pipe, I sank down onto the threadbare sofa feeling defeated and lost. He'd come to sit beside me, his eyes meeting mine as if he knew he was about to give me something special, and I'd hoped, just for a moment, that he might be right. I longed for escape, for something to wipe out all the feelings that tortured me. He'd placed the end of the short glass pipe between my lips, then pulled his lighter from his pocket, holding it beneath the bulb, heating the powder until it began to smoke.

'Breathe it in, slow and deep, Gem, slow and deep,' he'd said, smiling like the Cheshire Cat. I'd looked into his eyes and seen them filled with longing, envy even, and suddenly trepidation bubbled up inside me. I didn't know what it was he was offering, but I knew I was crossing a line. I could feel it. Sense it. But the thick white smoke curled slowly up through the narrow tube and I made my choice, breathed it in, and suddenly it didn't matter that it was wrong, stupid – dangerous even. It didn't matter at all.

It was only later, when I woke from the first deep sleep I'd had in months, that he told me what I'd done. I wanted to react with shock, but the truth was, I'd known deep down that I was being offered heroin, and I'd pretended not to realise because I needed to try it. I think a part of me had hoped for this moment, sure that at some point I would arrive here. It was inevitable. I was too useless to stop it.

But now Pandora's box had been flung open and I no longer had to imagine what it would feel like, how it might make every-thing better for a few hours. I'd let it happen, and from the second I'd opened my eyes after his visit, I had craved more, consumed by need with every waking breath. I'd held out as long as I could, but finally, two days ago, I had gone to his flat, let myself be sucked into the trap again, given in to my weakness. I was teetering on a precipice and I could not allow myself to do it a third time. It was too dangerous, too easy to love. If I let myself have this, it would be the beginning of the end for me.

It wasn't me I was holding on for. It was Drew. I owed him this much. I'd let him down time and again, but I wouldn't put him through seeing his sister spiral into an addiction with such irreparable consequences. This, I knew, was a world away from the codeine I was hooked on. There would be no way to keep up any sort of pretence that I was managing, surviving, and I wouldn't let Drew see me that way. I loved him too much to hurt him so deeply. And despite what Jason might think of me, this wasn't who I was. Not really. I wanted more for myself. To be a better person, make my time on this earth worthwhile. I just didn't know how to begin. As much as I'd loved the bliss of the escape, I knew the 'gift' I'd been given had only complicated things so much more.

I shoved the bottle of antidepressants back into the medicine cabinet, my fingers shaking as I somehow resisted the lure of the codeine. I needed it now more than ever, but I had to regulate my supply if I didn't want to run out before I could pick up my repeat prescription. I let my fingers graze the packet, my mouth dry, then, with a burst of determined energy, I slammed the cabinet door just as my mobile rang from the living room. I walked out the open bathroom door, picking up my phone from the table, seeing Beth's name flash up and frowning. Beth never called me. We weren't close, something I made no effort to change.

I pursed my lips, tempted to end the call, then sighed. 'Hello?'

'Gemma, it's Beth. I'm in hospital with Drew. He's... he's in a coma.'

The world seemed to fall from beneath me as the words rang in my ears. It was my fault. I'd known the last time I saw him how much I'd hurt him. I'd pushed him over the edge. It was my fault. My mouth was dry, my hands shaking as I gripped the phone. 'I'm coming,' I whispered. 'I'm coming right now.'

I ended the call, shoving my phone in my pocket, and ran to my dresser, pulling on a clean top. I spun on the spot, hesitating, feeling the tremors build in my body, needing, craving, even now. On shaking limbs, I strode back to the bathroom, flinging open the cabinet, not letting myself feel the guilt, the fear of what I was doing as I picked up the little white packet and pressed two tablets into my palm. Cramming them into my mouth, I stuck my head under the tap, swallowing them back before I could change my mind. I shoved the packet into my bag, then headed for the door, hoping I wouldn't have long to wait for a bus.

I had to get to my brother.

FOUR

BETH

The heart monitor beside the bed was silent, yet I couldn't take my eyes from the display, the evidence that in spite of appearances, my husband really was alive. I wished the nurse hadn't left me alone with him. I was afraid of getting too close, making it worse somehow. I'd always had a crippling fear of hospitals, something I'd tried to play down to Drew in recent years when I'd needed to take Cecilia in for treatment or surgery. And he'd clearly wiped my phobia from his mind, as he hadn't offered to take over, or even come with me.

Last year, when she'd gone in for her heart surgery, I'd played the part of the perfect mother. I'd been calm, steady, holding her hand right up until she went into theatre. I'd stood resolute, a stupid smile on my face, as they asked me to kiss her as they put her under. I'd done it without a word of complaint. I'd walked out of the room, leaving my daughter ready to be carved open on the table, strode past the theatre nurse into the corridor and promptly collapsed in a dead faint, chipping my front tooth on the tiled floor.

I ran my tongue over the uneven surface now, summoning the courage to move closer to my husband. I'd managed then because I had to, because that was my duty as a mother and it was unfathomable to consider letting Ceci go through it alone. But it had taken all my strength to hide my feelings and step up. I couldn't believe I was having to do this now. I wanted more than anything to see his eyes open slowly, see the dawning of recognition on his face and be sure that our time in this place, this room, with death and disease all around us, would be over soon and I could take him home.

I wondered if I should call his mum, Jacinta. She was a woman I'd always felt on the back foot with, though I'd barely got to know her, having only met her a couple of times in person. She came across as strong, loud and often quite hard, though Drew insisted she had a softer side. He and his sister had been born in England to an English father and a Greek mother, but after their dad died when they were children, their mother was ill for a time, and though she stayed on in their family home for several years, she'd returned to Greece when Gemma reached eighteen. Neither of her children had wanted to go with her, not feeling the pull to the country she still considered home. They had spent their formative years here, and England, in their minds, was where they belonged. I decided I would leave it to Gemma to make that call. I barely knew Jacinta, even twelve years after falling in love with her son, and it wasn't my place to tell her something like this.

I glanced back at the door, wishing someone would come. The nurse, a doctor, Gemma even, as awkward as that would be. I just didn't want to be here by myself. I was so afraid he'd suddenly stop breathing or have a seizure, and I would be expected to manage it – to know what to do.

'Drew,' I said, my voice barely more than a whisper. I reached forward, my shaking fingers hovering above his hand, nerves making them tingle. I took a deep breath and let my hand lower, curling around his, relieved to find it warm and full of life. *Hope*. I felt my throat thicken as a tear escaped the corner of my eye. 'Oh, Drew,' I whispered. 'What happened to you?'

I reached up to his face, cupping his cheek, the dark evening stubble rough against my palm.

'Babe, wake up,' I said, leaning close, ignoring the wires and tubes, trying to push my fear away and be what he needed in this moment. 'I'm here. I'm right here, Drew. Wake up. Wake up. Please wake up—'

I broke off with a sob, squeezing my eyes shut as I tried to compose myself. It wouldn't help anyone if I fell apart now. I moved away, reaching into my bag for a compact and a tissue, sighing as I saw the mess I'd made of my mascara, my face red and blotchy.

Hurriedly, I dabbed at my eyes, wiping away the traces of my weakness. I dropped the compact back into my bag as I heard footsteps in the corridor, and a moment later a doctor in blue scrubs stepped into the room. My stomach clenched at the sight of him, hoping he wasn't about to suggest taking Drew for surgery. What if they wanted to operate on his brain or something? What if he came out different, not the man I knew? I'd always loved how funny he was, how he could turn anything into a joke and make me laugh until I couldn't breathe. I loved his confidence too, his utter lack of shame in his successes. He was a man who'd come from very little but had worked relentlessly to change that. He was strong, unashamedly so, and his energy had been magnetising to me from the moment I laid eyes on him. It was true that in the last few years he'd complained more, but life with children, especially four of them, tended to have that effect, and I knew he was only blowing off steam. He didn't mean it. What if the Drew I knew, my perfect Andreas, was gone?

I felt tears begin to prick at my eyes again and blinked them away, standing up to face the doctor. He was only around Drew's age himself, I noted, no more than mid-forties and his light brown hair grew over his forehead, dangling in front of his glasses so he had to keep pushing it back. I wondered why he didn't just get it cut.

'Mrs Spencer-Rhodes?' he asked, clasping his hands in front of him.

'Yes, call me Beth,' I said, folding my arms across my chest. 'Is my husband going to wake up soon? He's going to be okay, isn't he?'

'I'm Dr Blaine.'

I nodded, waiting for him to answer me. Instead, he glanced around, then moved to one of the padded chairs, gesturing for me to sit down opposite him. It was the last thing I wanted to do. Now that he was here, I wanted answers and I wanted to get out of here. My body jangled with nerves, but I bit my lip, holding back the tidal wave of emotion, and took a seat, perched on the edge with my hands clasped tightly above my knees.

'I'd like to ask you some questions, if I may, Beth?'

I shrugged. 'Fine, yes, what do you need to know? I think his blood type is A positive, but I really would check first. It could be B, now that I think about it. He had an appendectomy six years ago, and broke his arm when he was nine or ten, but no other surgeries. He isn't on any medication, and he's had his well man check and everything was in order,' I said, my words hurried as I sped through the checklist I thought the doctor would want to know.

'And how long has he been having suicidal thoughts?' Dr Blaine asked, leaning forward, his bright blue eyes softening as they met mine.

'What?' I shook my head. 'I don't think you have the right patient,' I said, annoyed at him wasting my time.

'Mrs Spen— Beth, I mean,' he corrected, then cleared his throat. 'Your husband made an attempt on his life today. He was found in his office... with a rope around his neck.' His words were quiet, as if he was trying to tell me something he feared would shock me, but they merely confused me.

'You're mistaken,' I said, shaking my head. 'Drew isn't suicidal. He's not even depressed. He's not the kind of person given to self-pity. You don't know him. He's strong. He takes care of us. He would never do that – never abandon his family. He knows we need him!' My voice was growing steadily louder. 'He can't have—'

'I'm sorry, Beth, but he did. He was lucky to be found by his secretary, and more fortunate still that his neck didn't break, but as you can see from his current condition, there were some complications. It seems he was deprived of oxygen for some time before he was found. I have to be blunt with you, as difficult as this is for you to hear. Right now, it's impossible to know if or when he will come out of this. And if he does, we've yet to determine how his brain might have been affected. We'll need to do some tests, and I hope to have some good news for you once we've determined the level of activity in his brain.'

I shook my head. 'No... Drew couldn't do this... he couldn't,' I said quietly, those persistent tears springing to my eyes again.

'I'm so sorry,' he said, rising to his feet.

I glanced up at him, seeing the way his eyebrows knitted together, his eyes filled with genuine concern. He looked kind, sympathetic, and I couldn't fathom how this conversation could be about *my* husband. It made no sense.

He took a step back. 'I promise we'll do everything in our power to save him.' He pursed his lips, looking uncomfortable, then, with a final nod, he turned, striding out of the door.

I waited until the sound of his footsteps faded, then I jumped up, rushing to the side of Drew's bed, yanking down the sheet and the patterned hospital gown that covered his neck, gasping as I saw the unmistakable red ring, raw and weeping, running across his throat.

Anger ignited inside me as I absorbed what this meant. He'd *chosen* this. He'd made a conscious decision to leave us, to leave *me*, and put himself here. To waste the life he was so privileged to have. He'd thrown it all away, and that was a slap in the face to everything I held dear, the worst betrayal I could imagine. I dropped the sheet, turning away from him and pressing my hands to my face, wondering if I would ever be able to forgive him for what he'd done.

FIVE

GEMMA

The door to Drew's room was slightly ajar, and I pushed it open, seeing Beth hunched over the windowsill, her back to my brother, who lay sleeping in the hospital bed. No, not sleeping – comatose, I reminded myself. I clamped my teeth over the soft inside of my cheek, steeling myself as I stepped into the room.

Beth glanced over her shoulder, then, seeing me, turned awkwardly, folding her arms across her body. 'Did you know?' she asked, her brown eyes narrowing as they met mine. 'Did you know he was going to try something like this?'

I pressed my lips together. Somehow I understood instinctively what she meant. 'What did he do?' I asked, not taking my eyes from my brother, needing to know how he'd chosen to die. Drew had never liked mess; I couldn't picture him doing anything that might involve blood.

Beth pressed her hands to her face, but when she pulled them away, her eyes were dry, two spots of angry colour flushing her defined cheekbones. 'The doctor told me this wasn't an accident. He tried to hang himself, Gemma! And there's no way you didn't know he was planning it – the two of you tell each other every-thing, thick as bloody thieves!' she spat, her voice saturated with envy.

'Of course I didn't know he was going to do this. I would never have let him.' Even as I said the words, I felt deceitful. It was true, I hadn't known it would come to this, that he would ever take it this far, but had I known he was struggling? That he was feeling like he couldn't handle the responsibilities life had thrown at him, Beth's constant demands and expectations for only the best for her family? Yes, I'd known. I'd been surprised at how oblivious his wife could be, how easy she found it to ignore his struggles and brush his complaints under the rug. Drew was so good at hiding his pain, turning any situation around to make it about the other person, but wasn't it a wife's job to see through the mask and understand what was really going on? But then Beth had always been selfish.

She stared at me, her distrust written on her face, then glanced at Drew. Usually she carried an air of smug confidence that came with being rich and beautiful. She expected the world, Drew included, to bend to her whims, and after so many years of getting her own way, there was an arrogance that grated on me. The fact that she had swooped in and claimed half of everything my brother had worked for, never satisfied, always pushing for more, had made me take an instant dislike to her, and the years had only served to cement my opinion of her. But right now, she didn't look arrogant. She looked like a frightened little girl dressed up in her mother's designer clothes, the white silk shirt too large for her tiny frame, her eyes wide and fearful as she cast furtive glances at the bed. It was as if she'd been playing pretend and now reality had turned up to bite her. The snobbish, bossy woman seemed to have faded away, and in this moment, I could see right through her to her humble roots.

I knew she thought me cold. Anyone else might have hugged her, comforted her and made promises they couldn't hope to keep to make her feel better. But I had never known how to be that person – to offer platitudes and lies in order to make a situation more palatable. Pain, unwieldy emotions, anything of that sort made me run in the opposite direction.

I dropped my bag on the floor, ignoring the sound of Beth's

heeled boot tapping nervously on the tile, and walked towards my brother. He looked almost peaceful lying there, so still, and I reached out, touching his shoulder, remembering the last time we'd spoken, two days ago. Had this been my fault? Had I driven him to this point? Pushed him over the edge with my words, my actions? I'd known the moment Beth told me he was here that this was no coincidence. I'd felt it in my gut, the guilt, the absolute certainty that I was to blame.

I glanced over my shoulder at Beth, wishing she would leave. I wanted to be alone with him, talk to him, apologise and explain myself. Maybe he'd understand, lost as he might be. Maybe I could bring him back to me. I stared at his face and suddenly knew that if I lost him, I would never forgive myself. I would follow. There'd be nothing left for me here.

'Will he live?' I heard myself ask.

Beth didn't reply, and I turned to stare at her. 'Will he? Did they say he's going to wake up?' I demanded.

She shrugged helplessly, then looked down at the ground. 'I don't know what's going to happen,' she said, and I thought I heard a thread of anger in her voice. 'I don't know anything now.'

I stared at her, unsure what else to say.

'He *has* to live,' she said, suddenly squaring her shoulders and picking up her handbag from the chair in a flurry of energy, as if she'd remembered who she was supposed to be and stepped back into the character – the Stepford wife, the woman who always got what she wanted.

She fixed me with an angry stare and I realised she was planning to leave. I didn't know if I was relieved or disappointed in her.

She glanced at Drew, her face hard and determined. 'We need him to live,' she repeated. 'There's no other choice.'

SIX

BETH

I drove away from the hospital with an overwhelming sense of guilt, intertwined with relief. I'd felt as if I couldn't breathe in there, the walls too close, suffocating, crushing. Part of that need to escape, I knew, was down to the feeling of betrayal, knowing that all of this mess was because of a choice. *Drew's* choice. He had intended to leave me. To walk away from our marriage without so much as a conversation to explain what exactly it was about our life together that was so abhorrent. So terrible that he felt the need to—

I cut off the thought before I could finish it, squeezing the wheel tight, trying to breathe, to calm myself down. I wondered if he'd even bothered to leave a note. If Sandra hadn't found him in time, would I have been driving home as a widow right now? The idea was shocking, and as I turned onto a side road, I replayed the last moments we'd spent together at breakfast that morning, trying to recall if I'd missed something in my hurry to cajole the children into their uniforms and get their lunches packed.

Drew had made me a coffee, I remembered. Black and strong, just how I liked it. Had I thanked him? I couldn't remember, but I was certain that by now, he knew how much I valued those little gestures. After all, *he* hadn't thanked *me* for getting up twice in the night to settle Ceci after a nightmare, nor for spending the twenty minutes I would have liked to use for a shower helping Rufus find his lost topic book. Thanks were implied, and he hadn't seemed put out.

I'd told him my plans for the evening, what we would need to get organised, when I would have to leave for Amelie's swimming competition, and mentioned that he might make time to have a father–son chat with Tristan, see if he could figure out why he had suddenly transformed into the sulky, detached teenager I'd never imagined he would become. I was so sad that my sweet boy was slipping away from me. We'd always been so close. For the first three years of his life, it had been just the two of us, and we'd formed a bond so strong I hadn't imagined it possible that a time would come when our relationship might crumble to a collection of slammed doors and one-word answers, but it seemed that was exactly what had happened over the last few months. And as much as I pretended I was all right with letting him go, the raw truth was that my heart broke every time he walked away from me.

Drew had nodded, picking up his travel mug, the smell of coffee beans making my mouth water, then kissed me goodbye and left as I ran to help Ceci brush her teeth.

He hadn't said a word. Hadn't asked me to stop what I was doing and sit down so we could talk. Hadn't said a real goodbye even. That final kiss had been brief, nothing special to remember him by. There had been no sign, no opportunity for me to change his mind, and I could barely cope with my anger now as I thought of how unfair he'd been. He should have told me.

I slammed on my brakes, swearing loudly as a cyclist veered in front of me, then sat back, mouth agape, as he flipped me the finger, as if the fault had been mine. Had it? Had I been so wrapped up in my own thoughts that I hadn't seen what was right in front of my face?

My hands were sweating, I realised, some loud, irritating pop song blaring out of the radio, though I couldn't recall switching it on. I took a breath, holding on to the wheel, staring at the dash-board. Then slowly, ignoring the queue of traffic mounting up behind me, I moved the car forward again, scanning the edge of the road for a parking space. I needed to breathe, to collect my thoughts before I kept going. The last thing I needed right now was to get into an accident.

Spotting a space up ahead, I swung the car into it, turning off the engine and letting out a deep, shuddering sigh as I rested my head on the wheel. Was all this *my* fault? Had I been so oblivious that I hadn't seen the signs?

I closed my eyes, trying to think back over the past weeks and months, but I couldn't pinpoint a single moment when I'd thought we were headed for disaster. I'd thought we were happy. That he loved our life together. But right now, it was as if I'd walked in on him with another woman. He was like a stranger to me, the hurt he'd caused insurmountable. How could I ever tell our children that their father had chosen to leave them? The fact that he'd done this without so much as speaking to me, without bothering to seek help, go for counselling, try anything that might have made his apparently miserable life better was unforgivable. He'd taken the easy route out and now I was left having to clear up after him. However would I manage?

My phone rang from inside my handbag on the passenger seat, and I grabbed it, terrified that it would be more bad news. It was all too much. I looked at the screen and saw my home number flash up, and knew before answering that it would be my mother. She'd already called twice, double-checking what time I'd be home.

'Mum, hi,' I said, pressing the phone to my ear and leaning back against the headrest. 'I'm on my way. Is everything all right?'

'Oh, are you?' she said, the relief in her voice palpable. 'Yes, everything's fine, darling, but I am getting anxious about Daddy,' she said, referring to my father. 'He's due his medicine in a little while, but he won't remember to take it. How is Drew, love?' she added quickly, as if she'd suddenly remembered why she was there.

'He's... he's having to stay in. He's had an accident. Look, don't tell the kids anything – I don't want them to worry. I'm sure he'll be fine,' I said, wondering if I believed that or if I was just trying to play pretend.

I looked through the windscreen, watching the sky turning darker, the street lights shining down. Amelie should be showing off her trophy right now. I wondered how long it would be before she'd get another chance at the gold. If Drew would be awake to see it.

'I'm sure he's in the best place,' Mum said. 'Try not to worry.'

I heard a yell in the background that sounded like Amelie and hoped it wasn't another fight between her and Cecilia.

'I'll be back soon,' I said, cutting the call before I had to hear the familiar panic in my mum's voice as she tried to handle my daughters. As much as she wanted to help, it wasn't fair to expect her to manage all four children at her age. And she was probably right that Dad wouldn't remember his meds. He was so used to her doing everything for him, I doubted he remembered how to choose his own clothes anymore. She'd taken care of him ever since I was a child and he'd fallen from some scaffolding, breaking his back and injuring his head badly. He'd learned to walk again, though the process had been slow and painful, but he'd never regained his strength, nor been able to return to work. For as long as I could remember, he'd been a quiet man, kind and sweet, always sleeping in an armchair as my mum rushed around him, looking after me and my sister Daisy, picking up the slack. It wasn't fair for me to expect her to take on my responsibilities when she had enough of her own to manage. Chewing my lip, I turned the key and rejoined the stream of traffic.

It would have been nice for Gemma to offer to help out with the kids so that I could stay with Drew. I'd seen the disapproval on her face when I told her I had to leave, though I suspected she was glad not to have to make small talk with me, but I didn't know what else she expected me to do. Gemma lived a life free from responsibilities. She was able to sleep when she wanted, do what she liked, constantly moving from one minimum-wage job to the next with no thought of making a life for herself, no effort to better herself.

She had no one to care for, no duties that couldn't be left behind. She couldn't possibly understand what it meant to have the weight of responsibility I had to cope with on her shoulders. To have her judge me for choosing to leave my comatose husband in the care of doctors so I could go home and do both my job and his was quite frankly insulting. Besides, I knew as well as she did that she wanted to stay with Drew. She would never have left him, even if I'd begged her to trade places with me.

I pulled into my road, taking in the sight of the smart white townhouses, the tree-lined pavement and wrought-iron fences, though even the sight of the home I loved was unable to draw a smile from me today. There was something about coming home, knowing I lived here, that made my shoulders relax every time, a warmth spreading through me as I counted my blessings. But tonight, that relief was countered by unease. I didn't dare to consider my future, what might come next. I couldn't face it.

I parked up, trying not to let myself feel guilty for the fact that I wasn't by my husband's side, and headed inside, bracing myself against the noise that hit me as soon as I opened the front door. I paused, trying to separate the sounds. Ceci was singing at the top of her lungs from upstairs, a tuneless babbling melody with no real words that I knew would last for hours. Rufus was crying loudly, shouting something about a boat, and I could smell burning.

I dropped my bag on the hall table and rushed into the kitchen, seeing Mum bent forward with her hand on Rufus's shoulder, trying to console him, as smoke poured from the oven. I flung it open, coughing as I yanked on oven gloves and pulled a charred black thing from inside it. Mum turned, a frantic expression on her face, her eyes wide, as if she'd only just noticed the fire hazard igniting metres from her.

'Oh, Beth, you're back,' she said, her voice thick with relief.

'What is this supposed to be?' I asked, dropping the oven pan in the sink, hearing the angry hiss as the scorching metal hit the remains of the washing-up water. I flung the window wide.

'It was a pie... I'm sorry, love, I thought I'd feed the kids, but I got a bit distracted,' she said, nodding towards Rufus as he rushed across the room, straight into my arms. His hands were hot and sweaty, his face damp with tears as he pushed it into the comfort of my shirt, and I spared a fleeting thought for the state the white silk would be in when he pulled back.

'Hey, my darling, what's happened?' I asked, wrapping my arms around him. He was the quietest of my children, though often the most likely to find himself in mischief, and it wasn't often that he cried. I felt my stomach tense as I glanced sharply at my mother, hoping she hadn't frightened him by telling him that his daddy was in hospital.

'He said he was allowed to watch it,' Mum said defensively, a guilty flush spreading across her cheeks. 'But I shouldn't have agreed without checking with you first.'

'Watch what?'

'*Jaws*...' She flinched as her eyes met mine, my shock written on my face. 'Sorry, love... I didn't think. There was a lot going on.'

Rufus gave a moan against my shirt, and I squeezed him tight, sure that he'd be having nightmares for the next few nights at least. 'Why did you tell Grandma you could watch that, Roo? You know I wouldn't have said yes.'

'All my friends have seen it,' he mumbled, not lifting his face from my chest. 'I wanted to know what it was like. Max said it wasn't even that scary, and his dad lets him watch much worse things, but it *was* scary. It was horrible!'

I sighed. There was a lot I liked about the schools my children were enrolled at, but I couldn't deny there were things I wished they didn't have to be exposed to. Their friends all seemed in such a hurry to grow up, and I hated that the other parents couldn't seem to appreciate how fleeting these childhood years were. At eleven, Rufus was on the cusp of puberty, but I wasn't ready for him to rush into adolescence yet, leaving his childhood innocence behind. God knew it had been a disaster for my relationship with his brother.

'Sorry,' Mum said again, and I knew she meant it.

'It's not your fault,' I said, though I wished she'd asked me first if she wasn't sure. 'Rufus shouldn't have lied to you. You'll know better for next time,' I said, addressing them both, then forced a reassuring smile for my mum. 'You should get back to Dad – I'm sure he'll be wondering where you've got to. I'll call you a taxi.'

I sent Rufus to wash his face, promising we'd have another cuddle after dinner, then walked my mother out, wishing she didn't have to go. 'So what happened?' she asked as I pulled the front door to behind me, looking down the road for the taxi to appear. 'Is Drew okay?'

I shook my head, feeling tears spring to my eyes.

'Oh, love, what is it? Not his heart? I know how hard he works, and at his age—'

'No.' I blinked back the tears. 'It wasn't his heart. He... he did it to himself, Mum. They said he tried to hang himself.'

She gasped, and I grabbed her elbow, afraid that she might fall down the three steps to the pavement. 'Oh, Beth,' she whispered. 'Did you have any idea he might do something like this?'

'None.' I swallowed, wishing I hadn't told her. I craved her comfort, but I couldn't give in to it. I had to be strong. I couldn't let the children see me sobbing; it would frighten them. 'He's in a coma, Mum. They don't know if he'll wake up.'

She set her jaw, her eyes meeting mine. 'He *will*. It's Drew. He's strong – he'll make it through this, Beth. He will.'

I nodded, accepting the platitudes she needed to give, though I didn't know if I believed them. The taxi came round the corner and I sighed, keeping my hand on her elbow as I guided her down the steps.

'I don't want to leave you like this.' She frowned, glancing uncomfortably at the taxi.

'You have to. You should.' I forced a smile. 'Dad will be waiting, and besides, right now, there's nothing any of us can do but wait.'

She shook her head, reaching out to touch my cheek. 'This wasn't your fault. I want you to remember that, no matter what happens. This was Drew's choice. His alone. You can't let yourself feel responsible for his actions, Beth.'

'You should go, Mum. Thanks for everything.' I hugged her briefly, then stepped back, stiffening my shoulders. As difficult as it had been to see her reaction, I was glad I'd told her – I'd always hated secrets. But saying it out loud had made it feel all the more real. And I'd seen on her face just how much she wished she could stay. I wished it too. I hated having to ask for her help, but she always brought me comfort, made me feel like I had someone to lean on, and now that she was gone, I felt the weight of my responsibilities heavy on my shoulders.

I stood on the top step, waiting until I felt calm enough to go back in, needing a second to breathe, to press pause. The street was quiet, birds singing in the trees, and for a moment, I stood with my palm on the warm black lacquer of the door, pretending that nothing had changed. That I would walk inside and find the older children doing their homework, Drew reading to Ceci, the smell of a delicious home-cooked dinner filling the house, our home warm and safe and brimming with love. I sighed, brushing aside the childish fantasy and headed back inside.

'Tris?' I called, glancing into the mirror in the hall to make sure my eyes weren't red from suppressing my tears.

His music continued to blare, and I called again, louder. The music cut out, and a moment later I heard heavy footsteps as he made his way reluctantly down the stairs. I didn't want to tell the others about Drew, but Tristan was different. He was too old to mollycoddle, and I thought I should tell him that his stepdad was in hospital at the very least.

'Hi, darling,' I said, finding a smile for my handsome son, making an effort not to wince at the black eye he sported. I wished he would offer a smile in return, a hint that he was pleased to see me. After the day I'd had, I needed to feel close to him, to spend some time together and let his presence numb my fears over what was going on with Drew.

I thought over my routine, all the tasks I had to get through until I could have a moment of down time. 'Will you do me a favour and help Ceci into her pyjamas so I can sort dinner?' I asked. 'She's going to need to be in bed soon, and I still have to go through Amelie's homework with her.' I touched his arm, wanting to hug him but afraid it would upset him. He was too cool for hugs from Mum these days.

He took a step back, crossing his arms. 'You know, if you couldn't handle the responsibility, maybe you shouldn't have had so many kids,' he said coldly. 'Have you ever considered that we're not all here to serve you, Mum? That we might have other things we need to be getting on with?'

'Excuse me?' I gasped, shocked at his tone, though if his recent behaviour was anything to go by, this shouldn't have hit me so hard. 'Tristan, I'm not asking you to be a parent. Just to be a helpful member of this family. Your dad is—'

'Probably working late so he can avoid us,' he said, grabbing his trainers from the rack and shoving his man-sized feet into them. 'I'm going out. You'll have to figure it out yourself, Mum. Throw some money at the problem – that usually seems to work, doesn't it?'

'Tristan!'

He grabbed his jacket from the hook and turned, his profile hard and unfamiliar as he walked out, slamming the door behind him.

I stood frozen, the sound echoing in my ears, and willed myself not to burst into tears.

SEVEN

GEMMA

I squeezed Drew's hand, hating how it lay flat and unresponsive in my own, trying to ignore the insistent signs from my body that I was entering some kind of withdrawal, whether from chasing the dragon or just a consequence of the pills I'd crammed in before leaving my flat, I couldn't be sure. I was used to the side effects that came with my long-term reliance on codeine – the dry mouth, the stomach cramps that struck out of the blue. They were minor irritations compared to the relief the pills brought, but this felt different, more intense, and I was sure my body was trying to lead me down a path I couldn't allow myself to follow.

I glanced at the door, feeling ashamed and dirty as I released Drew's warm hand and reached for my bag, fishing around for the codeine, sliding the foil bubble pack from the cardboard sheath, running the tip of my finger over the pills one by one, counting them silently in my head, a habit I'd formed to keep me calm, though I knew it only made me look all the more crazy. I'd thrown a handful of miniature bottles of whisky into the inner compartment a few months back when I'd seen them lined up ready to throw out at work. The batch had been recalled and the supermarket had stripped them from the shelves, but I couldn't walk past without rescuing a few, just in case. It wasn't my first choice, nor even my second or third, but this was an emergency. I cracked the seal on one now, swallowing it back as I reluctantly returned the foil packet to the box without taking another pill.

A warmth spread through my veins, the whisky offering a moment of comfort. Nothing could compete with the feeling that came with the one thing I couldn't have though. No escape had ever been so blissful, so alluring. I knew I couldn't go back there, but it was all I could think about, always in my mind, even now. I was disgusted at myself. Why couldn't I be strong? I had never been strong...

I waited for the tremors to pass as I sat silently watching my brother, glad that he wasn't awake to see me. I knew he'd be disappointed, disgusted even. Drew had never been weak like me. He wouldn't have stooped so low as to let his whole life revolve around a bottle of pills, an escape from reality. Then again, here he was fighting for his life after hanging himself by the neck, so perhaps he had no right to judge after all. I shook my head, hating my thoughts, wishing for silence, longing to escape from myself. It was something I yearned for daily.

Leaning forward, I rested my head on the edge of the mattress, staring up at Drew's strong jawline, the dark stubble that coated it. Someone would have to shave him tomorrow, I realised. He didn't like a beard, said it made him feel unkempt. I sighed, hoping the hospital would provide the necessities. If not, Beth could bring his things in, and I would take care of him, the way he'd always done for me. All my life, it had been Drew who had stepped up for me when nobody else would. Drew who'd been my protector, the person I trusted with my life, who I would give anything for, *do* anything for. He had looked after me, watched over me, and when he'd met Beth, he'd instantly taken on the same role with her. Caring. Providing. Protecting. It was just in his nature to do it, and as far as I could tell, that would never change. He cared so much... too much, I thought now.

I took his hand again just as the door to his room swung open and a nurse bustled in, stopping when she saw me. 'Oh,' she said, her tone clipped and put out. 'I didn't realise you were here. You know visiting hours ended thirty minutes ago?'

I raised an eyebrow, fixing her with a look I hoped communicated exactly what I thought of her visiting hours. 'Thanks, but I'm not going anywhere,' I replied, turning my attention back to Drew.

'I'm afraid you'll have to. I'm sorry, I know it's difficult, but it's the rule, and it's not fair if we break it for you. You won't be the only one having to leave a loved one this evening.'

I ignored her, not wanting to waste my breath on arguing when I'd already made up my mind. She stood, her hand wrapped around a thermometer, staring at me as if she expected me to jump up and fall in line, then, with a huff, she turned and walked out, muttering something about going to get the ward sister. I didn't care. Let her come. Let the whole fucking world come. They weren't going to make me move.

A few moments later, I heard footsteps approaching, and my body tensed, rallying for a fight.

'Hi there, I'm the ward sister, Janice. May I ask if you're Mr Spencer-Rhodes' next of kin?'

'I'm his sister.'

'I see, right... I have his wife down as next of kin. I'm afraid visiting hours are over, my love, but your brother will be in good hands here. You can come back between eight and ten in the morning if you like,' she added.

I turned my head slowly to look at her, meeting her nervous eyes. 'Like I told the nurse, I'm not going anywhere. I'm staying right here with Drew. It's what he would want. I can give him that much at least,' I muttered.

'I really must insist.'

I turned my face away, my spine straight and stiff.

She sighed, clearly weighing up how far to push me. Finally she spoke. 'Right... well, I'm afraid I don't have a bed for you. If you're really determined to stay, you'll have to make do with the chair.'

I held back a smile, relieved that I'd won this battle and done right by my brother, for once. 'Believe me,' I replied, not taking my eyes from Drew's face. 'I've had far worse.'

EIGHT

BETH

I crept out of Amelie's bedroom, casting a final glance at her peaceful sleeping face, relieved that I'd finally managed to encourage them all to wind down after their hectic evening with Grandma.

Ceci was fast asleep in her own room, her arm wrapped around her pillow, her music box playing, soothing and soft. Ever since her stint in hospital last year, she'd been so much tougher to settle at night, needing me to stay with her, stroking her hair as the white noise filled the room, blotting out the sounds of the house, the road outside. She had no way of explaining what she was afraid of, but I could guess. Her fears were tinged with memories of nurses with sharp needles, doctors with deep voices who loomed over her speaking words she couldn't begin to comprehend.

I had had my own share of sleepless nights since her operation, the memories fighting to get free when I closed my eyes. It was getting easier for me now, but for Ceci, I knew it would take so much longer to process. I didn't mind waiting for her to drift off before I left her if that was what she needed. It was the least she deserved.

Rufus had ended up in my bed, crashing diagonally across the mattress an hour previously, and though Drew would usually carry him through to his own room when he came up, tonight he wouldn't be here to help. At the best of times, Roo made for a fidgety bedfellow. Tonight there would no doubt be nightmares after he'd watched that film. It was going to be testing, especially when I was already ready to collapse from exhaustion.

I tiptoed down the stairs, going to the front door and opening it, stepping out into the chilly night and staring down the street. It was past ten and Tristan still wasn't home. I'd called his mobile three times, but each time it went straight to voicemail, and now I didn't know if I should be angry or worried. Tristan had never been the type of child to get into fights at school, but yesterday, he'd come down to dinner sullen and silent, sporting a fresh purple bruise on his cheek, his eye swollen almost shut. I'd been shocked, devastated to think that someone had laid a hand on him, but he'd insisted it was an accident, refusing to tell me who had done it. It was obvious he was lying, but I didn't know how to get him to speak to me. If he was being bullied, I knew how hard it would be for a boy as strong and confident as he was to admit to it.

I'd sat at the dinner table, unable to eat, the little ones staring at their older brother as I tried to press him into telling me the truth so I could help. Then Drew's voice had cut across mine, telling me to drop it. Our eyes had met, and I'd wondered if I was letting my fears take over, becoming hysterical, so I did what he asked, shut my mouth, though I hadn't been able to stop thinking about it. I'd hoped it was just a one-off, a rite of passage somehow, but now it was late, and Tristan was nowhere to be seen.

The dark sky was cloudy, the air damp, and I could feel a storm building, the night thick with expectation and electric energy. Where *was* he? I felt sick at the thought of him lying beaten and broken somewhere. He'd done martial arts classes since he was young, but even I knew that in the heat of the moment, those learned skills might not stand up to raw aggression. And kids these days carried knives...

I walked back inside, my chest tight with terror. I wondered if I should call his friends' homes, speak to their parents, find out if he was there, but the notion made my stomach squirm uncomfortably. I didn't want gossip to start up about my family, my inability to keep track of my own son, and that was exactly what would happen if I picked up the phone now. Besides, his friends had curfews on weeknights – they would all be safe at home, and if Tristan had been there, he would have been given his marching orders by now. He should be here. The old wives' saying *bad things happen in threes* popped into my head, and I wondered if I was about to experience that myself. Tristan's bruised face, Drew's coma... What could possibly come next?

I walked into the kitchen, scraping off the dinner plates and stacking them in the dishwasher, wishing I'd done this before getting the kids to bed. Then again, it served as a reasonable distraction, and right now, that was just what I needed. Though Drew had worked long hours all through our relationship, he'd rarely spent nights away, and I'd never had to get used to being the only adult in the house. It felt different. Now, every little thing would be down to me to deal with, my job to fix. I was the sole parent, the sole protector, and the realisation made my mind instantly turn to everything that could go wrong. Drew was always the one who knew how to cheer Amelie up when she'd had a bad day at school, making her laugh with silly stories and jokes. He and Rufus shared a special bond, and I knew it wouldn't be long before they all missed his presence. Raising four children was a full-on job that between the pair of us we always balanced so well, but without him, I was lost, and already I longed for my teammate to fall back on.

I turned on the dishwasher, then ran a bowl of water to wash the fragile glasses and pans, and as I plunged a glass into the water, I was struck with fear that this might become my future. That if Drew didn't recover, I was going to be alone. A single mum with no income. The panic began to rise in my throat, and I tried to focus on the hot water against my hands, taking slow, measured breaths, working methodically. How would we survive if Drew didn't wake up? How would I feed my children? I could feel my heart racing as I realised I was in a situation I'd spent my entire life trying to avoid.

Although Drew had thrown himself into his work, he hadn't ever found the motivation, or perhaps the courage, to start his own business. Instead, he'd worked for his old school friend, Matthew, and together they'd built up *his* business. I was always saying they needed to come up with a partnership contract, at the very least, but Drew had maintained his stance that there was no need. He was paid generously, had a lot of input in the decision-making, and zero responsibility if it should all fall apart. And he trusted Matthew. I'd always felt uneasy about the arrangement, but Drew was right: he earned a more than comfortable salary, which paid for our Notting Hill mortgage and our children's schools and enabled me to stay at home rather than having to go out and find work, something I was immensely grateful for. But his choice to keep himself in the position of employee rather than entrepreneur meant that he had no claim on the business, no shares to sell. If he died, we would be left with nothing...

I took a breath, feeling the anger hot in my veins. Did he even care? Had he spared a thought for what his actions could cost his family? Or was he too selfish to think of what we'd have to face when he was gone? I felt my hand tighten involuntarily around the glass I was washing in the soapy water, my eyes squeezed shut as I heard the roar of blood in my ears.

A sudden stinging pain made me snap my eyes open, seeing the water turn claret.

'Shit,' I muttered, letting the shattered glass sink and pulling my hand back to see a long bleeding slice running along my palm. I grabbed a clean cloth from the drawer, holding it tight against my skin, hoping I wasn't going to throw up. What if I needed stitches? I couldn't go to the hospital now. How did people do this stuff, manage a family with nobody else to fall back on? I hadn't signed up for this life.

Feeling queasy, I pulled the cloth cautiously away from my shaking hand, sighing with relief as I saw that the bleeding had stopped and the cut wasn't too deep. It would be sore, but I would manage. But what if it *had* been bad? I thought again, my mind consumed with fear and fury.

I heard a key in the front door and turned, seeing the silhouette of my fifteen-year-old son through the glass before he stepped inside.

'Oh, thank goodness,' I muttered beneath my breath, glancing again at my hand before walking as calmly as I could into the hallway. I was determined to keep my cool this time, not wanting to do anything that might get Tristan's back up. There was no denying he was prone to oversensitive reactions these days.

'Hi,' I said as he stepped through the door.

He grunted in response, kicking off his shoes and tossing his jacket over the hook.

'It's quite late, Tris. I was starting to worry. Are you okay?'

'I'm fine.'

'I'm glad,' I said quietly, scrutinising his face for fresh cuts or bruises and feeling relieved when I saw nothing new. 'I missed you... Where have you been?' I asked gently.

'Out.'

I pursed my lips, watching the way he avoided my eyes, his head bowed low. I could sense his disappointment at finding me here waiting and felt sure he would rather have slipped in without having to deal with my attentions. But that wasn't a relationship I could accept. Not with him.

'Are you hungry? I could heat up some leftovers for you,' I offered, hoping to appeal to his stomach. He seemed to be constantly in search of food, and it was usually the best way to grab his attention.

He shook his head, still not meeting my eyes, already making for the stairs.

'Tristan,' I said softly. 'Won't you at least come and sit with me for a little while? I'd like to talk to you. We used to do that all the time, don't you remember? You always loved staying up with me after the little ones went to bed – said it was the best time to really talk without distractions. And there are some things you should know,' I added, wondering how I could begin to explain to him what was happening with Drew when I hardly understood myself.

'I'm not in the mood for a chat. And I'm not a child, Mum. Things change. It's just the way it goes.'

'They don't have to,' I replied quietly, disappointment flooding through me.

I watched his shoulders stiffen as he jogged up the stairs, his long legs taking them two at a time. I heard his door close, shutting me out, and closed my eyes, breathing in deeply. I didn't know how to get through to him, and I had an uneasy feeling that something was wrong, more than just the normal teenage dramas. This wasn't Tristan. The boy I had known would never have treated my feelings so carelessly. He had always been so loving.

I turned away, intending to go back to the kitchen, then paused, seeing his leather jacket on the hook. Without thinking, I slipped my hand into a pocket, pulling out the contents. A pack of gum. A pair of sunglasses. I put them back and reached into the other pocket before I could question the morality of my actions. A handful of paper – receipts for sandwiches, clipped cinema tickets from two weeks ago – and finally the smooth, hard form of his phone. I glanced up the stairs, knowing that I was crossing a line, yet feeling as if I had no choice. I was worried about my son – what mother could resist?

I glanced down at the lock screen, trying to figure out what he might use as a code. Remembering the one he'd created as a child for the family computer, I bit my lip, typing it in and subduing a smile as it unlocked. It was the date we'd bought his leopard gecko, Harry, when he was seven. The sweet-natured reptile still lived in a tank in Tristan's room, and I loved that a part of my son, however small, was still the excited little boy who couldn't wait to take care of his own pet.

My thumb hovered over the apps, unsure what I was even looking for. I clicked onto his emails, scrolling down, seeing very little. He clearly didn't use email much. I navigated to his social media, finding the accounts logged in but lacking in clues. A photo of him on a climbing wall, taken three months previously, was the last thing he'd posted. I clicked out, finally navigating to his messages, an act that made my stomach tense. I didn't want to do this, and yet now that I'd begun, I couldn't seem to stop. I glanced up the stairs again, listening for sounds of movement, sure that it wouldn't be long before he came looking for his phone.

There were a few messages from his friends, names I recognised, asking if he was coming to rugby practice, what was going on, why he'd missed a match. It looked like he'd left a lot of messages unanswered over the last few weeks. He hadn't told *me* he'd missed anything. That was the kind of thing I would have expected him to ask permission to do. Had he been going to any of his sports sessions? I made up my mind to call around his coaches in the morning and find out.

There were several messages in a row from his best friend, Guy, asking where he'd been, why he hadn't turned up to meet him, and I frowned. I'd assumed that in avoiding me, he was choosing to spend more time with his friends, but this didn't make sense. I scrolled back further, clicking on a message from someone he'd labelled only as X. As I scanned the short conversation, my heart froze in my chest.

The initial message from X read: *Come to Barnsbury at 10. Someone will meet you at the station and take you to him.*

Tris had replied: *I'm not sure I want to do this.*

X had responded with: *It will be fine. Smooth as, mate. Don't lose your shit. I'll see you soon.*

I stared at the screen, my palms sweating, panic coursing through me, noting that the date was over a week ago. I didn't know how my son had managed to do it, how he'd sought out the truth without coming to me, but there was only one reason I could think of that he would travel to Barnsbury. He had found his birth father. And he'd gone to visit him in prison.

NINE

GEMMA

Day Two

The incessant sound of talking and laughter from the nurses' station was grating on my nerves, and I rubbed the tight muscles on the back of my neck, trying to work out the aches and knots. I had somehow managed to fall into a deep sleep not long after the altercation with the ward sister last night – no doubt due to the painkillers making my mind swim and the shock of the day's events taking its toll. I'd passed out with my head resting on Drew's mattress, his hand clasped in mine as if I could hold on to him, keep him from slipping away somewhere I couldn't reach him.

Sometime after midnight, I'd woken with a start to find that a different nurse had come in, along with a group of serious-looking doctors, muttering low assessments between themselves, none of them making any effort to bring me into the conversation. I'd heard words that made me sit up straight – *scan... CT... brain activity* – but when I'd pushed for answers, I'd been blanked. They'd clearly been told that I wasn't the next of kin, and it rankled that they would withhold information from me when it was obvious that I was the only person who cared enough to stay.

After fifteen minutes or so, they'd left in a flurry of aftershave and energy, and as irritated as I was, I was relieved that they seemed to be doing something – they hadn't given up trying, and I was grateful for that. By the time they'd gone, I was wide awake, and as the hours ticked by – a patient screaming out for pain relief every now and then, the sounds of nurses wheeling medication trolleys up the corridors, Drew's monitors beeping, peppering my thoughts with anxiety – I lost any hope of getting any more sleep. Instead, I worried. I waited. And I tried to pretend that my mind was entirely occupied with my brother, rather than being drawn back to the cravings I couldn't seem to subdue.

The sun had been up for an hour or so, and part of me had expected that after his long deep sleep, Drew might open his eyes, yawn and smile, surprised but happy to find me here. That this awful night could be forgotten and we could go back to how things were before. But of course, life didn't work that way. I was stupid to even hope. I cradled the mug of coffee a kind healthcare assistant had brought in for me, nibbling at a corner of toast, though my stomach protested, having gone far too long without food. I kept trying to force it down though – I needed to keep my strength up for him, to keep going, as hard as this was. He would have done it for me.

My phone rang from the bedside cabinet, and I reached for it, seeing Beth's name and feeling a rush of anger. It was the first I'd heard from her since she'd walked out last night, and though I had no wish to speak to her, I still found it hard to believe she had waited so long to call and check on her husband. I accepted the call, tossing the cold toast back onto the paper plate and leaning back in my uncomfortable chair.

'Hello?' I said, hearing the cool anger in my voice and doing nothing to hide it.

'Gemma, hi, it's Beth. Are you still with Drew?'

I'd told her last night I would stay with him. Not that she'd made any attempt to offer. Nor had she asked if I would look after the kids so she could trade places with me. I would have refused, of course – I couldn't have coped with leaving him – but the fact that she hadn't suggested it made me think even less of her, if that were possible.

'Of course I am,' I replied, hearing the background noise of my nieces and nephews, shouts and laughter and traffic. 'Where are you?' I asked pointedly. Not that I wanted her here with me, fussing and pacing and making the situation all the more stressful, but still, it was coming up for nine and she clearly wasn't in any rush to get to the hospital.

'On the school run. Late,' she added. 'Rufus, wait! Look left *and* right, for God's sake, there's a bike!'

I bit my lip, considering cutting the call so I didn't have to listen to her trying and failing to multitask.

'How's Drew doing? Any change?' I heard her ask, keeping her voice low in a way that made me sure she hadn't told the children yet.

Part of me could understand that. I didn't know how I would approach the conversation if it were down to me. I'd never been good at knowing which details to share and which to hold back. I'd put my foot in it multiple times in the past when the kids had asked me to explain something, and I still hadn't forgotten the look on Drew's face when he caught me fumbling my words after Amelie confronted me, asking what would happen if her sister died on the operating table during her heart surgery last year. Would Cecilia go to heaven? Or would the fact that she'd purposely smashed Mummy's favourite vase when she hadn't been allowed a biscuit be enough to make her get sent to hell?

I'd been blindsided, wanting to say whatever she needed to hear but knowing that if she were anything like I was as a child, she'd see straight through a lie. I'd settled on the truth, what *I* felt was the truth anyway, and told her that of course Ceci wouldn't die that day, but when she did, hopefully as an old lady, I didn't think there was any place she would go. That I believed that after death, there was nothing, and things would be just the same as they had been before we were born. No awareness. No fear. Simply gone.

Amelie had nodded, looking far older than her years, and then left the room, quiet and lost in her thoughts. I'd been pleased with myself, sure that I had handled the tough question well, replying honestly, yet not morbidly so, but then Drew had given me a talk-ing-to about the concept of sugar-coating, and I'd vowed to keep my opinions to myself from then on. I clearly wasn't cut out for parenting.

'I don't know how he is,' I replied, glancing at Drew now. 'They won't tell me anything. He's still not woken up, if that's what you're asking.'

'But what are they doing? Has he been for the scan they mentioned?'

'No. And like I said, they won't tell me anything. Why don't you call the desk and ask the nurses? I'm sure they'll answer your questions.'

'I have, twice but there was no answer.'

'Welcome to my world,' I muttered beneath my breath.

'What was that? Sorry, it's so loud out here. Ceci, hold my hand please, darling! Sorry, Gemma, what were you saying?'

I sighed. 'You need to bring in some things for him. Shaving stuff. Pyjamas. He shouldn't have to be in this awful hospital gown. He would hate it.'

'Oh, of course, yes, I can do that.' There was a pause, and I wondered if she had hoped to avoid coming back here so soon.

'Good,' I said, breaking the silence. 'I have to go.'

'Home? Or are you staying at the hospital?'

'I'm not going anywhere,' I said, rubbing my temple with the tips of my fingers, wishing she would stop talking and leave me in peace.

'Right,' she replied awkwardly. 'I'll speak to you soon then. Call me if you think of anything else he might need.'

I hung up without replying, slamming the phone down hard on the mattress, glancing at Drew, half hopeful that the impact would have disturbed his slumber, shocked him into consciousness.

He didn't so much as flinch. I shook my head, feeling dizzy

with exhaustion, a bitter taste in my mouth as I replayed the conversation in my head.

'If there's anything else he needs,' I muttered, vitriol coating my words. It was too little and far too late.

I stood up, folding my arms as I walked over to the window, looking out over the car park at the people arriving at the hospital. I wished Beth could understand how badly she'd messed up. If she'd asked that question weeks ago, cared about Drew's needs even a little bit, perhaps he wouldn't be here now.

And I wouldn't be stuck in this room waiting to discover if my brother, the one person in this world who cared about me, would live or die.

TEN

BETH

I hung around outside the school gates far longer than I should have, pasting on a false smile as I chatted to the other mothers, agreeing to meet up for a yoga class or a coffee date soon. I felt a fraud, making small talk, smiling brightly, my hair done perfectly, my outward appearance unruffled as my husband lay in a coma across town. I knew it would come out eventually, but I was in no rush to reveal the humiliating truth. That Drew, the handsome, confident man I had always been so proud to call my husband, would rather die than spend another day with me – that the life I loved was in jeopardy. And though I knew I should be there by his side, doing my duty despite his betrayal, the truth was I was terrified to go back to that hospital room.

Sandra, Drew's secretary, had called before I'd even had a chance to brush my teeth this morning, asking after him and explaining that she was doing her best to contact Matthew but that he was away on a wellness retreat in Thailand, where phones weren't permitted, and she was finding it hard to get hold of him.

I was disappointed to hear that he wasn't around – I wanted to speak to him. He saw Drew every day in the office and the two of them were good friends, always looking out for each other, going to play tennis or for a quick pint after work. I wanted to hear

Matthew say that he hadn't known either, that he'd been just as blindsided by what Drew had done, so that I could stop feeling like I'd missed something crucial, something obvious that could have prevented it from happening. Matthew would understand. If he'd known Drew was struggling, he would have told me, but he'd never said a word. I'd arrived at the school feeling shaky and desperate for distraction.

I laughed along with Martha as she told a story about her window cleaner catching her getting dressed and flashing her a wink, how she hoped it meant that she still 'had it', and then I had to congratulate Julia, whose daughter Raya had predictably taken Amelie's trophy at the swimming competition last night. I made up an excuse about a family emergency, pretending I wasn't crushed that Amelie's opportunity had been stolen from her by none other than her own father.

I'd have stayed there all day pretending, wasting time, had they been willing, but one by one they rushed away, talking about appointments with decorators and personal trainers, fittings for new clothes, until at last I found myself alone and knew I could put off the inevitable no longer. I took the longest route back home, making a checklist in my mind about what to pack for Drew. I couldn't make up an excuse not to take a bag for him, but I was afraid that once I set foot in his hospital room, I wouldn't be able to leave. If Gemma wanted to go and get some rest, she might expect me to take over her vigil, and I couldn't. I just could not do that.

I'd assumed he would have woken by now, but the fact that he hadn't made me feel like I was stuck in some sort of limbo, unsure which direction I was about to be pulled in. I parked in a space across the road from the house, and after dithering for a few moments, using an old tissue to rub away at a spot of dirt I'd been meaning to clean off the windscreen for weeks, I got out and went inside. I could hear music coming from the kitchen as I opened the front door, and I sighed, annoyed that Tristan hadn't bothered to turn it off before leaving for school. I bet our neighbours, a retired couple to the left and a single female artist to the right, rued the day we had moved in and destroyed their peaceful existence.

I walked into the kitchen to turn off the stereo and stopped, seeing Tristan hunched over a mug of coffee, a book open in front of him on the countertop, a pastry on a plate beside it. He looked up, a flash of guilt crossing his still boyish features, and I folded my arms, instantly annoyed that he'd obviously decided to play truant. I knew I should never have trusted him to leave the house last. He refused to walk with his younger brother now that Rufus had joined him at secondary school, and I accepted that, not wanting to force him to have to take care of Roo. I was happy to let Tris walk in with his friends, making a detour myself to make sure that Rufus got there safely, but I couldn't believe he would be so sneaky. He'd put his school shoes on right in front of me, and I'd assumed he would leave as soon as he'd packed his lunch.

He cleared his throat, wiping at the sugar on his lips with the back of his hand. 'What are you doing here? I thought you had an exercise class,' he said, having the good grace to close the novel, his fingers tense as they gripped the cover.

'I could ask you the same thing. Why aren't you in school? You're an hour late!'

'I... I felt sick.'

I glanced at the sticky bun half eaten on the plate beside the mug of coffee, and his eyes followed mine. He didn't say anything, and suddenly my mind went to the fears I'd been having lately, the suspicion that he might be being bullied. Why else would he be here? Tristan had always loved school and had never been the type to skive off. He was so conscious of rules, and I'd never had to worry about him falling in with the wrong crowd, letting me down. If he was avoiding his responsibilities, there had to be a good reason, and it was my job to discover exactly what was bothering him. The unsettling messages I'd read the night before still played on my mind, but I couldn't imagine how, or indeed why, he would have searched out his biological father. Drew had been his dad for so long now, and we never spoke of Lee. There had to be another explanation for the texts, and I was determined that today I would find out what it was.

I felt my anger fade as I walked around the breakfast bar, replaced by motherly love and concern. I pressed a hand to his forehead, more as an excuse to touch him, to remind myself that he was real, than because I actually believed his flustered excuse. My fingers lingered on his cool skin and I had to stop myself from moving closer to draw him into my arms.

'Take the day off then,' I said gently. 'You can set up camp on the sofa and I'll make you some soup in a bit.'

'Don't you have to go to your dancing thing?'

'Zumba? No, not today. It... it was cancelled.' I thought of Drew, of Gemma waiting for pyjamas, a razor. What difference did it make if he had a bit of stubble now? He could grow a full beard and he wouldn't know. He'd made it clear he didn't care about anything anymore. Why should I rush around waiting on him when my son, my sweet firstborn, needed me so much more and was actually conscious enough to appreciate my efforts?

I managed to form my mouth into a smile, taking my hand from his forehead, brushing his hair back from his face. His eyes were guarded, cautious, and I wasn't surprised. It wasn't like me to ignore school, classes, responsibilities. I knew what it took to make it in life, and sitting around watching TV while your classmates overtook you wasn't going to cut it. But to have my son to myself for the day, to finally get him to open up... I couldn't throw away such a chance. And though I hated to admit it to myself, perhaps avoiding the hospital was part of my motivation.

I let my fingers move gently to the bruise on his cheek, waiting for him to look up at me.

'Tell me what happened,' I urged gently. 'Are you having trouble with the other boys at school? Because you know I can always go and speak to the head; their parents too. You don't have to deal with it alone, Tris – you can always rely on me.'

His face hardened and he stood so fast I thought he was falling, ducking away from my touch and grabbing his backpack from the floor by the bar stool. 'You know what, I'm feeling better. I think I'll go in after all. I'll see you later.'

'Tris, wait!' I said, kicking myself for being so impatient. I should have waited until he was ready to talk before trying to prise answers from him. 'Don't go. I... I have to tell you something. About your dad.'

I paused, watching his face closely, wondering if I'd see a flash of guilt, if he'd assume I meant Lee, not Drew.

He paused in the kitchen doorway. 'What about him?' he said, his voice bored, cold.

I faltered, unsure how to explain now that I finally had his attention. 'Tristan, something happened to him at work, and... There's no easy way to say it, but you're old enough to know the truth. I don't want you to tell your brother and sisters though, okay?'

His face blanched and he took a small step forward. 'Is he...?'

I took a shaky breath. 'He's in a coma. He has been since yesterday evening. I don't know what's going to happen.' I was trying to be as honest with him as I could manage. I felt numb as I spoke the words, surprised at how I could say such things without falling apart. Perhaps because it still felt so unreal. The Drew I knew would never have been in this position. It didn't feel like *my* life, *my* husband.

'What happened to him?' Tristan asked, his lips trembling as his eyes met mine.

I stared back, not wanting to say, yet unable to lie to his face. 'He made an attempt on his life, Tris. Don't ask me why, because I just don't know. But they think... they said that's what happened.'

He swallowed, looking down at his shoes, frozen as he let my words sink in. I worried that I had frightened him. Had I made a mistake in telling him so much? Maybe I should have held back, not been quite so honest, made up an accident to explain the fact that his father was in a coma. It had been a terrifying thing for *me* to hear; I shouldn't have put that on his shoulders too.

Slowly he raised his eyes to meet mine. 'Will he be okay?' he asked, his voice hoarse.

'I... I don't know, darling. They're doing tests, I think. They're trying their best.'

He nodded, and for a moment he looked like the little boy I recognised, his eyes wide and fearful, glistening with the tears he refused to give in to. I stepped forward, intending to hug him, but before I could reach him, he lurched back, holding his hand up. 'No,' he said, his voice full of venom. 'Don't touch me.'

'Tristan...'

He spun without another word, and I watched, my heart breaking, as he stormed out of the house, slamming the door behind him.

ELEVEN

GEMMA

My head snapped up, my heart thumping hard in my chest, as two men walked into the room. I jumped up from the chair, realising I must have somehow fallen asleep again. My neck ached and I could smell the sweat on my clothes, my body still feverish, withdrawing from the stupid mistake I'd let myself make again. It had been more than sixty hours since I'd given in and turned up at Jason's door asking for just one more try of that mysterious glass pipe, and I was surprised that I still felt as rough as I had yesterday. Even the codeine hadn't taken the edge off the symptoms, though I'd swallowed more than I ever normally would to try and dull the ache. I'd hoped it would have got easier by now.

'Oh, sorry to startle you, miss,' the closest man said, pausing as he took in my reaction. 'We've just come to take the patient down to radiology.'

'For a scan? Can I come?'

'I don't see why not,' he began, before a woman's voice interrupted from behind him.

'I'm afraid that won't be possible. Only next of kin allowed unfortunately. I'm sure you understand.' I gathered from her dark blue uniform that she was the ward sister for the day shift.

'His wife isn't here,' I retorted as the woman stepped around the two men, who looked more than a little uncomfortable to be caught in the middle. 'I, however, *am*. I'm his sister, and he'd want me to go with him.'

'I'm sorry, but it's not possible. Now, gentlemen, let's not delay. The radiologist is waiting.'

They nodded, avoiding looking in my direction as they unlocked the wheels of Drew's hospital bed and guided it slowly towards the door.

'There's a nurse waiting for you by the desk. He's got Mr Spencer-Rhodes' notes and will accompany you.'

They muttered in muted agreement, and I watched, feeling out of control, like a trapped animal. The room seemed too big, too empty without Drew here, and I turned from the vacant bed space to find the ward sister waiting expectantly.

'They'll be quite some time,' she told me. 'And it's my understanding that you've been here all night. This might be a good time for you to pop home. Get some rest. Eat something. Have a nice hot shower.'

I shook my head. 'I'm not leaving.'

She shrugged infuriatingly, as if she didn't much care either way. 'Gemma – that is your name, isn't it?' When I didn't respond, she continued. 'Look, your brother might be here a while. Days, weeks, months even. We don't know yet. And you're going to burn out if you don't take care of yourself. It's helpful for you to visit, but he's not conscious right now, and he won't thank you if he wakes up to find you exhausted and ready to collapse. I know how hard this must be for you, but you have to find the strength to walk away. To trust us to take care of him.'

I shook my head. 'I'll go down to the café. Get a coffee or something,' I said, unwilling to admit how desperately I wanted to leave the empty room now that Drew was gone from it. 'But I'm not going home. Not yet. I have to wait, to see if—' I broke off, and the sister nodded, her eyes softening.

'Okay then. Maybe step out and get some fresh air. It's very stuffy in here,' she added, and I wondered if she could see the sheen of sweat on my forehead. I longed for a long soak in a deep bubble bath, but there was no way I would leave Drew here alone.

I waited for her to go then picked up my bag, half scared to leave for fear that they wouldn't let me back onto the ward when I returned. I felt guilty for walking away, but the ward sister was right: it made no difference to Drew. It did to me though. I couldn't shake the thought that it was partly because of me that he was here. My failure to fight against the addictions that had controlled my life, to be the person he needed me to be. I loved him more than anything, but had I been there for him once in his adult life? I couldn't pinpoint a moment when our relationship hadn't revolved around his need to make things okay for me, and me leaning on him harder than he could cope with. I'd broken his spirit, given him no sign that I might be ready to turn my life around, despite knowing the pain I caused him every day. He had always cared too much, and I had let him, and now we were here. I couldn't walk away even if I wanted to. My guilt was a chain attached to his hospital bed, forcing me to step up and for once in my life be the one to take care of him.

I walked quickly down to the café, nervous energy coursing through my body, making me fidget as I stood in the long queue. I ordered a sandwich and a coffee and took them out into the cool morning air, where I sat on a bench, putting them down beside me. Then I reached into my bag and pulled out a pack of cigarettes, lighting one and breathing in deeply, tilting my face up to the clear blue sky. It felt like I hadn't been outside in days, rather than the mere fifteen hours it had really been. I felt dirty and ill, my body aching, my head thick and throbbing.

I tried to watch the flow of people coming and going from the hospital, focus on the sound of the old people chatting by the taxi rank, the ambulance sirens echoing from somewhere nearby, but my thoughts kept travelling back to Drew, in there somewhere where I couldn't get to him. What if he woke up inside one of those awful MRI machines and panicked? I would hate it if it were me. I would feel so trapped. If the tables were turned, he'd never have let them take me without him by his side. Once again, I'd let him down, been too weak to fight for him the way he always had for me. I wasn't the sister he deserved. It made my stomach churn to think of how much he had been hurting, how many opportunities I might have missed to stop him ending up here.

I took a last deep drag of my cigarette then dropped the butt on the pavement, stubbing it out with the toe of my trainer, ignoring the loud tut of the woman on the next bench. I shoved the untouched sandwich packet into my cavernous shoulder bag, glugged down the scorching hot coffee and headed back inside. I felt too far from him out here, as if anything might happen and I wouldn't be there to stop it.

Instead of heading straight up to the ward, I detoured towards the radiology department, glancing through the double doors, hoping to see something that might bring me comfort – Drew sitting up on the bed, talking and laughing, or even lying there where I could check on him – but there was nothing. The corridor beyond was empty, and when I tried the door, I found it was locked, operated on a buzzer system. Defeated, I took the lift back up to the third floor, making my way back to Drew's room and slipping inside without being seen by the nurses. I slumped down in the chair beside the empty bed space and waited.

Where the hell was Beth? It had been ages since we'd spoken on the phone, and I knew the kids would have been dropped off at school long ago. She should be here by now. The fact that she wasn't made me all the more certain that my views on my brother's wife were entirely accurate. I had seen from the very beginning of their relationship how attracted she was to his money, his success. It has been Beth who had insisted they buy a house in one of the most expensive roads in London, rather than do as Drew suggested, which was to buy in the countryside so he could commute in and have a far more manageable mortgage to fork out for. I hated how she pushed herself forward in every situation, every event, always desperate to be seen, acknowledged, envied. She never earned a penny off her own back, but she had no qualms about insisting that Drew work himself to the bone to buy her a brand-new wardrobe every summer and winter, enrol the kids in the most expensive schools in London, pay through the nose for everything that would bolster her ego and make her forget that she was nothing but a poor little girl from a grotty two-bed terrace in East London. She had always been a fraud, and the fact that she couldn't even be bothered to show her face now made me hate her all the more.

I pulled my phone from my pocket, checking if I'd missed a call from her. I hadn't, but there was a message. I clicked to open it and felt my stomach roll.

Got some more of the good stuff. Come over tonight if you want it. No more freebies. J.

My finger hovered over the reply button. *If you want it?* He knew full well that I did. I could hardly think of anything else. Getting a cab over to Jason's house and letting myself go, of giving in to that ultimate state of freedom, however fleeting, was all I wanted to do – and I hated myself for it.

I glanced up, hearing noises outside the door, and a moment later, Drew was wheeled back in. I shoved my phone into my bag, standing to see him. His long dark eyelashes fanned out across his olive cheeks; his full lips remained slack and unsmiling. Disappointment hit me, and then I felt instantly stupid. What I had expected, I couldn't say, but somehow I'd thought that he would have woken, that they would have fixed him and he would be himself again.

The porters gave a brief nod in my direction and then backed out of the room before I had the opportunity to grill them, and as they left, I glanced up to see Beth slip past them into the room, a black leather holdall slung over one arm.

She'd made time to wash and style her hair, I noticed, and to put on a full face of make-up. She looked perfect, and somehow that made me uneasy. I hadn't even brushed my teeth since I got here. How could she spare a thought for lipstick at a time like this?

'How is he?' she asked breathlessly. She remained by the door looking uncomfortable, and I wanted to scream at her: *Go to him! Talk to him! Do something to show that your marriage is more than just an act, for fuck's sake! Be his wife!* I was fizzing with rage now that she was here, disgusted that she looked so put together, that she wasn't strong enough for this. Did she think *I* was? Of course not, but I stayed because it was the only thing to do. He should have made *me* his next of kin; he should have known she would let him down.

I turned my face away from her in disgust, sinking back into the chair and reaching for Drew's hand. Beth fidgeted but didn't move closer, instead dropping his bag on a table beside the door. 'There's fresh pyjamas in there, shaving stuff and aftershave. Maybe the nurses can—' She broke off as a doctor entered, a nurse at his side.

'Mrs Spencer-Rhodes?' He put out his hand towards me and I shook my head, nodding towards Beth. Beth, who should have fought tooth and nail to be where I was sitting, to be holding his hand.

'Ah, my apologies. You must be the sister. He's lucky to have such support around him.'

I nodded in silent agreement, taking his proffered hand and wondering if finally I had an ally.

He smiled professionally as he turned to Beth, shaking her limp, manicured hand then moving to the foot of Drew's bed. 'Well, I'll get straight down to business,' he said, his sparkling eyes meeting mine. 'There's some good news and some not so good news.'

'You mean bad news,' I muttered, unable to match his smile.

'Not nearly as bad as I had expected. As you know, Andreas's brain was deprived of oxygen for several minutes. We were unsure if we would see any brain activity on admission, but when after resuscitation we found that he could breathe without a ventilator, we had more hope.'

I flinched, realising that they would have been aware of this last night but hadn't told me. If Beth had been here, if she'd bothered to call, she could have saved me a night of pure terror wondering if he would be a vegetable. I glanced at her now – her expression was unreadable, showing no trace of emotion.

'This morning we have conducted an MRI, and I'm relieved to tell you there is no evidence of brain damage.'

'So he's going to be okay? He's going to wake up?'

'Well, that's where the not so good news comes in. The fact that he has yet to regain consciousness is... a concern. We would have expected him to rejoin us by now, but he hasn't responded to stimulus, his eyes have not opened, and there is no reaction to sounds or commands.'

'What does that mean?' Beth said, glancing from Drew to the doctor. 'Surely if there's no brain damage, he should wake up soon?' I could see hope in her eyes, her need to be rid of this place, to go back to her old life where she could brush all her issues under the carpet and keep on playing pretend.

'And he might.' The doctor nodded. 'The next few weeks are going to be really important for your husband. We'll be monitoring him very closely for signs of consciousness, and if we're lucky, he will wake up.'

'And if he doesn't?' I asked, my hand gripping Drew's tighter. 'If he's still like this in a month?'

The doctor sighed. 'The truth of the matter is that the longer Andreas stays in a coma, the less likely it is that he will wake up. His brain activity will diminish, and his body will struggle to function without intervention.

'He'll be a vegetable!' Beth cried. 'He'll be stuck here in this hospital unable to talk, to be a father to our children, to even sit up, and I'll be left trying to clear up the mess he left behind!'

The doctor and I both stared, shocked into silence at her hysterical outburst. Of course she would immediately think of herself, how hard this was for her, what she might have to endure. Even now, even with him lying here in a coma, she still couldn't scrape together enough empathy to feel for him. To apologise for putting him here. I felt a wave of guilt as I remembered that the blame wasn't hers alone. I'd played my part. I'd pushed him too far, too often, and perhaps it had been my actions that had been the final straw. I knew I was guilty. But I was here. And I was prepared to be here for the rest of my life. Beth couldn't say the same.

The doctor cleared his throat, speaking at last, the twinkle in his eyes gone, his mouth tight and unsmiling. 'It's possible. There are many questions and complications on the road ahead, but,' he added, 'we have every reason to be hopeful. Speak to him as much as you can. Keep holding his hand.' He looked at me. 'These seemingly small things can make all the difference in a case such as this. Keep hoping, and I promise we will do everything we can to bring him back to you. The nurses will be repositioning him periodically and massaging him to help prevent blood clots and bed sores. They can show you how to massage his legs if you'd like to help.'

'Thank you.' I nodded, my resolve hardening even further as he turned, leaving us to absorb his words.

Beth stood silent, staring after him, her face pinched. I could hear her breathing, heavy and fast, but I ignored her, having no wish to play into her panic and drama. It didn't help at all.

After a while, I could hear her breathing begin to slow as she finally got a grip of her emotions. She looked over at me, almost embarrassed as she opened her mouth to speak. 'Do you want to go home for a bit and get some rest?' she asked, folding her arms, rubbing her hands up and down the tops of them nervously.

'No. I'm fine here.'

'Are you sure?'

I nodded, refusing to be drawn into that argument again. Why did everyone keep trying to get me to leave? I wondered if I should offer her my chair so she could take my place, hold his hand – after all, I had been with him all night – but I didn't want to let go. I didn't trust that she would make a good substitute. When he was dressed up in a suit for work or a Christmas party, smelling of expensive aftershave and looking his best, she could never seem to keep her hands off him, holding on to him with a sense of ownership that had always put my teeth on edge, but now, I noticed, she kept her distance, giving the impression that the mere idea of touching him repulsed her, never getting too close, never leaning in to kiss his cheek. She was nothing but a show pony, there for the good times but useless when he really needed her. Not a real wife.

I ignored her. I'd spent all morning wishing she would come so I could find out what the hell was going on, but now that she was here, I just wanted her to go. Instead, she dragged a hard plastic chair from beside the wall over to the opposite side of the bed and sat down in it. She was seated too low to reach him even if she had wanted to, and again I felt a flash of guilt that I hadn't been willing to give up my own chair.

We sat in silence, her eyes flicking between her lap and the bed, her legs crossing and uncrossing as she fidgeted uncomfortably. Nobody came in. Nobody broke the silence. I had nothing to say to her. Nothing kind anyway. Every now and then Beth cleared her throat and my entire body tensed, half expecting her to try and have a heart-to-heart, ask why I thought he had done it. I was surprised she hadn't brought it up yet, but then she had never accepted the notion that I might know him better than she did, that the two of us might have secrets he had never shared with her. I was relieved when no words came. That was a conversation I wasn't prepared to have with her. It would be far too messy.

Finally, after what felt like hours, she stood up. 'I have to go,' she said, not meeting my eyes. 'I'm picking Ceci up early for speech therapy.'

I glanced at my watch, seeing that she'd barely made it through two hours. And she hadn't said a word to Drew the whole time.

'You're leaving already?' I exclaimed, though a part of me was glad I could have my brother to myself again.

'I have to. Ceci can't miss her appointment. Besides, I don't think it's making any difference my being here. Look at him, Gemma. He's completely out of it – he doesn't have a clue we're even...' She broke off with a sigh, turning her face from him and making for the door.

'Have you told the kids?' I asked.

She paused, looking back at me, her expression unreadable. She was guarded with her emotions, and that was something I understood. I was the same. 'Tristan knows he's here. I told him what's happened.'

'Was he okay?'

She shook her head. 'Not really, no.'

I chewed on my bottom lip, feeling tense. 'I could speak to him, if you like?'

'You?' She raised an eyebrow, as if the suggestion was utterly ridiculous.

'If you want me to. I know you've been having a tough time with him lately.'

She stared at me, her eyes curious, and I looked away, embarrassed, trying to hide my guilt – my anger.

'No, that's okay. I'll talk to my son.'

'If you think that's best.'

'I do.'

The tension had grown thick in the room, and I found I couldn't look at her now.

'I can give you a lift home if you like... or to the station,' she offered, and I knew she would be thinking of the inconvenience of having to drive so far out of her way for me.

'No, I'm not leaving him,' I said, resolute. 'I'll stay.'

'You have to leave sometime, Gemma. He doesn't even know you're here.'

She turned, disappearing through the door before I could respond, and I stared after her, amazed at how easily she could just walk away.

TWELVE

BETH

The golden leaves crunched beneath my feet, spiralling through the cool air as they detached from the centuries-old trees before cascading to the ground. My legs burned from exertion, my heart thumping, my skin clammy beneath my jacket, but I didn't slow my pace as I marched through Hyde Park. The liberation of being out here – freed from the suffocating claustrophobia of the tiny hospital room, where I'd felt crushed by the lingering threat of death and despair – was undeniable. I couldn't decide which emotion was stronger in this moment – guilt or relief.

It wasn't that I'd lied when I said Ceci had an appointment. She did, and I would never have skipped out on her therapies, knowing how vital they were to her progress. Two years ago, she had been stuck at the babbling stage and I'd carried a secret fear that she would never speak, not that I'd let on about my concerns to anyone else. I'd been desperate to hear her voice, to know what she needed and to help her get as far as she was able in life, and to do that without talking was going to make the world all the more complicated for her to navigate. But more than any other reason, I wanted her to talk for *me*. I needed to be able to converse with her, to *understand* her, and I had thrown myself into making it happen.

We'd moved from one speech therapist to another. Drew had complained it was a waste of time, but I knew Marissa wasn't pushing Ceci, wasn't trying hard enough. She didn't care, that was the crux of it. She had no invested emotion in my daughter and it showed.

As soon as I'd found the new specialist, Lina, sourced after hours and hours of research on the internet, I knew it had been the right choice. Within two months, Ceci had begun mouthing words, and now, two years on, she had a hundred or so words in her arsenal and was improving all the time. The sound of her voice made my heart simultaneously break and swell, and even now I had to hide how much it moved me when she asked for a simple glass of water or raised her head to say goodnight as I tucked her in bed. Every word she spoke was a reminder that being pushy, not being afraid to expect more, demand a better service, was in the best interests of my family. I was right to insist on the highest possible standards. It was no less than I expected from myself.

A yellow Lab carrying a long drool-covered branch rushed past me, whacking me across the leg. I bent down to rub the bark chips from my tights, tutting when I saw the pull in the knee but pasting on a polite smile as the dog's owner shouted an apology, jogging past without pausing to see my reaction. I straightened up, continuing along the path.

I hadn't lied to Gemma. Cecilia *did* have speech therapy today, but she also had a recently appointed teaching assistant who was young and vibrant and eager to immerse herself in her education, and since she'd come to the school, I'd found her so willing to step in that I hadn't minded letting her. She was the first TA I'd felt I could truly trust, and knowing that Cecilia loved her too made it feel less like I was letting her down when Ruby took over, rare as those occasions were.

I still carried the brunt of the responsibility not just for Ceci's care, but for Amelie, Rufus and Tristan too – when he let me – but even taking such a small step and allowing someone to help me was enough to make me feel like I wasn't good enough. Not strong enough to do it all alone. And, I thought now, crossing the path to avoid a group of tourists taking selfies in the shade of a majestic oak, not nearly strong enough to be the abandoned wife of a man in a self-induced coma.

I'd felt the judgement from Gemma the moment I'd walked in, the anger behind her clipped words. She expected more from me, but what that was I couldn't tell. It was clear that she didn't want me there, but the fact that she wasn't prepared to leave the room for even half an hour so that I might be alone with my husband had only fed my frustration. The doctor had said we should talk to him, let him hear our voices, but the things I had to say weren't things I wanted an audience for. I wasn't about to forgive him for what he'd chosen to do. I wanted to rage at him. Demand answers he couldn't give. I needed to tell him how he had broken my heart, and how I couldn't understand why he had made this choice without ever indicating to me that he was even struggling. I had a lot I wanted to say, but none of it would come with Gemma's piercing brown eyes watching me like an eagle about to strike. Short of having her thrown out though, I didn't know what I could do about it.

I knew she didn't think I was good enough for Drew. She'd been cold with me since the day we'd met, giving me the once-over before striding past muttering 'It won't last' as she headed to the bar. In the months and years following that awful first meeting, she'd never apologised for her cool welcome; if anything, she'd held on to whatever assumptions she'd made about me on sight, despite the fact that I knew Drew had told her to get over herself and give me a chance. We would never be close, and I was fine with that. But right now, she was a barrier between me and my husband, and it was abundantly clear that she didn't want to give me a scrap of power over this situation. I'd always been the intruder as far as she was concerned, and now she would sit by his bedside and show me all the ways I was letting her brother down.

A large measure of her response to me, I was certain, was down to jealousy on her part. They had been a pair, a perfect little twosome, closer than any sibling relationship I'd ever known, mine with my own sister included. They had lost their father young, their mother had left them to go back to her home country and their isolation had only pushed them closer together. My arrival into Drew's life had ruined that, though I was always conscious of trying to include Gemma, make suggestions that Drew should take her out somewhere, just the two of them. I preferred it that way, and I knew she would much rather see him alone than at a dinner party or some group gathering, where, if I was honest, she would have stood out like a sore thumb.

Neither Drew nor I had grown up in the circles we mixed in now, but we had adapted, educated ourselves in how to dress, what to talk about, how to behave without making a spectacle of ourselves. Gemma, though, refused to let go of old habits or make the slightest attempt to better herself. She was stubbornly resolute in her attachment to her identity, dressing in frumpy old jeans, tattered shirts and sweatshirts, rarely wearing make-up or taking care of herself, moving from one dead-end job to the next. Drew had worked hard, propelled himself into a new life, and no one could have blamed him if he'd chosen to distance himself or leave her behind, but he never had, never would, and as much as I found it hard to relate to Gemma, I had always grudgingly respected his dedication to her.

I stopped, pressing a hand to my stomach where a stitch stabbed through me, then moved to the side of the path, sinking onto a bench. I knew I should be feeling something else right now. I should be crying, devastated, but I just couldn't seem to get past the anger. It boiled inside me, corroding my thoughts, pulsing through my veins. It consumed me. And until I had answers from Drew, I didn't think I would ever get past it.

I slipped my jacket off, laying it neatly over my lap, and stared out at the lake, watching a couple of toddlers throwing bread to the fat ducks, their mothers hovering close. I toyed with the run in my tights, poking at the nylon with my manicured nail, making up my mind to go home and change before going to pick the children up.

I would continue to let myself be pushed out by Gemma, not because I thought she deserved to be there more than I did, but because I just couldn't face playing the doting wife to a man who'd cared so little for what his actions would do to me. And because right now, in this moment, I hated him. And I didn't know how I could ever forgive myself for that.

THIRTEEN
GEMMA

'I really must insist. This can't go on.'

I folded my arms, glaring at the night-shift sister in the doorway. I could feel instinctively that this time she wasn't going to back down. It was just gone 9 p.m. and it had been a long, trying day. The last thing I needed now was her coming in, guns blazing, ready for a row I didn't have the energy to win. She continued speaking, her hands on her hips, beady eyes laser-focused on my face. 'You've had next to no sleep, hardly eaten and you don't have more than a handbag with you. I'm sorry, but the last thing we need is you collapsing because we didn't send you home.'

I opened my mouth to argue, but she continued her rant, holding up a hand to shut me up. 'Now, I know it's difficult. And I know you want to do everything you can to help your brother. But right now, the best thing you can do for him is to go home. Come back in the morning if you like. But you have to leave now.'

I sighed, looking down at my lap. Part of me wanted to keep fighting, to see how far I could push my luck, whether she'd actually call security, but I was afraid to make myself unwelcome here. If they banned me from coming altogether, I didn't think I would cope. And if I was honest, I knew she was right. The smell of my own stale sweat was everywhere, and I felt sick with hunger. Every muscle in my body ached from so many hours hunched over Drew's bedside, and the thought of going home to a hot shower and my own bed was unbearably tempting.

'You'll call me?' I said, hating the tone of defeat I could hear in my own voice. 'If there's any change. Anything at all.'

'I'll call his wife now and make sure she's happy for me to do that. And if she is, then yes, I'll call you. But I'm not expecting much to happen tonight. Go, Gemma. Get some rest.'

I raised my eyes to meet hers. I could see she knew that she was wearing me down, but I didn't have the strength to argue any more.

'Fine. I'll go.' I stood up, leaning closer to Drew, his freshly shaven face smooth. I'd let the nurses change him into his PJs, but I'd insisted on shaving him myself, sure that he'd prefer it that way. I didn't want them messing up and cutting him. The bruises around his throat were still angry and dark, and part of me hoped he would sleep a little longer, just until they had faded. I wanted to protect him from having to see them, being reminded of that moment. He needed to move forward, not back.

I brushed a kiss on his cheek, whispering a goodbye, then picked up my bag, striding past the sister without looking at her so that I didn't have to see her satisfaction at having won.

It felt wrong to be leaving him, and yet I'd been driving myself crazy in the silence of that hot, cramped room, waiting hour after hour for something to happen, someone to arrive who knew how to fix him, how to bring him back from wherever he had gone. The withdrawal I'd been experiencing seemed to have faded now, but I was far from being in a good place, emotionally or physically. I couldn't stop thinking about what would happen if he died. If he didn't come back to me. How easily I would slip away too.

I walked through the hospital, my footsteps quickening as I approached the main doors, the evening air sweet-smelling and cool as I finally made it outside, heading for the bus stop. I fished around in my bag, relieved to find enough change for a ticket, and climbed on board, glad to find the bus relatively empty. I was conscious of how I must look, and I knew I smelled awful. In the hospital, it hadn't seemed to matter. It had felt almost like a badge of honour, a declaration of how much I cared, but now, I felt dirty and disgusting, and as I took my seat – the furthest I could manage from the other passengers – I found myself blushing. Beth would never have treated herself so carelessly. Even now, with her husband clinging to the edge of life, she still found time for lipstick and perfume.

I knotted my fingers in my lap, staring out of the window, shocked to find everything unchanged, the world continuing though mine had frozen. It made me angry to see people talking in the street, shopkeepers locking up for the day, children riding their bikes along the pavement. I sat stiffly, willing the bus to go faster, until finally it turned the corner into my road and I pressed the stop button, walking towards the doors as the driver pulled over. I muttered my thanks then crossed the road, finding my keys at the bottom of my bag and letting myself into the building.

My flat, if you could even call it that, was on the second floor, and I jogged up the stairs hoping not to bump into any neighbours. Not that I was particularly friendly with any of them, but still, I wanted to get cleaned up, and the idea of making small talk right now was enough to make me quicken my pace.

Once inside, I dropped my bag on the table and headed straight for the bathroom, kicking the door shut and stripping off, throwing the stiff, sweat-crusted clothes into the laundry basket. I turned the shower on hot and stepped under the stream, sighing with relief as I let it run over my aching body. I felt tense, despite the soothing effect of the water, and knew that feeling would stay with me for however long it took for my brother to come back. I scrubbed at my skin as if I could wash away the mistakes I'd made, shampooed my hair twice, and finally, feeling the water turn cool, stepped out, pink and raw and feeling marginally better as I wrapped myself in an oversized towel. I rubbed my hair roughly dry, then pulled a comb through the tangles and opened the bathroom door in a haze of steam.

'Hey.'

I stifled a scream as I instinctively stepped back, wrapping my arms tight around my towel-covered body. 'Jesus Christ, Logan! You nearly gave me a fucking heart attack!'

'Sorry.' He grinned, his eyes mischievous and entirely unapologetic as they raked over my body. 'I let myself in.'

'I told you I want that key back.'

He shrugged, still smiling, and I walked past him, opening the fridge and pulling out a beer, making no attempt to offer him one. I slipped a covert glance in his direction, noting with irritation that he looked good – fit and strong and sexy as hell, his brown hair flopping over his forehead. I took a swig of cold beer and put the bottle down on the counter. 'What are you doing here, Logan?'

'I wanted to see you.' He stepped closer, slipping his fingers into the knot of my towel, his knuckles grazing my bare skin. 'You haven't returned my calls. I missed you.'

'I'm sure you have other options.'

His eyes, blue-green and piercing, fixed on mine and I found I couldn't look away.

'Look,' I said, 'I have a lot going on right now. Can we do this some other time?'

'Do this?'

'Talk. If that's what you need to get some closure.'

'And what if I don't want closure? Come on, Gem. We're good together. You know we are,' he said, stepping even closer. I could smell his skin, clean and masculine, as his strong, broad chest pressed against mine. I closed my eyes, clenching my jaw. I didn't have the energy to fight him, to fight this. And he was right, we had been good together.

We'd met in a bar a year ago and clicked instantly. But he was from another world, nothing like mine. His family had a country house and spent Christmas in the Bahamas. And as much as I knew he wanted me, we weren't right for each other. I wasn't going to change the way Beth had. The way my own brother had. I wasn't going to pretend to be something I wasn't in order to fit in at snooty garden parties. I knew who I was and I was painfully aware that there would come a time when Logan saw it too. Realised just how much he'd been roughing it with me. So I'd ended it. He needed someone from his own class. And I, quite frankly, was a mess. A ticking time bomb of disaster. I liked him too much to inflict that on him.

His hand swept across my collarbone, up my neck, and I felt my skin erupt in goose pimples, a shudder of desire rocking through me. I couldn't have him. I knew that. But how good would it feel to let myself go and give in to it for just one night? That promise of release, the escape from my pain.

'I miss you, Gem,' he repeated, his words smooth as honey. 'Don't you miss me?'

He didn't wait for an answer as he lowered his head, his mouth hot as his lips found mine, urgent, hungry. I let myself be guided backward, my shoulders pressing against the cool metal of the fridge, his kiss deepening as he pushed against me. He deftly released the twist of the towel, letting it drop to the floor, his hands moving expertly across my waist, my breasts. I closed my eyes, needing it, needing him. But it wasn't fair. Not to him. He deserved better. And I couldn't do this.

I gasped, breaking the kiss, pressing my hands to his chest, breathing hard. 'Stop,' I panted. 'No.'

'Gem...'

'No.' I pushed away from him, bending to pick up the towel, wrapping it around myself with shaking hands. 'You have to go.'

'You're lying to yourself. You *want* this.'

I shook my head. I wasn't an idiot. Of course I wanted him. I had done from the moment we'd met. But we didn't belong together and the quicker he realised that, the better.

'I can't. I can't do this. I just can't,' I repeated, shaking my head.

He stared at me, his chest rising and falling fast, his hands squeezed into fists as if he were trying to stop himself from reaching out for me again. 'You're throwing away something good, Gem. Something that could be really fucking good if you'd stop being so stubborn.' He turned, crossing the floor in three strides and heading out without a backward glance.

The door slammed behind him and I let out a breath, picking up my beer and taking a deep swig. I waited until my breathing had settled then carried the bottle over to the bed and let the towel fall to the floor.

Slipping between the blankets, I opened the bedside cabinet drawer, pulling another pack of codeine from it. I dropped a couple into my palm and swallowed them down with the beer, then stared at the pack before popping out a third pill, shoving it into my mouth, needing the escape it would bring.

I grabbed the remote, switched on the tiny TV to some sitcom then leaned back into my pillows, trying not to let myself give in to my thoughts. I craved oblivion and hoped it would come soon.

FOURTEEN

BETH

'But I want Daddy to do it! He promised he would help me!'

I pressed two fingers to my temples, surreptitiously massaging the tension headache that had been building steadily over the last few hours, as Rufus stood stubbornly in the middle of his room, Lego strewn all around him. The solitary walk in Hyde Park had been the last moment of silence I'd claimed today, and ever since, I had felt like I was being pulled in a thousand different directions, so much to do, so many tears, complaints, responsibilities, problems, and everyone looking to me to solve them.

The ward sister had called just as I'd stepped through the front door from the school run to tell me that Gemma had finally gone home and to ask permission to share Drew's information with her. I'd been half tempted to say no, just to assert control over the situation. He was my husband, after all, and I'd felt like an intruder since the moment he was taken into hospital, in large part because of Gemma. But she had done what I was unable to manage, and including her in the conversation kept the pressure off me, the need to be everything to everyone at every bloody minute, so I'd agreed. I'd then felt the instant weight of the ward sister's expectation as she repeated that Gemma would be spending the night at home. She hadn't asked me directly if I was coming back in, but I knew it was implied. She expected me to come. What wife wouldn't be doing everything in her power to be by her husband's side as she waited to hear if he'd live or die?

Perhaps, I thought wryly, a wife who suddenly had the responsibility of four children to care for by herself, who had nobody to ask for help and not enough hours in the day to complete the never-ending to-do list. Even if I'd wanted to, finding the time to go and hold a vigil over my comatose husband was pretty near impossible.

I helped Rufus into his pyjamas now, though he was perfectly capable of doing it himself. I couldn't remember the last time I'd got him ready for bed. I had expectations, routines, and if the children fought against them, I felt it was my role to remain firm until they gave in. Learning to be self-sufficient was for their own benefit, and I was always prepared to stick to my guns and help them take on these important lessons, no matter how much they might complain. They didn't need babying. But tonight, I was done, beyond exhausted, and I just wanted to turn out his light so I could have a moment of peace.

I was annoyed too, I silently admitted, the irritation combining with the exhaustion simmering inside me, making me feel ready to snap at any minute.

I had managed to take Rufus to his karate class, having missed his trombone lesson last night, but it had meant dragging Amelie and Ceci along too. Tristan had disappeared up to his room straight after school, and though I should have been able to rely on him for a bit of support, I just didn't trust him to do the job. There was a time when he would have done anything to help me, but not now, and I couldn't have relaxed leaving his sisters in his care. It had meant that Amelie had missed swimming again, and I hadn't had time to go through any of their homework yet. I was burned out and starving, and now Rufus wouldn't go to bed because he had suddenly seemed to realise that his daddy had disappeared.

I supposed I was lucky I'd managed to make it this far fobbing them off with excuses, but as hard as Drew worked, he'd never been the type to miss family dinners or bedtimes. It had been inevitable that they would notice sooner rather than later. I was also hyper-aware that with Drew missing, my spending so long settling Ceci at bedtime was leaving the other three to their own devices far longer than I was comfortable with. Drew would usually pop up to read Amelie a story while I lay in the dark room getting Ceci to wind down, and I felt horribly guilty that I was being pulled in so many directions. But letting Cecilia's routine go was out of the question. It would only cause more problems in the end, and I could sense that even the subtle changes in our routine this week were having a much bigger impact on her than on her siblings.

'I can help you with it, Roo,' I said, determined to give him some undivided attention. I glanced uncomfortably at the Lego kit and the complicated instruction booklet in his hand, then took it from him, flicking through the pages, frowning as I tried to understand the steps.

'You can't. You don't know how. I need Daddy.'

I bit my lip, trying not to show how hard I was struggling to keep my emotions in check. Of course he needed Drew. So did I. But he wasn't here, because he'd chosen to leave me. To leave his children.

I stared down at the booklet so as to avoid Rufus's scrutinising gaze, my hand shaking as I realised there could come a time when I might have to tell my children that their father was dead. And even if it didn't come to that, he could be gone weeks... months, and who knew what he might be like if – or when – he came around.

The thought made bile rise in my throat. What if Roo and his daddy never sat side by side on the carpet working through a Lego project again? It was unfathomable. What could have been so awful about Drew's privileged life that he would put his own children through such unimaginable pain? Destroy their innocence, their childhoods with one selfish move? I looked up into Rufus's expectant face and realised I couldn't keep pretending. I had to tell him something at least.

'Sit down, baby. Sit with me,' I said, sinking onto the rug beside his bed and pulling him onto my lap. He was too big to be held this way, but I ignored the strain in my back as he curled into me, still so young despite appearances. Just a little boy missing his daddy, I thought, a lump forming in my throat. 'I have to tell you something and I need you to be brave.'

'Why?' he asked, looking at me with round eyes, his lower lip trembling. He looked so much like his daddy, his big brown eyes framed by thick black lashes. His full lips and high cheekbones.

I sucked in a shaking breath. 'Because I don't want you to be afraid. I don't want you to worry. That's Mummy's job.'

'Okay.' He gave a tiny nod, his hand gripping my shoulder.

'Okay.' I chewed my lip, half wishing I hadn't broached the subject, yet knowing I had to go on. 'Daddy is going to be away for a little while. Maybe a few weeks. He... he hurt himself at work and he has to stay in hospital so that the doctors and nurses can make him better.'

'Did he break a bone?'

'No.'

'Get a cut? Tristan got a paper cut last week and he said a bad word.'

'No, not a paper cut, I don't think.'

'Can I see him?'

I shook my head. 'Not yet. He needs to sleep for a little while. And—' I broke off, scrambling for excuses. I rubbed his back, my mind racing. 'Do you remember when your friend at school got chickenpox?'

He nodded, his face instantly more animated. 'Joseph, yes! He got sent home from school and we weren't allowed to go and play with him for ages... weeks!'

'Because he was contagious, right?' I reminded him.

'Yes, and he said that he was covered in really itchy spots, even inside his mouth and he couldn't eat and he wasn't even allowed to go to karate.'

'Exactly. Well, the doctors say that Daddy needs time... so that he's not contagious. I can visit because I'm a grown-up, but children can't go... not yet anyway.'

'So you're immune?'

'Yes.'

He nodded sagely. 'Will you tell him I miss him? And will you tell him that I'm sorry if he has spots in his mouth?'

'I'll tell him.'

He nodded, looking slightly more mollified.

'Are you sure you don't want my help with this?' I asked, holding up the Lego booklet.

He shook his head. 'No. I'll save it. It will give Daddy something to look forward to. Tell him that too, okay?'

'Okay.' I kissed the top of his head. 'Into bed then, sweetheart. I'm going to go and let your sisters know what's happening so they don't worry,' I said, easing him off my lap and standing up, my back cracking as I did. I watched him climb under the covers, then turned towards the door, dreading the conversation that I had to repeat again, hoping that the girls would understand and hating that I had to lie because the truth was just too awful to burden them with.

The doorbell ringing woke me with a start, and I sat bolt upright on the sofa, scrabbling around on the coffee table for my phone to check the time. The room was dark, and a pile of unopened letters scattered to the carpet as my hand bashed against them. I held my phone close to my face, squinting as I saw that it was only just gone half past nine.

I groaned, feeling shaky and disorientated as the bell rang again, and jumped up, cursing under my breath. If whoever it was woke Cecilia, there would be hell to pay.

There was music coming from upstairs, I realised as I padded down the hallway. Tristan. Still awake and still avoiding me. He could have made the effort to come down and answer the door at the very least, I thought, frowning as I flung it open.

'Took your time. I was about to shimmy up the drainpipe.'

'Daisy! What are you doing here?' I cried, practically leaping into my younger sister's outstretched arms. She wrapped me in a tight hug, her wild curls pressed against my cheek. She smelled of home, of familiarity, and I didn't want to let her go.

'I heard you might need a hand,' she said softly, pulling back to look me in the eye.

I ran my tongue nervously over my front teeth, blinking back tears as I stepped aside to let her in. She bent down, picking up a small suitcase from beside her feet, and my heart leaped.

'You're staying?'

'I thought I might. For a week or two at least.'

'But... you have your work, your own stuff, Daisy. You don't need to—'

She cut me off, taking my hands in hers, her dancing eyes sincere as they met mine. 'I want to. Mum called this morning and I knew you'd never ask. But luckily, our darling mother is always prepared to interfere on your behalf.'

'She shouldn't have.'

'I don't mind.' She glanced past me, looking up the stairs as the indecipherable rap music filtered down, thankfully at a more reasonable volume than usual. 'Is that Tris?'

I nodded, pursing my lips. 'He's holed up in his room. Won't talk to me.'

'And the others?'

'Asleep.'

'Good.' She parked her case at the bottom of the stairs and took my hand, guiding me into the living room and pulling me down onto the sofa, her body angled towards mine. It had been months since I'd last seen her, and I didn't know why, but her sudden appearance made me want to break down in tears. She was right – I would never have asked for her help. She lived in Newcastle with a neurotic flatmate and a full-on life. She worked long hours, having set up her own small business as a website designer, and when she wasn't working, she was volunteering at soup kitchens and involved in fundraising events for projects in her local community. All her endeavours left her with little time for babysitting for me, or long family visits. I missed her, but I understood how busy she was.

We'd been two peas in a pod growing up, as close as sisters could be, and had shared both our secrets and our wardrobes during our teen years. She remained one of my favourite people, and despite the distance, we were still close – we spoke on the phone regularly. Our lives were both equally full and yet so incredibly different that we no longer managed to spend nearly enough time together. I missed her. But to have dragged her down here under such awful circumstances made seeing her now feel bittersweet.

'Now, before you start, I know what you're going to say, but I've figured it all out,' she said, offering a reassuring smile. 'I've got my trusty laptop and I'm going to work from your spare room when the kids are at school. Mum said you were struggling to figure out all the extracurricular stuff for them, and how to get back and forth to hospital without worrying them. I know it's not perfect and I can't fix everything, but I can help. And I'm going to. I'm not taking no for an answer, okay?'

'You're sure you won't get snowed under with your work? I can't risk you losing clients because of me.'

'Beth, I'm sure. I promise I can handle it. Besides, I might be willing to give up my business to come and live in your swanky house. You can employ me as your nanny or something.'

I smiled, squeezing her hand. I knew she didn't mean it. She loved her life in Newcastle, her friends, her volunteer work. The fact that she would press pause on all of that to come and help me out was more than I could possibly have hoped for. 'Thank you,' I said softly.

She nodded, then took a deep breath. 'So, how bad is it?'

I sighed, looking into her grey eyes. 'What did Mum tell you?'

She flinched, and I saw the answer written on her face. I gave a small nod. 'She's not prone to overexaggeration.'

I wrapped my arms around my stomach, squeezing tight as if I could hold myself together.

'He tried to end it, Daisy. Put a rope around his neck and stepped off his desk. If it hadn't been for his secretary...' I shook my head and paused for a moment. 'How could he do it? Never mind to me, but to the kids? His own children having to deal with the consequences of his actions... How could he?'

She shook her head. 'I don't know. But he wouldn't have done it lightly, sis. I mean, he must have been in so much pain. I know how much he loves you. For him to have done this, he must have had a good reason.'

I brushed away a tear that had escaped the corner of my eye, my anger returning in an instant. 'Loves me? No... I don't think he can. Not anymore. He couldn't have hurt me this way if he cared at all about me.'

'We don't know what he was dealing with, Beth. We just don't know.'

'And if he doesn't wake up, we never will,' I added quietly.

FIFTEEN

GEMMA

Then

The moonlight streamed through the small rectangular window onto the bare wooden floorboards, the knots, as dark as spiders, seeming to move as I shrank closer against the wall. My feet were icy cold as I tucked them beneath the thin pale pink nightgown I'd been given to wear. I slipped off the damp-smelling threadbare blanket, the only soft thing in the tiny room, and moving slowly so as not to make the floor creak, cracked open the door, listening. I counted to two hundred, my breathing shallow as I strained my ears, then finally, pinching the inside of my wrist for courage, I opened it fully, stepping out onto the landing. The thought of creeping through the big dark house in the middle of the night, the consequences if I got caught, made my stomach roll, my hands clasped tightly around my teddy to stop them from shaking, but I had to find Drew. I needed him with me.

Ignoring the hunger pains in my stomach, the sparks of light behind my eyes as I breathed through the dizzying head rush, I clutched my teddy beneath my chin, my cold feet slow and silent on the carpeted stairs. There was a smell of cigarettes and sour perfume that seemed to permeate the walls of this place. Nothing like the way my real home had smelled.

The kitchen had been a constant source of mouth-watering scents, Mama always busy, always creating some delicious dish, her black hair piled on top of her head in a messy bun, her floral apron smeared with chopped tomatoes and carrying the faint whiff of garlic, no matter how many times it had been washed. It made no difference how busy she was, how many pots she had bubbling on the stove – if I pushed my face into her apron needing her love, her attention, she always stopped, her hands sliding beneath my armpits, lifting me up to her hip, her dancing brown eyes always pleased to see me. Not like the people who were paid to take care of me now.

I pushed away the thoughts of my old life, hating the memories for daring to surface, not wanting to compare those moments, those feelings of safety and warmth, with the world I'd been catapulted into now. It hurt too much to remember.

Social services had told Rod and Jan, our foster parents, that they couldn't foster two children in the one tiny room, so they had lied and said we'd share the big room, but it hadn't happened. Once we'd arrived, Rod had kept the big room as his private space and I'd been given the box room – barely more than a closet.

In their twisted way, they staunchly insisted on following their interpretation of the rules social services had set and refused to let Drew share the small room with me, repeating the social worker's declaration that it was too small for both of us. Instead, Drew was left to sleep wherever he fell. He often came into my room while they were downstairs watching TV. He'd lie on the thin blanket, his arms wrapped round me for warmth, and whisper stories to me, familiar tales our own parents had shared with us back when we'd been oblivious to the pain that lay ahead. Sometimes he fell asleep with me, but then he would get in trouble, though I couldn't understand why Rod and Jan were so comfortable breaking some rules but not this one – or why we couldn't sleep in the big room we were supposed to have been given, in a proper bed. I always begged Drew to stay with me, but he wouldn't, instead sneaking out before they came up and punished him.

Now, I slipped downstairs, shivering in my nightgown. They had never given me the warm pyjamas I'd brought from home, nor the suitcase my mum was supposed to have packed for me. I had nothing of my own here, save for my school uniform and the clothes I'd turned up in. I pushed open the door to the dining room and paused, clinging tighter to my teddy as I heard a low growl from the darkness beyond, goose pimples rising up all over my body. I flicked on the light, closing the door behind me so as not to alert Rod and Jan, my fingers gripping the handle.

Drew lay curled up on the rug under the dining-room table, Duke, a small black-and-brown dog with a rough coat, lying beside him. I didn't know why the animal hated me so much yet seemed to love Drew. I'd never been a big fan of dogs, and Duke had only made me all the more wary of them. He'd bitten me on the arm our first week here, and since then, he'd snapped at me twice more. Rod had said it was my own fault for invading his space.

Duke growled again, and I stepped back, my hand trembling on the door handle, ready to run, but Drew, disturbed by the noise, raised his head and issued a command to the dog then crawled slowly out from under the table. I watched him move, his dark hair dull with dirt, his shoulder blades sticking out through his T-shirt. He rose to his feet, rubbing the sleep from his eyes, and his stomach growled loudly.

'Gem, you should go back up,' he whispered, touching my cheek, cocking his head to listen for movement above.

'I don't want to,' I whispered back, eyeing Duke nervously.

'You have to be brave, Gem. Mum said we just need to be brave. We'll be home before you know it.' His ten-year-old shoulders stiffened as if he could fool me with his show of bravery. I could feel his tension, his pain. It was as deep as my own.

'I want to go now. Let's just go, Drew – we can run away. You can find the way home, can't you?'

He shook his head. 'There's nobody there, Gem. You know

that. There's nowhere else to go. We have to wait. Mum needs us to wait.'

He turned, heading through to the kitchen, Duke at his heels. He didn't bother to ask if I'd eaten. Neither of us was ever offered dinner.

I followed cautiously, careful not to get too close to the dog. Drew pulled open the fridge, and though I glanced over my shoulder, frozen with fear, my mouth watered too. He reached in, pulling out a pack of plastic-looking cheese squares, unwrapping one and holding it out to me. The dog stepped closer, sniffing with interest, but Drew put it in my hand. 'They won't notice one missing. Eat it then go back up. You need to sleep, Gem. Okay?'

'Okay.'

'Promise?'

I looked down at the cheese, not wanting to agree but unable to resist. I nodded, then lifted it up, the smell filling my nostrils, making my stomach rumble loudly. I didn't hesitate, just shovelled it into my mouth, chewing hard, my eyes half closed. It was gone too quickly and I wished I could ask for more.

'What about you?' I asked, looking up at him as he watched me, his eyes dark and serious, just like Daddy's had been.

'I'm fine. Not hungry.'

'Drew...'

'You promised,' he said.

'I know I did.'

'It's only a few hours until morning. I'll walk you to school. Just a few hours, Gem. You'll be okay.'

I nodded, clenching my teeth together in determined silence. I felt his eyes on my back as I turned, walking back through the house of shadows to my cell of a room, closing the door softly behind me so that those people, those awful, awful people, wouldn't suspect me of wandering at night. I hated them. Hated this place, this life. I wanted to be home, sitting on the kitchen floor as my mummy rushed around, the sound of sizzling butter hitting the hot pan, humming a tune as she cooked. I wanted it so much I could hardly breathe.

Slowly, I lay back down on the hard floor, pulling the blanket around me, the taste of the cheese turning sour on my tongue. I should have shared it with Drew. Should never have let him talk me into taking it. I was greedy, selfish. If they found the empty packet, they would punish us, make us miss breakfast to teach us not to steal. I rolled into a ball, sick with fear and guilt. I wanted my mother so much it hurt.

I thought about what the social workers had told me, and what Drew had explained after they'd gone. My mummy was poorly. She had lost her mind after my daddy had died so suddenly, and she wasn't fit to care for us. I was only six, but I wasn't stupid. I understood what they'd said. What I didn't understand was how she could choose to lose her mind when me and Drew still needed her. How she could just let us be taken away from her, from our home. How she couldn't be bothered to try for our sake.

Drew said I had to forgive her, that it wasn't her fault, but I saw how much he struggled too. He was better at hiding it, but he felt the same as I did. He missed her and wanted to go home. But he hated her too. He had to. Because I couldn't be the only one to feel like this. I had to share it, and Drew was the only one who could understand those feelings. Hate and love. Longing and despair. Pain and hope. I didn't think I'd ever be able to untangle one feeling from another again.

SIXTEEN

Now

I woke gasping for air, choking on my sobs as I clawed my way upright, staring blindly into the darkness. Gripping my throat, I tried to suck air into my constricted lungs and was rewarded with a cool fresh breeze, chilling the tears on my cheeks. Slowly, as my vision adjusted to the darkness, I saw the window cracked open across the room, the familiar surroundings of my studio flat, and with a rush of relief, I felt my heartbeat slow, my tears already running dry.

I pressed my hands to my face, wiping it with disgust. During my waking hours, I never cried, never broke down – I couldn't have, even if I'd wanted to. Those emotions were locked away inside a box with no key, out of reach – not that I ever went looking for them.

I still had a clear memory of the last tears I'd willingly shed. It had been the night they'd come to take me and Drew from our mother. I'd begged her to stop what was happening, but she'd stayed resolutely silent. As the social worker had taken my hand, pulling me towards the front door, she'd turned away, let it happen, and I could still recall the intense feelings of shock that had hit me in that moment – the disbelief that she wouldn't fight for us. She'd let us go without a care for what we were going through, what we might have to endure while she wallowed in her grief. She had lost her husband, but I'd lost my daddy too.

I had sobbed all the way to Rod and Jan's house, begged the social worker to take us home, but she'd ignored me too, flipping through her paperwork as if she could excuse her actions by playing the professional, pretending that what she was doing was nothing but a job. I'd hated her more and more with every mile we drove. And that hate had turned my devastation into something dark and bitter. Something that would no longer let the tears come.

I didn't know if I'd cried during those six months in the foster home. Logically, I knew I must have done, but I couldn't remember. After I'd got free of that place, those people, I'd blocked out the pain for a long time. But at night, when the dreams came, I lost control. Those tears, so easily fended off during the day, found their way to the surface in my nightmares. Those memories I refused to acknowledge became my reality when I slept.

It had started in my teens; just once in a while I would wake shaking and crying, certain that I would open my eyes and find myself back there, six years old, starving and skinny and more scared than I had ever been. Over the years, the dreams had come more and more frequently, catching me off guard when I was least prepared to cope with the aftermath. Sleep, the escape I had once relied on, was fast becoming something to fear. Was it any wonder I craved something more, something to take away the pain, the memories, the fear?

I leaned over, flicking on the lamp, swallowing a sip of warm, flat beer from the bottle on the bedside cabinet. The digital clock read 6 a.m., and I picked up my phone, checking for calls from the hospital and seeing none. I was due to do an early shift at the supermarket this morning, and I'd already missed a day without bothering to call and explain why I hadn't shown up. What I was going through right now was none of their business, and I didn't want gossiping tongues wagging about my private life, taking bets on whether or not Drew would pull through as they stacked tinned beans on the shelves.

I knew I should show my face and get on with the work, but as I climbed out of bed, pulling on a T-shirt and a pair of half-clean jeans, I realised my decision was already made. I had to get back to Drew. Right now, work was the least of my worries. Let them fire me if they wanted – I could always find another shitty job. And if Drew didn't make it through this, it wouldn't matter anyway.

Nothing would.

SEVENTEEN

BETH

Three months earlier

The smell of sautéed garlic mushrooms filled the kitchen, making me salivate as I rushed around the room tidying away the children's discarded toys. My red dress was tight, clinging to my body, and I caught a glimpse of my reflection in the dark window and smiled. It had been hand-made especially for me, and it felt expensive, made me feel like a Hollywood starlet as I moved from surface to surface clearing the mess, my heels clicking against the floor.

I knew Drew missed our date nights out at nice restaurants, the soft music and relaxed atmosphere. We'd once spent every Saturday night at a different place, drinking wine long into the night as we talked and laughed with nowhere to rush off to. We'd had so few responsibilities back then, so much energy to offer one another. My mum had been happy to take Tristan for an evening, far better able to cope with one child than she was with the brood I had now, and we'd enjoyed the freedom of going out for a romantic evening, just the two of us, making the effort to create quality time together. It had been so important to me that he see me not just as a mother but as a woman too.

But life couldn't stay the same and I wouldn't have wanted it to. I loved that we had more children now, a busy, noisy family that never left room to be lonely. Drew had commented more than a few times about how it felt like I didn't have time for him anymore, moaning about me being too wrapped up in the children, their activities, rather than making time for us, but as I tried to explain to him, we were just in a different stage of our lives. I had no doubt that we would get back to that sense of freedom when the children were grown. We had years ahead of us, I often reminded him. He just needed to be patient.

All the same, I always tried to make an effort. The weekly night out had been replaced by a monthly dinner for two in our kitchen, the Michelin-star food exchanged for my home cooking and a few candles to make it feel romantic. I made a rule to have the kids in bed and to change into something a bit special, to show him that of course I still had time for him, still thought of how I could make him smile at the end of a working week.

And if I were being honest, I far preferred it this way. I was relaxed here, knowing my children were sleeping within earshot under the same roof. I didn't have to keep my phone on the dinner table, tense with expectation of the inevitable panicked call from a babysitter out of her depth and struggling with a meltdown from my younger daughter. If Ceci ever woke and found me gone, she would scream until all the children were wide awake, and I couldn't expect any babysitter to deal with that – it was too much for *me* at times and I was their mother. Not that a live-in nanny wouldn't have been a welcome addition to the family, but that was different. A nanny would grow to know the children as well as I did. She would be trained and prepared for the challenges that might come her way, rather than some teenage girl trying to earn a bit of pocket money for a few hours in front of my TV, eating my snacks, hoping for an easy job. This set-up may not have been Drew's first choice, but marriage and parenthood were about compromise, adapting, and goodness knows I'd had to do my fair share of *that* over the years.

I had rushed the kids through their baths and bedtime stories, silently crossing my fingers that it would go smoothly and feeling grateful when it had. I'd showered, styled my hair, done my make-up, cooked a meal and was still on my feet now, having been up since 6 a.m., and still Drew hadn't shown his face. It was now ten to eight, and he hadn't even bothered to send a text to say he was running late.

I swept a pile of plastic bricks off the table into a storage tub, dumping it on the floor, then rushed over to the hob, picking up a wooden spoon, tutting as I stirred the sauce. If he wasn't back in the next five minutes, it would all be ruined.

I poured myself a glass of wine, taking a deep sip; then, hearing a key in the front door, I felt my tension dissipate, my spine relaxing. Taking another sip, I pasted a smile on my face, determined not to start this evening on the wrong foot.

Drew walked into the kitchen and I felt my expression grow tight, the smile stretched and pinched as I took in his slumped shoulders, the heavy eyelids.

'Shit,' he said as he glanced from me to the stove. 'Date night! Damn. I'm sorry, Beth, I completely forgot.' He rubbed his fingertips deep into his eye sockets.

I held the smile, turning back to the pan. 'I was getting worried,' I said, keeping my tone light. 'Thought I might have to eat all this by myself.' I gestured to the steak in the pan – Drew's favourite. He always forgot I hated red meat, but I bought it because he loved it.

He managed a half-smile in response, and I felt a wave of disappointment. Sometimes I felt as if I had five children, not four and a husband. More and more often I found myself having to cajole and encourage him to be present and cheerful, to acknowledge the effort I'd made as if he were a sulky, self-involved teenager. I already had Tristan's mood swings to endure; I didn't need another hormonal male to contend with. It wasn't that I minded putting in the effort – I enjoyed doing things to make him smile – but I needed him to meet me halfway, and lately I'd felt like I was nagging him to do what should have come naturally.

Compliments and thanks had to be dragged out of him – at times it was like pulling teeth.

'I'll just change my shirt while you serve up then,' he said, turning without waiting for me to respond and heading upstairs. I pressed my lips together, trying not to feel hurt that he hadn't bothered to kiss me, hadn't even seemed to notice my new dress. I should have put on my old tracksuit with the holes worn through in the armpits. I doubted he'd even look at me long enough to notice. It made me wonder why I bothered when he didn't seem to care.

I sighed, swallowing down my hurt and resolving to keep trying, to make this evening a good one as I served the food, then refilled my wine glass, taking a gulp, my eyes closed as I tried to summon some energy. Fridays always felt never-ending.

I heard footsteps and turned as Drew came in wearing a fresh shirt and smelling of aftershave. 'Looks good,' he said, glancing at the food on the table.

'Sit down,' I said, gesturing to his place. 'Do you like my dress?' I asked, determined to lighten his mood. I twirled flirtatiously, throwing him a playful look over my shoulder.

'Very nice. Looks expensive though.'

'So it should,' I said, laughing. I poured him a glass of red and then sank into a chair, relieved to finally sit down. 'So, how was your day? I take it there was a problem that held you up at the office?'

'Nothing major. Just paperwork. Where's Tristan?'

'Sleeping over at Guy's house. And the little ones are fast asleep.' I waited for him to look at me, but his head was down, staring at his plate as he cut into his steak.

I speared a potato with the tip of my fork, trying to think of a way to break the ice, get him to loosen up and stop brooding. I was a bit put out that he'd been so late because of a bit of paperwork. Surely it could have waited until Monday? No one would be working over the weekend to do anything with it anyway, and he could easily have spared a few minutes to call me. I chewed slowly, hoping he'd take the hint and give me a bit more back – fill the awkward silence – but he didn't. He looked lost in his own world, and I knew that if we were going to rescue this evening, it would have to be up to me.

'Amelie came first in her race,' I said, cutting a tiny morsel of my steak and swirling it in the pool of Diane sauce before popping it in my mouth. 'She won a little trophy, and when she went up to get it, she made a speech! You should have seen her – she was so sincere, thanking her swimming instructor, you and me, her teachers. I had to bite my tongue to keep from laughing.'

Drew looked up, offering a small smile. 'You'd think she's going for the Olympics the way she carries on.'

'Well, she may well have a shot in the future. She's very good. You should try and finish work early so you can come and watch her next time. You'd be amazed at how far she's come since you last saw her swim.'

He grunted in response, picking up his wine glass and taking a sip. I could see his attention already sliding back to his plate and realised he must be tired. I knew *I* was – it had been a long week, and it wasn't over yet. Saturday was our busiest day, with all four kids being ferried to their sports and music tuition, not to mention all the homework their schools gave them to complete every weekend. But I hadn't made all this effort to let tonight go to waste. I wouldn't be accused of not giving my husband the time he deserved. Besides, I thought, smiling softly as I looked at him across the table, he was still as gorgeous as the day I'd met him, still had the most beautiful smouldering eyes, those strong shoulders that seemed ready to lift anything the world could throw at him. I still wanted him, even all these years on.

'We could have pudding in bed if you like?' I said, waiting for him to look back up at me. 'I made your favourite.'

'Chocolate mousse?'

I nodded. 'Uh huh.'

His brow creased. 'Beth, we really need to have a conversation.'

'About what? Don't say the dress; I knew you'd bring it up.' I sighed, glancing down at myself. I'd been half expecting this reaction. Lately he'd become obsessed with the impact on the environment every time I got a package in the post, or came home with surprise gifts for the children. It was a wonder he hadn't changed his diet yet, shunning steak in favour of lentils and mung beans in order to save the planet. I had tried to take his concerns on board, but it was just one little dress. And it was pure silk – that couldn't be bad for the environment!

'You never complained about me treating myself before. And it's not like it's for my benefit. It's supposed to be a treat for you. And anyway, it will last for years. That's the benefit of buying quality – it's not throwaway fashion. I'm sure it's more sustainable when you think of it that way.'

'It's not—'

'Mummy!' Ceci's voice reverberated through the house. 'Mummy! Come!'

I jumped up, anxious to get to her before she woke fully and I got stuck settling her back to sleep for the next hour.

'I'll make it up to you,' I said, smiling. 'How about you grab that pudding and I'll meet you upstairs... and if you're lucky, I'll let you take the dress off for me. Will that do?' I winked, already heading for the door.

'Beth, I—'

'Five minutes, okay? I'll see you up there,' I said, blowing him a kiss as I rushed to settle my daughter, certain that I would be able to find a way to take his mind off his new obsession.

EIGHTEEN

Day Three

My phone beeped with a text and my stomach dropped as I yanked it from my pocket, pausing in the middle of the corridor, causing a nurse to bump into me. She muttered a disgruntled apology as she continued along the hall, but I couldn't manage a reply, too focused on checking the message. I stepped to the side of the corridor, unlocking my phone and reading it under my breath.

Everything is fine here. Amelie and Rufus are making cakes for their daddy. Tristan's gone out with his friends and Ceci and I are snuggled on the sofa with a pile of books. Take your time. I know you're struggling with not being able to be everywhere at once, but I can handle this. Love you. D xx

I gave a shaky sigh, grateful to my sister not only for taking the reins at home, but for giving me an update. She understood even without my having to say it out loud just how anxious I was about not being there with them. I'd always been the one to wipe their tears, mediate their arguments, take them to classes and keep their young minds busy. It was my job to care for them, to make sure they didn't miss out on opportunities, and already I could feel my standards beginning to slide.

I was so tired. It had been many years since I'd had to sleep alone, and the past two nights without Drew had been the longest of my life. I could barely sleep, couldn't relax, every creak of the pipes convincing me that there was an intruder in the house. I hadn't realised just how safe I'd felt until he was gone, and all of a sudden, I was imagining danger everywhere. My sanctuary, the home I'd envisioned spending the rest of my life in, now felt far too big, the children's rooms too far from my own when all I craved was closeness. Every time I drifted off, I would wake what felt like almost instantly, my mind racing as I thought of what my life would be if Drew didn't come out of his coma. Or if he did but chose not to continue in our marriage, to walk away from the life I'd thought we both loved. Having Daisy in the spare room had helped, but it wasn't the same as having my husband there, and as angry as I was with him, I longed to hear him breathing beside me as I lay in the darkness.

I put the phone back in my pocket and continued up the corridor, turning towards Drew's room. I'd called last thing before going to bed last night, and again early this morning, but the nurse had told me that so far there'd been no change, good or bad, and I didn't know how to feel about that. It felt like we should be doing more, trying something else rather than waiting for things to play out with no control, no way to influence the result.

I opened the door to his room, my stomach sinking as I saw Gemma already sitting by his bed, her hand resting on his in a gesture that looked almost territorial. I wondered if that was her intention. Glancing at Drew, I was shocked to see a long tube inserted into his nostril, snaking off towards a purple pump attached to his drip stand.

'What's that?' I asked, stepping into the room and moving to the foot of the bed.

'Feeding tube. Didn't they tell you?'

I shook my head. 'The nurse mentioned they were starting feeds, but I didn't realise... I didn't think...' I drifted off, feeling stupid. Of course she had meant tube feeding. How else was he going to eat? It had to be the shock and tiredness making my mind work so sluggishly. A cannula still ran from his wrist, hooked up to a bag of saline, hydrating him. He looked so small, so unlike the man I had married.

I had a sudden urge to slap him. To walk right over to him and hit his face as hard as I could. He couldn't sleep through that. He would *have* to come back, to end this limbo of waiting and finally give me some fucking answers. I wanted to scream and yell in his ear, to force him back, because I didn't know how much longer I could take this.

I gripped the plastic footboard and tried to breathe, using my old trick of counting to ten in my head and finding the effect less than satisfying. Finally, I loosened my grip and pulled up a chair. 'How long have you been here? Have the doctors done their rounds yet?'

'A couple of hours. And no, not yet.'

'He looks thinner already. That... that can't be good, can it?'

She shrugged. 'I don't think there's anything that can be described as good about this situation.'

I nodded. 'Tell me about it. I had a stack of bills come through this morning and I've no idea how I'm going to pay them. Did he tell you he took out a loan for the car? I thought he'd paid for it outright. And I'm supposed to pay the balance for Tristan's school trip to New York next week and now I don't know if he should even go. Should I cancel it, do you think?'

She stared at me, eyes wide. 'Should you cancel it?' she repeated, her tone caustic. 'Of course you should! I can't actually believe you would even consider sending him now. How does your mind work, Beth?'

I opened my mouth to defend myself, but she continued, her eyes dark and terrifying as they stared me down. 'How can you be thinking about bills and money when your husband is lying here in a coma? He could die and you're still not interested!' Her voice was growing steadily louder. 'God, Beth, I knew when I met you that you only had eyes for his money, and I guess you've just proved me right, haven't you? No wonder he tried to hang himself. It was the only way he could be free of you and your money-grabbing mitts!'

I slammed my palm on the arm of my chair, shaking with fury, shocked that she could be so cruel. 'How dare you! You have no idea about our marriage, none whatsoever. And you might not get it, but money *is* an issue. I have four children who need paying for. Am I supposed to just pretend we can live on fairy dust? Life isn't that simple, Gemma – we can't all manage with a minimum-wage job and a studio flat. I have to put food on the table, and that means I have to find money to pay for it. Drew knew that, and he did nothing to protect us before deciding to leave us high and dry!'

'They need food, yes, but not steak and caviar. Can Rufus even go to sleep without his organic matcha tea?'

My mouth dropped open. I was stunned by the venom in her tone. It was hard to fathom that she was talking with such contempt about her own nephew. My sweet little boy. What the hell did it matter what tea he liked to drink? Was she really that petty?

'And don't even try to pretend it wasn't you who insisted on moving to the most overpriced area in the country. Don't act like it was Drew's choice to send them to those snooty up-themselves schools so they could learn how to be snobs and look down on the rest of us peasants. It was *you* who piled on the pressure, year after year, always wanting more, needing to show how far you'd come by showing off. I mean, fuck, Beth, even their names are your way of showing us how wonderful you think you are.'

I shook my head, swallowing back a bitter taste, hating the confrontation yet needing to defend my children. 'I don't know what you mean. What could possibly offend you about their names?'

She gave a snort. 'Tell me, how many Amelies and Cecilias are there in each class? How many darling little Rufuses? You picked those names because you wanted to fit in with the yummy mummies at the school gates. To be invited to brunch and Pilates and pretend you were one of them. But you and I both know you came from nothing. You would think you'd be grateful for the luck you've had since meeting my brother, but you're never satisfied, are you? You want so much from him, but what do you give him in return? Because from where I'm standing, it's clear that he got the short end of the stick. You can dress up in your designer clothes, wear your fancy perfume all you like. You're still just council-house trash playing pretend, and if you think your snobby friends can't see straight through you, you're more deluded than I thought.'

I stared at her, wide-eyed and sick to my stomach at her vile accusations. Then slowly I rose to my feet, blinking back tears, determined not to give her the satisfaction of having made me cry. I'd always known she didn't like me, but I had never realised just how much. It was awful to see this visceral hatred pour from her, pinpointed directly at me. All I had wanted was a moment alone with my husband, so that I might begin to try and make sense of what was happening. To look into his sleeping face and say the things I could never voice with her here. But no, she couldn't even give me that. She was always here, *always*, and she was too selfish to see that she was making this situation so much harder for me in order to make herself feel like a hero. I knew she wanted him to see her face first if he opened his eyes, to claim she had been there for him, letting the unspoken words – that I had not – hang in the silence.

I opened my mouth, trying to think of something to say, but nothing came. I was too angry, too frustrated, sure that it wouldn't matter what I said – she would never leave. Instead, I picked up my bag and, with my head held high, walked out, leaving her alone with my husband.

. . .

I stood on the doorstep of my mum and dad's house, the home I'd grown up in, and realised I couldn't recall the last time I had visited them here. Since Drew and I had moved to our dream home after our wedding, and especially in the years after we'd begun to grow our family, it had just seemed to make sense for them to come to us instead. We had the space, the light, airy kitchen where we could sit and chat over a pot of tea, and besides, the children would have been climbing the walls to have been crammed into my parents' tiny living room, with none of their toys to keep them occupied. I always offered to pay cab fares for them to save them driving across town, and always used the same trusted taxi company, but now that I thought about it, I realised I should probably make time to come here once in a while too. As much as this place felt like it belonged in another world, it was still a part of my story, and no matter what Gemma might think, I wasn't ashamed of that.

I pressed the bell with a sense of nostalgia as I heard the familiar chimes, glancing at the pristine flowers in the hanging basket beside the door. Mum had always prided herself on keeping things neat and tidy, insisting that a small house didn't have to be a messy one. She had green fingers, but the tiny paved courtyard out the back, with barely room for more than the bins, was all she had to work with. It hadn't stopped her from filling pots with tulips and roses though, collecting unwanted plant pots from her neighbours if they had them going spare, never ashamed of asking for a cutting or a few seeds if she saw something a bit special she wanted to grow for herself. She'd made her own fertiliser using banana skins and old vegetable peelings and God knows what else, and when I'd taken her a bag of manure after the children had been on a riding lesson during a week in the country, you'd have thought I'd brought her a suitcase full of diamonds from the way she'd reacted.

There was the sound of a bolt being drawn back behind the door, and I pinched my cheeks, trying to bring some colour to them and hide the evidence of my tears. I still couldn't believe the things

Gemma had said to me, the shock still as visceral as it had been in the heat of the moment.

'Beth! Hello, darling, what a lovely surprise,' Mum said, enveloping me in a hug, her lips pressed to my cheek, guaranteeing a lipstick smear. I wrapped my arms around her, holding on an extra few seconds, needing the steadying certainty of her comfort, the smell of her perfume making me feel safe and warm. She held me tightly, her hand moving in slow circles on my back, and I knew she would never be the first to end the embrace. In all my life, I couldn't remember a time when she had been the first to pull back. She'd never made me feel like these moments were an inconvenience to her – that she had too much to do to stop and have a cuddle.

I eased away from her, and she looked at me with a quizzical expression, concern etched on her creased face. 'Come in, love – we're letting the heat out standing here on the doorstep,' she said, ushering me in and closing the door. She rearranged the draught excluder along the bottom, the same one she'd had since before I was born, and I hung my jacket over the banister then went into the living room.

'Hi, Dad,' I said, not in the least surprised to find him sitting in his faded winged armchair opposite the fireplace, his small round glasses sliding down his nose, his newspaper spread over his brown trousers.

'Bethy! Now this is a treat. Come here and give your old dad a kiss!' he said, his face lighting up as I approached.

'Less of the old, thank you,' Mum chided, folding her arms. 'As I've told you before, if you're old, then *I'm* old, and I'm not ready to throw in the towel on life just yet.'

'Try vintage,' I teased. 'Has a far better ring to it.'

Mum stuck out her tongue and I felt myself smile, glad that I'd made the decision to come. 'I'll pop the kettle on. Biscuits?'

'No thanks,' I said, sinking into the chair beside Dad's as she left the room.

He reached over, taking my hand. 'Your mum told me what's

been going on, angel. I was sorry to hear it. Doesn't bear thinking about,' he said, his voice shaking.

I dipped my head. 'Thanks, Dad.'

He nodded, leaning his head back against the chair. He'd never been much of a talker, especially when it came to the big stuff, but even so, I'd always been sure that I had his support. He showed it in other ways. When I'd been dumped by my first boyfriend, he'd brought me a bunch of flowers handpicked from his uncle's allotment. When I'd failed my driving test on the first try, after working a Saturday job for a year to pay for the lessons, he had baked me a ginger cake and we'd sat in silence side by side on the sofa, drinking tea and eating thick slices, our shoulders pressed together. He hadn't had the words to comfort me, but it hadn't mattered. I'd known in those moments that I wasn't alone, and I felt that same solid energy now, the love he tried to pass through his fingertips as they gripped my hand.

I let myself sink into the warmth, the familiar comfort of this tiny living room, the porcelain-blue wallpaper, still there after more than three decades, the old sideboard filled with cheaply framed photographs of me and Daisy as little girls, bruised knees and knotty hair, Dad sitting on a picnic blanket in the park with both of us on his crossed knees; Mum holding my hand as I took my first steps across this same carpet, which had looked old, the colour indecipherable, even back then. There were school dresses and sports days and Christmas mornings, a scrawny plastic tree and chipped baubles, a few small, hard-earned gifts but a lot of smiles. It had never been about the presents here.

I heard Dad's breathing slow, his grasp on my hand going slack, and smiled as I turned to see his eyes closing. Mum walked in and glanced at him, then winked at me as she handed me my favourite mug, filled with strong sweet tea, the way she'd always made it for me. These days I almost exclusively drank coffee, made by my fancy espresso machine that Drew had bought on my insistence when I'd realised I was the only mum still using a cafetière.

It had been Rufus's first term at school when I'd been invited to join the weekly coffee mornings. It had soon dawned on me that most of the parents already knew each other from nursery or toddler ballet classes, and I'd felt like I was being left behind, so late to the party I'd practically missed it. I'd chosen to keep Rufus home with me until he started school – neither Daisy or I had been sent to a nursery or preschool, and I'd just assumed that as a non-working mum, it was the best thing for him to be with me. I'd felt so stupid when I'd realised that every other child in his class had been going to private Montessori nurseries since they were two years old, and had immediately taken Amelie in to be registered so as not to make the same mistake twice.

The school mums had taken pity on me being the new girl and invited me to join them at their meet-ups, a fact I was beyond grateful for. We took it in turns to host a morning, and thankfully, mine came last, so I had a chance to see what the others were offering and make sure my own home was up to standard. I'd assumed I could make a pot of fresh coffee and open some Tesco Finest biscuits, but once I'd seen the frothy lattes, and the tiny, perfectly made pastries, ordered in from independent bakeries everyone but me seemed to have heard of, I'd known I had to up my game – and fast. It had been more than seven years since that first coffee morning, and I still cringed when I thought of how I could have let myself down if it had been my turn first.

I took a sip of my tea, reflecting on how much I'd missed a decent builder's brew, and sighed. I wondered if Gemma was still at the hospital, sitting beside my husband with her smug righteousness.

Mum put her mug down and I looked up at her. 'You told Daisy,' I said.

She nodded. 'I won't apologise. You need your family right now. I only wish your dad and I could do more, but it's difficult. Daisy doesn't mind. She wants to help.'

I nodded. 'She's with the children now. They like her.'

'Have you seen him?'

I looked down at my mug, running my fingertip along the sunflower painted on the side. 'Yes. Just now. There's no change.'

'That doesn't mean there won't be. He needs time.'

I nodded. 'Maybe. Gemma was there again.' I took another sip of my tea then looked up, meeting my mum's warm eyes. 'I wish she'd leave me alone with him for a while. She...' I paused.

'What?' Mum pressed, her voice patient and kind.

I sighed, glancing at Dad, sleeping soundly in his chair, his glasses steaming up on the tip of his nose as he snored gently. 'Just... memories, I suppose.' I shrugged, thinking of the way Gemma had spoken to me, accusing me of being after Drew's money, reminding me of my roots as if she thought I should be disgusted with myself.

I looked down at my lap, clasping my mug for comfort as I began to speak softly. 'I remember you having a cup of hot water with an Oxo cube for dinner. I had finished the food on my plate and I was still hungry, but I knew I was better fed than you and I couldn't ask for more. It happened a lot. I remember Daisy and me sleeping with you and Dad to keep warm because we had no money for the heating. The frost on the living-room window on the winter mornings...'

'What else?' she asked quietly, her eyes glistening with unspilled tears. 'Tell me what else.'

I shrugged. 'The names the kids at school would call me when I undressed for PE and they saw my too-small vest and holey socks. The fact that I couldn't afford to go to any of the after-school clubs. I wasn't invited to birthday parties because I never took a present, and the other children thought I was mean.' I caught myself, seeing the look on my mother's face. 'I knew I was loved, but I knew we were poor too, as much as you and Dad tried to protect me from that. I couldn't have *not* known.'

I placed my cup on the table and sat back, looking at the photos across the room, the little girl who'd been so grateful for the home-made cake and the second-hand doll for her birthday. Who'd watched her classmates go off to the school disco in sequinned dresses that she could only dream of.

'I had a happy home and I'm grateful for that. I am. But is it so wrong that I wanted to offer my children something different? To make sure they had full bellies and opportunities to do anything they wanted? If you and Dad could have chosen to give us more, you would have too. I know you would.'

My mum didn't reply. She sat still and silent for a moment, and I worried I'd said too much. Finally she reached forward, taking my hand between hers, a tear rolling down her cheek. 'I didn't know you noticed me not eating dinner.'

'I noticed.'

She shook her head, giving a shaky sigh. 'Darling, you aren't wrong to want the best for your babies. We all do as parents. We would do anything to take away their pain. Your children are well fed. They're warm. They go to the best schools and they have a beautiful home.' She paused, glancing at Dad as she seemed to mull over her next words carefully. She looked back at me, her hand tightening on mine. 'What else could they need?'

Our eyes met as I waited for her to say more. Slowly it dawned on me that she wasn't making a statement, but asking a question.

'They are loved... they know that I love them.'

She nodded. 'Do you remember what Daddy used to say when you were small? Love is spelt T-I-M-E. It can't be given with words or gifts or opportunities. It's not that simple. We had nothing when you were children – we couldn't even afford books. No holidays to foreign countries. No clubs or expensive Christmas presents. But you knew you had love, a family you could always rely on. There was no pressure to be something else. You were accepted, just the way you were. Of course I wish we'd had a little more money, that you didn't have to feel hunger, and no one could deny that we had our struggles. But we were always in them together – we always had time for each other, and I think that matters more than anything else to a child.'

I felt her love as she spoke and knew that although I didn't want to admit it to myself, there was a part of her that could see what I couldn't. That as much as I wanted the best for my children, as hard as I tried to get it right, perhaps I was letting them down. Getting it wrong. Missing the most important part.

She smiled, releasing my hand. 'You're a good mother, Beth. And a good wife. I don't think anyone could deny the truth in that.' She handed me a pink wafer biscuit and I took it wordlessly, wondering if she was right.

I dug my fork into the steaming pile of mash covered in thick glossy gravy and shovelled it into my mouth, sending out a silent thanks to the lovely lunch lady who'd insisted on feeding me, since Drew certainly wasn't going to be taking advantage of the meals just yet. The purple tray was laid out on the table in front of me, two thick sausages and a heap of fat peas making my mouth water. In a covered bowl to the side of the plate was a huge helping of plum crumble. After days of having no appetite, I had suddenly found myself ravenous, and this act of kindness couldn't have come at a better time. I ate quickly, nervous that a nurse might come in and tell me off for accepting the food, my eyes flicking between Drew and the door.

It had been a morning filled with conflict, and I felt emotionally drained and shaken, needing the calories from the fatty food to suppress the adrenaline still pulsing round my body. Sandra, Drew's secretary, had turned up not long after Beth had left this morning, still upset and traumatised from having found him half dead, unsure what she was supposed to do while she waited to hear if he would wake up. I'd read between the lines as she told me that she'd finished dealing with Drew's correspondence and cancelled all his upcoming meetings with clients, but that she didn't know

what to do now, and Matthew still hadn't got in touch despite her
leaving dozens of messages at the retreat and with his wife. There
had been an unspoken question in her fractured sentences that had
been impossible to ignore. She wanted to know if she still had a job,
if she needed to start looking elsewhere. Matthew already had his
own secretary, and without Drew, she was surplus to requirements
for the time being.

I'd been angry at her for being so selfish, coming here under
the pretence of caring, and had sent her packing, then spent the
next hour fuming that Matthew hadn't had the decency to call. He
had to have heard the news by now; there was no retreat on the
planet that wouldn't disturb him under these circumstances. Why
hadn't he had the decency to jump on a plane and come and see
Drew straight away? With friends like that, it was no wonder Drew
had ended up here.

I swallowed the last bite of sausage and immediately flipped
the lid off the pudding bowl, breathing in the scent of custard and
cinnamon. I picked up the spoon, needing to keep eating to distract
myself from the spiralling thoughts that plagued me. My mind kept
returning to that awful argument with Beth this morning, guilt
making my stomach tense as I pictured the look on her face before
she'd walked out.

It wasn't that I hadn't meant what I said – I had. But if Drew
were awake, if he'd heard me laying into his wife like that, I knew
he'd be furious. He would never want me to challenge her about
her faults, even if we both knew it needed saying. I'd been relieved
when she'd walked out, glad not to have to sit in awkward silence
with her again, but the fact that I'd made her feel too uncomfortable to stay made me uneasy. I couldn't understand why she
wouldn't fight for him. If I were in her position, I'd be here every
minute of every day, talking to him, doing everything I could to
bring him back to consciousness. As his wife, didn't it tear her apart
to know that her husband, the man she was supposed to love more
than anything, had tried to kill himself and she'd never even known
he was struggling? I didn't want to believe she was only in it for his

money, but the way she was acting right now, I couldn't see another alternative.

I swallowed the last bite of pudding, pushing the tray aside and leaning back against my chair, pressing a palm to my uncomfortably swollen abdomen. I already regretted eating so much and was sure that the next few hours would be wholly uncomfortable, but it had seemed impossible to stop. Why I could never seem to restrain myself, I didn't know. I sighed, looking over at Drew. 'Now look what's happened. They gave me a man's portion and I've eaten the lot. You could have done me a favour and shared the burden.'

I paused, watching as I always did for some kind of response, but Drew slept on. I glanced at my watch. It was still four hours before the doctors would be back on their afternoon rounds. The nurses were doing regular checks, taking his temperature and hooking up fresh bags of formula to his feeding tube, repositioning him in the bed, but nobody was doing anything big. There was just a lot of muttering about 'wait and see'. I couldn't help but wonder if they would be so patient if it were their own brother in his place.

My phone rang from inside my bag and I tensed, hoping it wasn't work. I moved sluggishly out of my chair, over to the windowsill where I'd left the bag, hoping the annoying high-pitched ring would disturb Drew. It didn't. I fished it out and saw Tristan's name on the display. For a moment I considered not answering. Just waiting until the ringing finished then turning my phone off.

'Hi, Tris,' I said, not managing to hide the weariness in my tone.

'Are you there? Is he awake?'

I took a breath and lowered myself down to sit on the windowsill, staring out at the pale blue sky. 'I'm here, yes. But there's no change. Not yet.' I wasn't surprised he was calling me to ask rather than speaking to his mother. I knew Beth would talk to him like a child if he summoned the courage to bring his fears up with her. She couldn't get to grips with the fact that he wasn't a little boy anymore. He was changing rapidly, and the control she thought she had over him was nothing but an illusion. I heard him make a strange noise and hoped he wasn't going to cry.

'He's going to die, isn't he?'

'No... no, I really don't think it will come to that,' I said, unwilling to accept that it was a possibility. 'He'll be fine, Tris. They said he still has brain activity, which is a very good thing. They aren't giving up and neither should we.'

There was a long silence. 'This is my fault, Auntie Gem.'

I closed my eyes tightly. I had half expected this from him, but even so, it made me sick to think he was trying to take the blame for something so out of his control.

'Don't say that. Don't even think it. This is not about you.' I gripped the phone, feeling my anger rise as I thought of Beth again. She'd spent all Tristan's life training him, corralling him, reprimanding him for being anything less than perfect. She expected so much from all her children, and the result was that she'd raised a brood of hyper-critical humans with low self-esteem. They didn't know how to function without praise, and the minute something strayed from the plan, they tore themselves to pieces, unable to accept failure. I'd seen these traits in all of them, even little Ceci. It broke my heart and made me want to shake Beth and make her see what harm she was causing. It was too much, too intense, and with Tris, it had me scared. He was at an age where something like this could destroy him, and I could not let him blame himself for this when his mother was the one who should be burdened with that guilt.

'It's true,' he pressed. 'You know it is.' His voice cracked and I heard him sniff.

I shook my head, lowering my voice though I knew it was silly. Drew wasn't listening. 'What I know is that your dad's problems are far deeper than anyone realised. This isn't something that happened out of the blue – it's been building for a long time. You don't understand everything, and that's okay. You don't have to. But don't you dare blame yourself.'

'Auntie Gem, I—'

'Tristan,' I interrupted, cutting him off, unwilling to get into this deeper. I wasn't about to spill Drew's private stories to anyone. We'd always trusted each other, kept secrets, just the two of us, and besides, it wouldn't help. Talking about the past wasn't going to bring him back to me now.

'Look,' I sighed, feeling weak and exhausted, craving a long nap after the early start and the heavy meal, 'I promise you, you aren't to blame, but there are things you can do to help make it easier on your dad when he wakes up. You know what I'm talking about. You can't keep on as you have been. I mean it, Tris. You're heading down a bad path.'

'And what about *you*?' he asked, his tone hardening. 'Will you do better? It's not just me he has to worry about, is it?'

I bit my lip, staring across the room at Drew, feeling the desperate longing to lose myself, the effort of trying to fight it wearing me down. 'Yes,' I whispered finally. 'I will. I am... I'm trying.'

He gave a snort and I felt his derision without his needing to say another word. 'I mean it,' I said quietly. 'I have to go.' I hung up before he could reply, leaning back against the window, hoping I hadn't just lied to my nephew.

TWENTY

BETH

I was just climbing out of the shower, wrapping an oversized towel around myself, when the bathroom door opened, Daisy holding the house phone, her fingers pressed to the mouthpiece. 'Sorry,' she said. 'It's Drew's boss. I thought you'd want to take it.'

I nodded, reaching for the phone and sinking down to sit on the edge of the bath as Daisy retreated, rushing downstairs to where I could hear the children arguing over what music to put on.

'Matthew,' I said, my voice shaky, unsure if I was ready to speak to him about what had happened. I hoped Sandra had told him everything she knew so I wouldn't have to go into detail.

'Beth,' he gasped. 'Oh my God, I've only just heard. I just got back to the hotel in Bangkok and picked up my messages. I am so sorry I wasn't around. I feel like a complete idiot for missing everything here. I can't believe I've been off meditating in the middle of nowhere while—'

'It's okay,' I breathed, finding it strange to hear his voice. I had never formed a separate friendship with him, only ever speaking to him when he came somewhere with me and Drew. To hear him speak made me half expect to look up and find Drew there, ready with a quick joke on his lips, a smile on his face. Knowing that wouldn't happen caused a jolt of pain to run through my belly.

'You couldn't help it... you couldn't have known,' I said, waiting for him to agree. Needing him to tell me that of course he hadn't had a clue about Drew's intentions.

Matthew sighed. 'You're right. I mean, I knew he was going through a tough time... and partly that was my fault. You know I tried to figure out another solution, but business is business and sometimes there's no way to get around that.'

'I'm not sure what you mean?' I said, frowning. 'Did you two have a falling-out over a project?'

'No, no, I mean the redundancy. I never wanted it to come to that, but things were slowing down and I knew Drew had what it took to start again. I thought he'd be fine.'

'You made him redundant?' I shook my head, not understanding. 'The day it happened?'

'No, Beth. It was two months ago. I thought you knew... He said he'd told you. He had four weeks left to go before his contract ended. I—' He broke off, sounding uncomfortable. 'I offered him a decent package.'

I gripped the phone, stunned. 'Are you serious? You're telling me that after all the work he put into that business, everything he did to get it off the ground, working himself to the bone night and day, you thought you could just give him the push because you didn't want to have to keep paying him? He's as much a partner in that business as you are! He might not have a contract to that effect, but you know he's more than an employee. He's the reason you even *have* a business, Matthew! Are you seriously saying you were just going to throw him out?'

There was a long pause, then I heard him sigh. 'He was still my friend. I would have helped him start something of his own. It just couldn't continue the way it was. It wasn't viable. I'm sorry, Beth.'

'Yeah, so am I. I had no idea why he would have done what he did, but now it's beginning to make more sense. His best friend used him for all he could and then tossed him out in the cold.' My voice was trembling with rage.

'Don't you put all this on me!' he said, his tone hardening.

'Drew has been in a bad place for a long time. Yes, I played my part, but you have too. You're not an innocent party here, Beth, and there's no way you can kid yourself that you are. We all saw how much he was struggling.'

'*Who* did?' I demanded. '*Who* saw? Because nobody bothered to talk to *me* about it. Certainly not Drew himself!'

'Are you sure about that?' he asked quietly.

I slammed my hand against the button, ending the call, my chest rising and falling rapidly as I tried to stop myself from screaming out loud and frightening the children downstairs.

I jumped up, catching my reflection in the mirror, meeting my wide, shocked eyes. My cheeks were pale, my lower lip trembling. Drew had been on the precipice of losing everything he'd worked for. He'd given his all to Matthew, to that business, and had it snatched from him by the person who was supposed to be his best friend. He must have been so worried about how we'd cope financially – how we'd pay our mortgage, the kids' school fees, fund the lifestyle we'd grown comfortable with – and yet he'd never said a word.

For a moment I imagined just how hard that must have been for him. I didn't know why he'd kept it all locked inside, why he'd left me in the dark when it was my life in jeopardy too. I might have been able to help somehow. I almost felt sorry for him until I remembered what he'd done. He'd known the mess we were in, but in the end, he hadn't stayed to help us find our way out. He'd taken the easy option out and decided to leave me to pick up the pieces.

TWENTY-ONE
GEMMA

Then

I stared after Drew as he walked away from me, wishing I could call him back and yet knowing there was no point. I'd tried that before and it made no difference. I watched his back, his white school shirt creased, his hair longer than Mummy would have liked, unbrushed and matted at the back. If he turned and saw me still here, he would be annoyed, and I didn't want to upset him – it wasn't fair to do that when I knew he had no choice but to leave me.

I bent down, picking up my backpack, a dull black thing Jan had got from the market. Two of the three zips were already broken, and I was frightened of what would happen when the third went the same way, because I was sure I would be blamed. I slipped the straps over my shoulders, the oversized bag sliding down to hit the backs of my thighs as I turned reluctantly from the gate of Drew's school to walk to my own.

When we'd lived with Mummy and Daddy, this had been my favourite part of the day. Mummy had walked us to school every single morning, her warm hand wrapped around mine, strong and safe. We would come here to drop Drew off, and there would be an

almost embarrassing scene of hugs and kisses before he rushed off
to join his friends. And then she would smile at me, and together
we would walk up the long leafy lane to my own school. I'd loved
every minute of it. Listening for the birds in the trees above us.
Looking for squirrels running across the path. I would let go of her
hand and dart in and out of the little tracks that ran behind the
bushes, worn clear by the hundreds of children who did the same
every day, the paths too small for the adults to access.

Now, that lane, the place I'd once loved above everywhere else,
was the most frightening place in the world. Jan had grabbed me
hard by the chin on my first school day with her, little drops of spit
flying from her mouth and hitting my face as she yelled instructions at me. 'If anyone asks, you tell them I walked you right to the
gate, you hear me? You tell them I took you to school. Do you
understand?'

'But you will, won't you?' I had replied, confused.

'Ha! At that time in the morning? I don't bloody think so, do
you?'

I hadn't understood what she meant, but it soon became clear
that she thought it was a fine arrangement for Drew to take me
most of the way, and then for me to walk the last bit alone. I knew
why she'd told me to lie. I was only six, but even I knew I shouldn't
be here on my own. The lane that had felt so safe, so fun to explore
and play in, was now filled with dangers I couldn't see. I never
went through the tracks behind the bushes now, too terrified that I
might not come out. I didn't stop to hear the birds. I ran, though my
chest hurt and my backpack rubbed blisters on my shoulders, I ran
even when I thought I couldn't keep going, too afraid to stop, sure
that I would be attacked by a fox, or something far worse.

I faced the lane now, casting a look over my shoulder, wishing
as hard as I could that I would see Drew, or my mother, or even my
daddy, though I knew he was dead. Drew said wishing made
anything possible, but I'd made so many over the past few months,
and not one of them had come true. Maybe I was the reason, unde-
serving of the magic everyone around me seemed to believe in. Or

maybe it was all just a lie, made up to make children feel better. But it didn't. It only meant I was more disappointed when nothing changed.

I grabbed the straps of my backpack so they wouldn't slide off my shoulders and took a deep breath, then began to run. There were other children playing in the bushes, making dens and running in and out of the little tracks that ran behind them where the grown-ups couldn't go. I could hear them laughing and I felt jealous that they could do it when I no longer could. I passed mothers pushing buggies and talking in relaxed, happy voices and I hated them for not being my mother. Not seeing that I'd been left with nobody to care for me the way a mother should. I felt their eyes on me and wanted to ask for help, but I couldn't bring myself to do it. I was afraid they would brush me off, pity me, and then nothing would change and I'd be even more different from the other children.

I emerged into the playground, the school looming on the far side, relieved to have made it out into the open. The sky was blue, and as I stood beneath a tree, trying to catch my breath, I saw Julie Hannagan doing hopscotch a little way off. I stared at her, watching the way her neat plaits bounced as she jumped, her red-and-white-checked dress spotless, her shoes so shiny you could see your face in them. I used to have those things. Now I was dressed in a baggy bobbled grey skirt, a polo shirt that was more yellow than white, and ugly, too-small black plimsolls that hurt my feet. I knew that everyone was looking at me, could see that I was someone not worth their time. I wasn't even worth my own mummy's time. All the same, Julie had been my best friend before Daddy died. We'd held hands at playtime, made up games together. She'd invited me over for dinner and her mum had given us chocolate ice cream, every time, even if it wasn't a Friday. I missed that. I missed her.

I dropped my bag on the ground, willing her to look up and see me. There must have been some power in the way I was staring, because she suddenly glanced my way, her eyes meeting mine. I was too afraid to smile, but I hoped it wouldn't matter, that she would come over, we would play, and for a little while I could pretend everything was as it should be.

She stood unmoving, still looking at me, and then a girl I didn't know, with a high ginger ponytail and a green checked dress, ran over to her, laughing and shouting happily. I felt my stomach tense as I watched her steal Julia's attention, the pair of them turning away from me, hand in hand as they ran off to play. I nodded to myself, knowing that I'd lost one more thing today: the hope of keeping anything from the life I'd once had.

I picked up my backpack and, trying to make myself as small as possible, walked around the edge of the playground, finding a spot to sit on the wall, deep in the shadows, where I couldn't see them and they couldn't see me. I tucked my knees beneath my chin and waited for the morning bell to ring.

TWENTY-TWO

BETH

One year earlier

I checked the holdall for what felt like the fiftieth time since I'd packed it, rifling through the contents to make sure I'd remembered Ceci's favourite nightdress and the storybook I always read to her before bed. She wouldn't sleep without it, and the thought of being stuck far from home without it made my palms sweat, my stomach rolling with nerves. I felt utterly out of control whenever I thought about what was going to happen today, a feeling I couldn't bear, and so I'd done the only thing I could think of and taken control of the things I did have a hand in. The timetable I'd typed out on the computer was stuck to the fridge door, colour-coded, explaining where everyone should be and what time Drew would have to leave to make it to each activity. The children had been given tasks, and I'd told them which pieces of homework I expected them to finish after they came back from school. I'd packed their lunches and their sports kits, and everything was laid out in a row by the front door, different-coloured Post-it notes stuck to each one so there could be no confusion.

Drew walked into the bedroom now, his face creased as he

picked up his watch from on top of the dresser, buckling it around his wrist.

'Did you see that Amelie's swim is at five instead of half past today?' I said, not looking up as I continued to rummage through the holdall.

He frowned. 'I saw the timetable.'

'Maybe I should print another copy before I go to take with me? Then if you get confused, you can call me.'

'I won't get confused. I can read a timetable.'

I glanced up at him and he rubbed his eyes, looking weary. If he'd slept anything like as badly as I had, I couldn't blame him for feeling tired. I'd been up half the night wondering how I was going to cope with Ceci once she realised she wasn't allowed to eat breakfast before her surgery. I knew she wouldn't take the news well, but there had been no point in preparing her before today. She would only have got herself into a state. Drew leaned heavily against the dresser, knocking over a bottle of expensive perfume.

'Careful,' I warned, nodding towards it.

He glanced at the bottle, picking it up with a sigh. 'I'm not sure we should be focusing on all the clubs and classes today, Beth. Haven't we got enough going on without worrying about swimming training and music lessons? It's going to be a hell of a day as it is.'

I shook my head. 'It's important. We need to stick to our routines. It's the best thing for the children. Besides, it will take your mind off Ceci.'

'I don't want my mind taken off her. It won't work anyway. I mean, Christ, Beth. Our daughter is having heart surgery and you're fretting about your timetable. Shouldn't I be there with you?'

I shook my head. 'We discussed this. Someone needs to be with the other children.'

'Your mum can come over. She won't mind.'

'But she won't be able to get them to their classes! Ceci is going to be in the hospital for at least five days after her surgery. They need you to keep things normal for them. I don't want them to be scared.'

He shook his head. 'I'm not talking about that; I'm talking about today. They know what's happening, Beth – they aren't going to be focused on what they're doing until they know she's okay. None of us will. Don't you think we should just take a break from it all and let them have a day off? They won't suffer from one missed day.'

He rubbed his hands over his face and I wished he hadn't chosen now of all times to pick apart my plan. I was anxious enough as it was.

'I'm exhausted, Beth,' he continued. 'It's just so much. It never stops. The kids must feel it too. They have to be tired.'

I looked at him, wondering why he had to make this more difficult, why he couldn't just pull his weight without making it into a massive drama. It was always this way when I asked him to do anything extra, to pick up the slack when my plate was too full. He'd try and figure out a way to skip the things that were important, and the children would miss out.

Next week I would be back home, sharing the driving, taking over the school run, putting them all to bed. It was *one* week, and it wasn't like I was heading off for a holiday. I was dreading the next few days. I hated hospitals, hated that I had to take my baby girl in and hand her over to strangers who were going to spend the afternoon cutting into her tiny body. The idea that I would kiss her goodbye and it could be the last time I got to see her – that a surgeon in blue scrubs might come and find me and I'd know from the look in his eye that they'd failed – that thought swam through my mind every time I allowed myself to stop, even for a second. I was only holding it all together because I had to, but if Drew pushed me now, I knew I'd crumble.

I stood up, picking up the bag and slinging it over my shoulder. 'Stick to the schedule,' I said, my voice firm. 'It's for the best. For all of us. I don't want them to fall behind.'

I stared at him, waiting for him to nod, needing him to agree before I could bring myself to leave.

He sighed then gave in, dipping his head in defeat. 'Behind who?' he asked.

I didn't bother to reply as I ran down the stairs, calling for Ceci to come and get her shoes on. I didn't have time to pander to him when I already had so much to do.

TWENTY-THREE

BETH

Day Four

'Amelie, watch out for that bike please!' I yelled as my daughter
zigzagged across the path, making a game of hopping over the
cracks in the pavement, with no awareness of anything going on
around her. She glanced over her shoulder at me, her chin covered
in chocolate ice cream, a wide grin on her face, and I resisted the
urge to pull the pack of wipes from my bag and clean her up.

Sundays were supposed to be for homework. Catching up and
getting through the things we hadn't managed to complete during
the week so we could start afresh each Monday. At least that was
the theory. Tristan had tennis. Rufus had his extra maths tuition.
Ceci and I had her reading to practise and Amelie had a play meet
in which everyone spoke only in French, the idea being to push her
forward and give her the edge for when she started secondary
school next year. It was run by a Parisian woman who charged
through the nose for the privilege of putting out a few art supplies
and worn-out toys in her garden room, and so far, I was uncon-
vinced Amelie had picked up even the basics. All the same, I didn't
want her to be the only one among her friends who was left
behind. Every week I turned up and paid the fee, ignoring my

daughter's complaints about how boring it was and how the woman didn't make any sense, all the while trying to keep Ceci from running past me into the house, where I would have to spend the entire hour negotiating with her to leave. It was always a nightmare, and it took all my energy to get through the to-do list.

But not today. I'd called round cancelling their commitments. Just for this week, I'd told myself. Next week they would be back to normal. I couldn't have them missing out. I tried not to think about how I might pay for these things though. Now that I knew the secret Drew had been keeping from me about his redundancy, everything was in jeopardy. Maybe Matthew would change his mind now that he understood what his choice was costing us. Surely he wouldn't want to put Drew through losing the job he loved now that this had happened.

Besides my new financial worries, a part of my spur-of-the-moment decision was also the conversation I'd had with my mum. Her words had played on my mind all night as I lay alone in the darkness of my room, staring at the ceiling trying not to think about the empty space beside me. *Time*. Every day, from the moment I opened my eyes until the second I went to bed, was spent doing things for my children, and yet did they ever have the gift of uncomplicated, uninterrupted time with me?

I had lain there trying to think of the last memory I had where I'd been with them without thinking of where we were heading next, what task we had to get through, which class we needed to get ready for. I had been stunned to realise that I couldn't think of more than a handful of fleeting moments. The hugs given in passing. The stories hastily read before bedtime, my mind always half out the door, my attention split in a thousand different directions. There were conversations in the car, chats over the dinner table, but real, undivided quality time? Time with no pressure, no homework or lesson or goals? I couldn't think of anything.

Mum's words had hit me hard, but on top of that, I didn't know how to access Drew's accounts. He had always transferred whatever I needed to pay for the children's classes, clothes, days out, food. I felt ignorant when I realised I didn't know how to sign into his online banking, and I couldn't even find his bank card to take out cash. It had to be with him at the hospital, I assumed. I knew there must be a simple solution, paperwork tucked away some-where either at home or at the office that would give me the details I needed, but the whole situation was overwhelming, and the more my account balance dwindled before my eyes, the more terrified I became at the thought of what I'd do when the last few hundred pounds had gone, absorbed so easily by the routines I'd always taken for granted. I'd never had anything to do with money, and the idea of paying bills, contacting the bank, made me want to stick my head in the sand and wait for someone else to fix it. And now I had no idea where the money would be coming from. Had Drew been looking for a new job? He had to have known how lost I would be without him. He just hadn't cared enough to do anything about it.

'You're melting.'

I glanced up to find Daisy looking at me, her expression filled with concern as she watched me closely. 'Sorry, what?'

'Your ice cream. It's dripping all over the ground.'

'Oh.' I looked at it, wishing I hadn't bought it. I wasn't hungry.

'I'll eat it,' Rufus said with a hopeful smile, hopping in front of me.

'Where's yours?' I asked, distracted.

He patted his belly, licking his lips. 'All gone. Yum!'

'Oh fine, go on then,' I said, handing him the cone. 'But don't come moaning to me if you get a tummy ache.' I wiped the sticky side of my hand on my jeans and watched as he rushed off to join Amelie, Ceci hot on his heels as they made for the playground. Tristan was already in the park, sitting on the fence, his ice-cream wrapper screwed up on the ground beneath his dangling feet, his head bowed as he stared down at his phone as if it held all the answers to life's big questions. If only it were that simple.

Daisy linked an arm through mine. 'This was a nice idea,' she said. 'It's good for them to let off some steam.'

I shrugged. 'I wanted to spend some time with them, but they're more interested in the slide than being with me. I'd hoped to make it a fun day, you know, take their minds off Drew being in hospital, not nag at them, but look.' I pointed to Tristan's wrapper. 'They make it hard for me not to moan at them when they don't bother to think.'

'How about I be the baddie so you don't have to?' Daisy offered, flashing me a wink.

'Tris!' she yelled suddenly, sounding strict and scary – nothing like her usual laid-back self. He looked round, a scowl on his face. 'Litter! Does it go on the ground or do you know better?'

He gave a huff but dropped down from the fence and picked up the wrapper, stalking off in the direction of the bin. She smiled victoriously. 'I could get used to this. Did you see how he respected my authority? Born leader.'

I sighed, leaning my head against her shoulder. 'Thank you. For being here. I know I haven't said it, but I'm glad you came.'

'I know.' She gave my arm a squeeze. 'I'm enjoying spending time with them. Haven't seen much of Tris though. Is he always holed up in his room so much? He's a proper teenager now, isn't he?'

I nodded. 'I'm worried about him,' I said as we came up to the fence, leaning our elbows on it. I kept one eye on Ceci as I spoke, watching as she ran to the far side of the park and sat on one end of the see-saw, bouncing lightly and singing to herself.

'Do you remember his dad?' I asked, suddenly needing to confide in her.

'Lee?' She made a face. 'Hard to forget. Selfish bastard. He's still serving his sentence, isn't he?'

I nodded.

'You're not thinking Tris is anything like him, are you? Because I really don't believe that. You've raised him to be a good boy, a good person. He's nothing like his sperm donor. You know that, right? This is just hormones.'

'He's different, Dais... he's not my boy anymore. Something's changed and I can't figure out what it is.'

I scratched my fingernail into the wooden fence, my stomach rolling with anxiety. 'I think he's been searching for him,' I admitted, not taking my eyes from Ceci.

'For Lee?'

'I think so, and he's at an age where he's so easily influenced. It might be cool to have a dad in prison. He might think he's something to live up to.'

Daisy shook her head. 'Does he know what Lee did?'

'We don't talk about it,' I admitted. 'It's not that I've tried to hide it from him, but he's never asked. I think years ago I mentioned it to him – not the details, of course, just that he was in prison – but I don't know if Tristan would even remember that conversation now. If he looked him up though, he could find it all easily enough. I'm sure it would be online somewhere.'

I tried to picture what Lee might look like now, after fourteen years behind bars. He'd been the bad boy I'd made the mistake of falling for, thinking I could change him, rehabilitate him, if only I could shower him with enough love. He'd never made any pretence about who he was. He'd been raised by a single mother who'd let him run wild, expelled from three schools before he stopped bothering enrolling for new ones. He'd spent his teenage years getting into fights, proving his worth to the friends whose opinions he valued so much, and though he'd been kind and loving towards me, I never felt like I could grasp hold of him. He was always disappearing in the night, ignoring his phone for days on end and getting picked up by the police for scrapping in the street.

He'd loved the thrill of the violence more than he'd ever loved me, and it had taken too long for me to realise that. When Tristan was two months old, I'd presented Lee with an ultimatum. Settle down and be the father our son deserved or leave before Tristan was old enough to take on his baggage. He'd left that same day. Less than a year later, I'd seen his face on the news: he'd got into a fight on a train and killed a man, his self-control finally run dry. I had been sad, devastated that it had ended this way, and yet I hadn't been surprised. I hadn't trusted another man to get close to me or my son until I met Drew.

'I don't want Tristan to see him, Daisy,' I said, admitting my fear. 'To think that he came from a man like that. Lee never cared about him, not enough to give up his freedom to be a decent parent to him. I've never even had a letter asking how he's doing. I can't stand the idea of Tristan chasing after him, thinking he's deserving of his time and attention. I don't want him to get hurt.'

'He's a sensible boy, Beth. He isn't stupid.'

'I know he isn't. But he's changing. He's shutting me out.' I sighed. 'I miss him. It's hard to explain, but he and I were so close. Before I met Drew, it was just the two of us, and I never imagined we would lose that bond. We've always had this deep connection, and I've never felt like he was keeping secrets from me, but now...' I grasped for the right words, feeling an emptiness deep in my belly. 'I don't know... something isn't right.'

'Have you spoken to him? Asked if he's looking for his dad?'

'Not in so many words. I don't know how.'

She popped the last bite of her cone into her mouth and chewed thoughtfully. 'Ask him,' she said finally. 'Ask and then go from there. Even if he doesn't tell you the truth, you know him well enough to tell if he's lying. Don't pussyfoot around the issue. It does neither of you any favours.'

I pursed my lips, watching Ceci climb off the see-saw and run to join Rufus on the climbing frame. I hoped she wouldn't try and go too high. She'd got stuck last time we were here, and it had taken half an hour to help her navigate her way back down. 'Maybe you're right,' I agreed.

'Of course I am,' Daisy said.

I smiled, feeling a little better, and turned to give her a hug. 'Thank you.'

She hugged me tight, her long hair flying across my face in the breeze. I pulled some from my mouth as she eased back, and made a face. 'I'm going to get a hairball at this rate,' I said.

I turned back to the park, doing a mental check as I scanned the apparatus for each of my children. Ceci still climbing... Amelie and Rufus in the sand. I couldn't see Tristan at first, but then I recognised the light blue stripe that ran along the back of his jacket.

'What's he doing?' I muttered, frowning as I watched him. He'd gone out of the park through the far gate and was standing beside a thick-trunked tree about a hundred metres across the grass, half concealed from view.

'He's not smoking, is he?' Daisy asked, following my gaze.

I squinted, seeing a definite cloud of smoke wafting up on the breeze suspiciously close to him. I was about to reply when Tristan moved a step to the side and I saw that he wasn't alone. A man – early twenties, dressed in a baggy sweatshirt and cheap jeans tied at the waist with what looked like a length of frayed rope – was talking intently to him, his height giving him the advantage as he loomed over my son. I stared at his stubbled face, feeling my hackles rise, disliking him instantly. He looked mean, rough, his body coiled in the way I'd seen in those intimidating gangs that seemed to roam the streets, ready to fight at the drop of a hat. They lived and breathed violence.

Lee had been a puppy compared to these men. He'd killed a man with a punch, too hard and entirely unforgivable, but he had never carried a weapon. I would never have fallen for him if he had. But the man talking to my son now made me uneasy. I knew his type; I'd grown up avoiding boys like him, crossing the road to get out of their way. I couldn't imagine where Tristan knew him from or why he was speaking to him now. The crowds my children mixed in, our neighbourhood and their schools, didn't give them a lot of opportunity for encounters with men like him. Without intending to, I found myself reaching for Daisy's arm.

'I don't like the look of that,' she murmured, covering my hand with her own. 'D'you know him?'

I shook my head. Tristan took a step back, and I felt the tension release in my chest, proud of him for having extricated himself

from the situation without my having to tell him to. He turned
away, saying something I couldn't hear, but then the man grabbed
the collar of his jacket, spinning him back to face him.

I gasped, my fingernails squeezing tight against Daisy's hand in
my terror. He was clearly angry, and I felt adrenaline pour through
my body as I braced myself for the punch I imagined would follow.
I wished I could hear what they were saying.

'Oh my God!' I half shrieked. 'It's broad daylight, for goodness'
sake! Why isn't anyone doing anything?' I was already moving
around the perimeter of the fence. 'I'm going over there right now!'

Daisy didn't argue. 'I'm coming too.' She glanced back into the
park, then her hand shot out, gripping mine and yanking me back
before I could break into a run. I stumbled and caught the edge of
the fence to steady myself.

'Daisy!' I looked at her, feeling her grip tighten around my
wrist. Her hand was shaking. 'Daisy?' I repeated. There was a look
on her face that frightened me.

'Ceci!' she gasped, pointing a shaking finger across the park.

I looked to where she was indicating and felt instant terror, the
happy cries of the children in the park echoing around my head too
loudly, and yet somehow they seemed out of reach, as if they were
coming from some parallel world, a place where the scene I was
witnessing could never happen. I stared open-mouthed at the
horror I knew was coming, seeing my daughter on the climbing
frame dressed in the fluorescent pink jacket I always put her in so I
wouldn't lose her in a crowd. One hand was clutched to her chest,
her eyes rolling, her head thrown backward as she held on to the
rope with what looked like the very tips of her fingers.

For a moment time seemed to stand still, and then I heard
Daisy's scream as Ceci let go, her body free-falling, tumbling
towards the ground. I was already over the fence and halfway to
where she lay crumpled in a heap, Daisy's footsteps hitting the
ground as she raced after me.

'She didn't fall far,' a dog-walker called from over the fence. 'I
saw her – t'was just a little tumble.'

'She has a heart condition!' I yelled at him. I reached my daughter, rolling her onto her back, leaning close to listen for her breath. 'Ceci, darling, it's Mummy – I'm right here,' I said, only the barest tremble seeping into my voice, betraying the raw panic running through my veins.

'Oh God, oh my God! What should we do? What do I do?' Daisy cried, pacing behind me, her hands clasped tightly beneath her chin as she looked frantically from me to Cecilia. I ignored her, checking Ceci over, moving her into the recovery position the way I'd been taught on the first-aid courses I'd taken every other year since her birth. I looked up. Daisy was wide-eyed and panicked, biting her nails. Behind her, a crowd of children was gathering, and the dog-walker was staring at us.

'Call an ambulance,' I instructed. 'She's breathing, but she needs to get to a hospital now.'

Daisy nodded, pulling her phone from her bag with trembling hands. She dialled and spoke frantically down the line. Too fast, I thought. Slow down, speak clearly, breathe.

I stared at my daughter, feeling calm and controlled as I analysed the situation. Her lips were pale but not blue, her breathing shallow but steady. I would not panic. I would not let her down.

I leaned forward as I saw her move, her eyes flickering open. 'Hi, baby,' I said. 'You had a fall.'

She blinked. 'Ceci high. See me?'

'I did.' I smiled, stroking her hair back from her face. 'You went very high,' I agreed, reaching for her hand, which was cool to the touch. 'How do you feel, sweetheart?'

She sat up slowly, looking at the people surrounding us, pressing her hand to her chest. 'Ouch. Sore.'

I nodded, pressing my lips together, but didn't say anything.

Daisy put her hand over the mouthpiece. 'She's okay?'

'She needs to be seen. I don't know what happened.'

'They said fifteen minutes for the ambulance. There's been an emergency across town.'

I shook my head. 'I could walk to the hospital in five! That's not good enough.'

The dog-walker stepped closer to the fence. 'I have a van. I can run you over there now if you want? S'no trouble.'

Daisy shook her head, frowning at the suggestion. 'No. Thanks, but no.' She turned back to me. 'You're not getting in a van with a stranger, Beth,' she muttered. 'No way.'

I looked at Ceci, hearing the wheeze in her breathing, her little forehead puckering the way it always did when she was in pain. It was enough to make up my mind for me.

'Yes.' I nodded, meeting Daisy's eye, hoping she wasn't about to have a panic attack or something. 'I *am*. I have to.' I looked past her to the man. 'Yes please, if you're sure? I think it's the best option.'

Daisy opened her mouth, but I shook my head, lowering my voice as I looked from her to Ceci. 'It's not ideal, but we can't wait.'

She took a deep breath, her hands clasped tightly together. She looked so far from the strong, confident woman I knew, so scared and small. I wished I had time to comfort her. She'd never seen anything like this before. I, however, had, and I knew that I had to take charge of the situation. Ceci could plummet at a moment's notice, and I didn't want to be out here waiting for an ambulance that might not come for fifteen minutes. I needed her to be in a place where there were specialists, equipment, where she could be taken care of.

I stood, heaving her into my arms. 'Take the children home,' I told Daisy, seeing Rufus and Amelie still in the sandpit across the playground, oblivious to the drama unfolding. 'I'll take Ceci to hospital. It will be fine, but she has to go now. It can't wait.'

I pulled my daughter closer, frightened that her heart might stop, desperate to get her to the hospital before anything else happened. Then I froze, liquid fear trickling through my veins as I suddenly remembered Tristan and the man he'd been arguing with.

I gripped Ceci, my heartbeat thudding thunderously in my ears. 'Where's Tristan?' I looked behind me, unable to see him.

The spot by the tree across the field was empty, and there was no sign of either Tristan or the stranger. 'Tris!' I yelled. 'Tristan! Oh God, Daisy, where is he?'

She shook her head. 'I can't see him.' Her face was pinched as she stared at the place where he'd been just moments before.

'I can't just go... What if something's happened?' I cried, trying not to think of all the possibilities. My mind was racing, my thoughts turning dark as I recalled how many stabbings there had been in London recently, teenage boys the primary victims of the sickening, senseless crime. 'I have to find him.'

Daisy shook her head, touching Cecilia's back gently. 'You have to help *her*. You have to get to the hospital, Beth. I'll find him. I'll take him home,' she said, reaching for my arm.

'Daisy, I—'

'You can't be everywhere at once. You don't have to be. That's why I'm here.'

And why I need my husband, I thought bitterly. How was I ever going to raise four children alone? I couldn't do this. I shouldn't have to. This was never the deal.

'Beth, go. I'll deal with Tristan, okay? You're sure it's safe to go with a stranger?' she added in a whisper, unable to stop herself from checking one last time.

I blinked, feeling Ceci trembling in my arms, and glanced at the dog-walker, sizing him up, deciding that I trusted him – though, admittedly, I had little choice. His round face was warm, his blue eyes large and concerned. He had an ageing brown Lab sitting quietly at his feet.

'I'm sure,' I said.

I pulled away from her, making up my mind, silently prioritising Ceci's needs over my son's. I hated to do it, but I had no choice. Daisy would never know how to navigate the hospital, how to fight for Ceci to get the tests she so desperately needed. That was *my* responsibility. And while I was doing that, my son, my Tristan, could be bleeding to death somewhere. I had to trust that Daisy would find him. I had to get moving.

I turned resolutely towards the man. The safety of climbing into a van with a stranger was the least of my concerns right now. Besides, I thought as I hurried after him towards the gate, there were too many witnesses for him to try anything.

'Find Tristan!' I called over my shoulder as I climbed into his battered white C15 van. I saw Daisy nod and turn, already beginning her search, and stared through the windshield, desperately scanning for a sign of my boy.

The man shut the door carefully, put the dog in the back, then rushed around to the driver's side, climbing in beside me. 'Hold on, love – we'll be there in a jiffy,' he said, starting the engine and pulling away with reassuring confidence.

I held Ceci against my body and counted the beats of her heart as it thudded against my palm. I'd been forced to make a choice between my children. I just hoped I wouldn't live to regret my decision.

TWENTY-FOUR

Ceci gave a deep belly laugh as she lay back on the hospital bed, munching a slice of toast and jam and watching kids' TV. I tried not to pace as I waited for the doctor to come and see me and tell me what they'd found. She'd had an ECG, along with a blood test that she'd screamed blue murder about, and now I couldn't seem to stop my imagination running wild, thinking of all the horrible possibilities that might lie before me. The smell of disinfectant and alcohol hand gel made it impossible to relax, to forget that I was in a hospital. It was so surreal to think that a few floors below the room where I waited now, my husband lay unresponsive in a coma. How terrifying to have two members of my family under this same roof, their futures so tenuous, so uncertain.

I glanced at Ceci now, trying to feel reassured by the colour in her cheeks, her eyes alert and sparkling as she stared at the small screen above her bed. Daisy had texted to say that she'd taken Rufus and Amelie home but that she hadn't been able to find Tristan, despite searching for over an hour. She'd been on the verge of calling the police when I'd got a message from him saying he'd gone to see a friend and wouldn't be back for dinner. I was overwhelmed with relief to see his name flash up on the screen, but that relief had swiftly morphed into anger. He'd disappeared just when we needed him most, exactly like his father.

Stepfather, I reminded myself. Maybe Tristan didn't even care what happened to us. To his sister. More and more I felt sure he wasn't reacting in an appropriate way to the news about Drew. And the only reason I could find for his apparent ambivalence was that despite years of being raised by the man, he still didn't feel like Drew was his dad. Could it be possible that his loyalties lay with a man who had done nothing for him, nothing to earn his trust or respect?

I wished he'd been by my side when Ceci had collapsed. He knew the routines far better than Daisy – how to distract the others so I could focus on helping her, making sure they weren't afraid – and he was surprisingly calm in a crisis. When we'd had a power cut during a storm a few days before Christmas last year, Amelie had been beside herself with terror, the sound of thunder rumbling ominously through the dark rooms of our home. Rufus, though he wouldn't admit it, was scared too and kept asking for his daddy, who was stuck on the Underground, unable to get back to us. And Ceci had lost control completely, thrown by the unwelcome interruption to her evening. I was running between the three of them, attempting to stop Ceci from pulling her own hair out by the roots while trying and failing to comfort the other two, all the while hoping the lights would come back on and Drew would miraculously make it back in time to give me a hand.

Tristan, still my sweet boy back then, had taken control of the situation, finding torches and a battery-operated camping lantern. He'd set up a canopy in his room, draping sheets over his bookshelves and bed frame, and invited the little ones to come in – a rare treat. They'd crawled into the softly lit tent and he'd told them stories – funny ones, not scary ones – and even I had felt myself relax as Ceci lay across my lap, looking adoringly at her big brother, his deep voice soothing us all.

He could have been a huge help to her today as we deliberated what to do, but he was no longer the same boy who had made that safe little den in a thunderstorm. He didn't seem to care about anything anymore – had walked off on what was supposed to be a family day out, too absorbed in what *he* wanted to be bothered to help us out. Did he think we hadn't seen what was going on in broad daylight? Who he was talking to? He must think I was an idiot! I wondered for the hundredth time if the man he'd met by the tree was a friend of Lee's. He was exactly the type of person my errant ex-boyfriend would choose to have in his circle.

Tristan hadn't even asked about Drew since hearing about his condition, and it hurt to think that he didn't care. As angry and confused as I was about it all, Tristan had always worshipped Drew, and to see him shrug off the news, shut down and not even ask for an update made me even more sure that his head was being turned by something else. His biological dad would love nothing more than to have someone on the outside to do his bidding. If it wasn't for Tristan, I'd wish I'd never met Lee, but as stupid as my choice to be with him was, it had given me my firstborn, and even now, I couldn't regret that.

I stood up, walking around the bed, pressing a hand to Ceci's head and feeling the warm, healthy skin beneath my own. Surely if something was wrong with her heart, she wouldn't have bounced back so quickly? And yet what if this apparent recovery was just a mask and she was really ill? What if...

I didn't let myself finish the thought. I turned, opening the door to her room and looking out towards the nurses' station. Several doctors and nurses were there, looking over medical files and talking in low voices. A blonde nurse with pigtails looked up and smiled in my direction. 'Everything okay, Mrs Spencer-Rhodes?'

'Have my daughter's test results come back yet? Is Dr Bloom here today?' I asked, hoping to speak directly with her cardiologist. He'd known her since she was a baby and there was no one I trusted more with my medical questions.

The nurse walked over to me, glancing past me to look at Ceci and smiling. 'Dr Bloom is just going over the results now. He'll be in to see you and Cecilia in just a few minutes. How is she feeling?'

I shrugged. 'She seems okay now, but she definitely wasn't earlier.'

'Kids bounce back so fast, don't they? She's a strong girl.' She smiled, and I tried to mirror the expression on my own face. 'Is there anything you need while you wait for the consultant? Cup of tea?'

I nodded, more to give her an excuse to leave than out of a desire for a hot drink. My stomach was tense with nerves. I'd stayed calm, in control in the park because I'd had to. I wouldn't fall into a panic and shout and scream. That never helped anybody.

I felt sorry for my sister and knew it had been a shock to her to see both Ceci and Tristan in trouble, but a part of me was envious of her too. For her, this was all just temporary. She would go home and her mind would be her own again. Her life wasn't entwined with anyone's the way mine was. Her heart beat only for her. Mine was split into pieces, one for each of my children... and up until this past week, one for Drew too. I wasn't sure what had happened to that piece. It felt hard and cold in my chest, as if it had died the moment I realised how little he valued the life we shared. But I couldn't seem to find a way to cut it out, so there it remained, heavy and sharp, pressing against my lungs, making it hard to take a full breath.

'Beth?'

I turned towards the door and felt my whole body tense as Dr Bloom stepped into the room. He closed the door and gestured to the chairs by the window. Ceci didn't look away from the TV as we walked around her bed to sit.

'Tell me,' I said. 'What do her results say?'

He smiled, and I let myself feel a fragment of relief. He hadn't looked like this when she'd needed surgery last year. 'Her scan was clear. Her bloods too, with the exception of her sugars. Had she eaten before the episode?'

I thought back over the morning. Ceci had refused an ice cream, too excited about going to the park to eat. She'd asked for eggs at breakfast, but Daisy had cooked them, and she'd refused them on the grounds that they were different. I remembered thinking that we didn't have time to start again, and then Rufus had kicked his football against the bifold doors, and by the time I'd finished reprimanding him for what could have been a very expensive mistake, I'd forgotten to give her anything else. I was embarrassed to admit now that *I'd* been the reason she'd fainted. Low blood sugar. It didn't bear thinking about. I'd spent the past three hours pacing holes in my shoes, sure that my baby girl's heart was failing, and instead it was all because I'd been so wrapped up in my own worries that I'd neglected to make sure she ate. I knew how fussy she was, how distracted she could get when it came to food. I should have at least made her bring a snack in the car.

Dr Bloom had stood up and was giving Ceci the once-over with his stethoscope as I sat there overwhelmed with relief yet consumed with guilt and anger too. Yes, this was just a scare, but what if she *had* needed surgery? How would I have managed to take care of her, nurse her back to health and meet the needs of my other children without my husband to support me? Had Drew thought about moments like this when he made his choice? How I, already spread so thin that the concept of *me* time was laughable, would cope when my team was halved? Daisy wouldn't be able to stay much longer, as much as I knew she wanted to be here to help, and Gemma hated me too much to even consider how I might be struggling to keep my head above water. What would happen to us the next time one of them needed more from me than I could give? Because with four children, it was only a matter of time before I was thrown into a situation I couldn't handle alone.

'... so you can go home,' Dr Bloom was saying, a smile on his face as he patted Ceci on the shoulder. The blonde nurse stepped into the room, bringing in a cup of steaming tea and catching his words.

'Oh, lovely. That *is* good news.' She put the cup down on top of a cabinet. 'You enjoy your tea, Mum, and I'll have a chat with Dr Bloom and get your discharge notes all sorted.'

I nodded, rising from my chair. 'Can... can you keep an eye on her for just a minute while I pop downstairs?' I asked the nurse.

'Absolutely. She looks like she won't even notice. Good programme, Cecilia?' the nurse asked in a cheerful voice. Ceci didn't even register that she'd been spoken to.

I muttered my thanks, then left and walked briskly down the hall, pressing the button for the lift. I'd been so worried about how I looked to Gemma, what she thought of me – even though I knew she was wide of the mark – that I'd allowed myself to be cowed and shouted down. But the time for pandering to her and waiting for Drew to wake up and fix everything for me was over. I needed to take control of this situation, and to do that, I would have to accept that I couldn't let other people's opinions affect my actions. If Gemma thought she could bully me into submission, she was in for a shock.

TWENTY-FIVE
GEMMA

I tasted the sharp tang of blood on my tongue and realised I'd split my lower lip, all the nervous chewing and scraping of my teeth against the dry, crusted skin making it brittle. I dabbed at it with the edge of my sleeve, anxiety coursing through me, making it impossible to keep still. The longer I spent stuck in here, waiting for Drew to do something – *anything* that might indicate that his situation was changing – the more I felt myself sinking into panic. I couldn't handle this. I wasn't the right person to be here, sitting by his side waiting endlessly, and yet I couldn't seem to tear myself away for more than a few hours at a time.

Here, I was trapped. Life became some sort of limbo, time lost all meaning, but as hard as it was to watch the clock tick by hour after hour with no change, my hope dwindling, not being here was even more difficult.

Jason, like a match to kindling, had latched on to my weakness and hounded me every time I summoned up the courage to leave Drew's room. My phone never stopped ringing, the messages piling up; I didn't even bother to listen to them before pressing delete. I knew some were from work, but I didn't have the mental energy to sift through them. If I'd been weak before, it was nothing compared to what I was experiencing now. I'd run out of cannabis, and unless I bit the bullet and spoke to Jason, I would have to manage without until I could find another source. And I'd been taking too much codeine. I always tried to stretch out my supply, but what I had left was fast dwindling. I would have to call and tell my GP I'd lost them – had my bag stolen or something. She wouldn't believe me, but I had to try and convince her. I couldn't manage without.

So here I was, with no way of distracting myself, faced with the knowledge that all I needed to do to make the pain go away was to call Jason right now. Ask him to meet me. Bring the one thing I wanted – the only thing that could wipe out the mess going on around me and make it all better. I'd had his number ready to go on my phone more times than I could count, and the only thing that had stopped me from pressing that call button was the sleeping face of my brother lying on the hospital pillow, condemning me even without knowing my plans.

Drew had always managed to twist a situation, to find a way to blame himself for the terrible things I did. When I'd shoplifted a DVD I couldn't afford when I was fifteen, he'd sunk into a dark mood for days afterwards, talking about how I should have come to him, how he'd thought he'd made it clear that he was there for me. He'd assumed it was a simple fix – he would give me the money and it would all be fine, but it hadn't been about the money for me. It had been something else I couldn't find a way to explain to him back then. A fleeting thrill that had made life seem more interesting, blotted out the pain that lay constant and throbbing in my belly, the anxious need to be somewhere else, to run, though I never could understand where I was trying to get to. I didn't want his money, but he'd taken my theft as a personal failing of his own, and the look on his face had been enough to put me off ever doing it again.

I stood back up from the now familiar chair beside his bed, though I'd only been sitting there a matter of minutes, and reached for a comb, sweeping it through his thick, shiny dark hair, something I did almost hourly – just another anxious habit.

I paused in the act as I heard the unmistakable sound of Beth's voice in the reception area outside. I'd hoped, though I'd known it was a ridiculous wish, that she might stay away for a few days, perhaps just calling to check for updates rather than coming in to make things awkward. I hadn't spoken to her since we'd argued yesterday, and even though I knew I'd been harsh and should have kept my mouth shut, there was no way I was going to apologise for what I'd said.

I was tempted to pick up my bag and leave now – it wasn't like she would stay long anyway; she never did, and I could hang around in the café for twenty minutes until she felt like she'd done her duty – but before I could make up my mind, the door opened and she stepped inside. She ignored me completely as she walked up to Drew on the other side of the bed, looking down at him with a blank expression.

There was a strange energy about her – I could feel it radiating from her, her cheeks flushed, her eyes hard and shining as if she were ready for a row. She looked up at me, and for a moment, I hardly recognised her. There was nothing of the small, well-mannered woman who always seemed to be out of her depth, rushing to catch up with everyone around her. No sign of the little girl dressed up in Mummy's designer clothes and high heels. This Beth looked fierce, and for once, I had no idea what was about to come out of her mouth.

'Ceci is up on the children's ward,' she said in a clipped tone.

I frowned, taken aback and confused. 'Is she okay?' I asked. 'Is it her heart?'

'Not this time. Not that you care.' She stepped back. 'Either of you, it would seem,' she added, throwing a scathing look at Drew. 'I haven't come to argue with you, or to waste my time waiting for him to wake up. I have a thousand responsibilities, and do you know what? You had no right to tell me I'm wrong to worry about money, Gemma, none whatsoever. Walk a mile in my shoes and then tell me you think I'm a gold-digger. I've come to collect his wallet from the nurses, because believe it or not, I'd like to pay my electricity bill and put petrol in my car and food on my table, and I will not apologise for that.'

I shook my head. 'You're putting words in my mouth, Beth. You know that isn't what I meant. I'm not talking about the basics. I'm talking about your whole life. The pressure you put on him to keep making more, giving more, never stopping. Have you even asked yourself why he's here? Why a man in Drew's position, with what looks like everything going for him, would try and kill himself? Isn't that the kind of thing a wife should know? Did you even realise how much he was struggling?'

She folded her arms. 'Of course I didn't – how could I? He never told me! We were both busy – working, sorting the kids. Yes, it's never-ending, but that's what he signed up for. That's family life, Gemma!'

'No, Beth. That's a treadmill. An assembly line, working day in, day out to be something special. To produce a product that looks perfect on the outside so everyone can look at you and wish they had what you have. Your life, your home, your kids. But all those achievements come at a price. This is yours.' I glanced at Drew. 'And if he wakes up, I think you owe him an apology.'

The door opened and a nurse stepped in. 'Here's everything he had when he was brought in,' she said, handing a clear plastic bag to Beth. 'His wallet was in his pocket. I've left it in there for you. There's a set of keys too.'

Beth's shoulders seemed to relax, and I couldn't help but think she looked far happier now that she had his bank cards in her grasp. She looked up at me, her eyes blazing as they met mine, so different from the shy, uncomfortable expression she'd worn during our argument yesterday. 'If he wakes up, there will be an apology all right. But,' she added, turning to leave, 'it sure as hell won't be coming from me.'

TWENTY-SIX

BETH

I slammed the dishwasher door shut, turning back to face the mess of the kitchen, pasta sauce dried on the hob, toys and books and clothes seeming to cover every single surface. I'd told the cleaner not to come this week, embarrassed that I couldn't pay her, and I couldn't believe how little time it had taken for me to miss her. I felt like I'd spent hours moving from room to room, hoovering and tidying, and yet the house was still in chaos and I was running out of steam. I had Drew's bank card now, but I knew that whatever money was available in his account might have to last me a long time. I had the mortgage to pay, food to buy, and extras like a cleaner were luxuries I couldn't justify right now. Especially knowing that even if Drew did wake up, he didn't have a job to go back to.

Daisy was upstairs reading a story to Rufus and Amelie, and Ceci was already asleep, worn out from her adventures at the park and the hospital, no doubt. I was still filled with relief that it had just been a simple blood sugar imbalance rather than the beginnings of another issue with her heart, but despite her being discharged with the all-clear and instructions to make sure she ate her dinner, I still felt shaken by the day's events. I'd sent two more messages to Tristan, explaining what had happened with Ceci and telling him that I expected him back by half past nine, and now I couldn't stop clock-watching, counting down the minutes, hoping that he would do as I'd asked and come home, though he'd sent no reply to indicate he would.

I was shaking with exhaustion, with the adrenaline of having confronted Gemma, along with the comedown from the fear I'd felt rushing through the hospital doors with my daughter in my arms, unable to stop thinking the worst. I felt like I had run a marathon, and yet there seemed to be no end in sight. Was this what my life would be now? Plastering over the cracks, holding it all together and losing myself as a result? I didn't know how much longer I could keep going.

I ran a cloth under the tap, wringing it out and wiping the counters, not bothering to move things out of the way. What was the point? It would only be messy again by breakfast time tomorrow.

Daisy padded in, her feet bare, her long, wild hair tied up in a messy bun on top of her head, bringing a soft, uplifting energy with her. She shook her head, smiling as she took the cloth from my hand, taking over without a word. That small gesture was enough to make the tears spring to my eyes, my exhaustion making me weak and shaky. She scrubbed away the evidence of the last-minute dinner I'd thrown together, then tossed the cloth into the sink and picked up a bottle of oat milk that had been left on the side, putting it back in the fridge. 'They're both in bed,' she said over her shoulder. 'I told them they could read for a little while – is that okay?'

I nodded. It should have been lights out over an hour ago, but I didn't like to tell Daisy she'd taken too long getting them to bed – not when she was trying so hard to be helpful. I'd told Amelie we would be going to her swimming meet in the morning. Training began at 6 a.m., and the thought of turning up and making conversation with the other parents made me want to back out, but I knew I couldn't. If I was going to be alone, I was going to find a way to make it work. I had to, for their sakes. Amelie didn't deserve to fall behind because I didn't want to have to socialise. And maybe it wouldn't be that bad. I'd always enjoyed getting coffee and hearing all the gossip, planning a lunch or a shopping trip with my friends. Only, I realised now, I would have nothing to contribute to the conversation. I hadn't seen anyone or been anywhere these past few days, and I certainly wasn't going to tell them about Drew. And going for lunch was out of the question. I couldn't fritter money away; I had to be careful. I sighed, and Daisy turned towards me, pulling me into her arms.

'What a day,' she breathed into my hair.

I almost laughed, the tiredness making me giddy. 'You're telling me. Thank God you were there.'

She snorted. 'Fat lot of help I was. I've never felt so out of my depth.'

I shook my head. 'You were a lifesaver. I mean it.' I glanced towards the clock, biting my lip.

'Do you think he'll come back?' Daisy asked softly.

'He'd better. He may think he's all grown up, but he's only fifteen and he's my responsibility. He can't just disappear like that, no matter what the reason.' I sighed again. 'Today was supposed to be about me connecting with them. I honestly don't think it could have gone any worse.'

She smiled softly, squeezing my hand. 'It'll take time, Beth. From what I can see, they aren't used to having an afternoon of freedom. It probably went to their heads. Give it time. And maybe try not to make it into some big thing. Take the pressure off. Sit in the garden and just *be* with them, talk to them. Don't try and over-complicate it by making it something special – that's not what they need.'

I nodded, wondering if Daisy's lack of children was what enabled her to cut through the fog and see exactly what my own family needed. It was a little annoying to realise how right she'd got it, but I wouldn't let pride stand in my way. Time, however, might be more of an issue. There just didn't seem to be enough hours in the day to get through everything, and I wasn't about to let their schoolwork suffer. There were, after all, only so many plates I could keep spinning before some began crashing to the ground.

'He's home,' Daisy murmured as we heard the sound of the front door opening. 'I'll go and tell the little ones it's time to turn their lights out and give you a chance to chat, okay?'

'Thanks,' I whispered, nodding.

I stood waiting in the kitchen, hoping that he would have the courtesy to at least come in and let me know he was home before heading up to hide in his room. I listened, wondering if he was deciding how far he could push me, and then I heard his footsteps heading my way. He popped his head round the door, not bothering to actually step into the room. His entire body screamed resistance, and it was clear that he was annoyed at having been summoned back here. I wasn't going to apologise for that though. He'd put me through hell today.

'I'm home,' he grunted.

I nodded. 'I see that. Have you eaten?'

He made a non-committal noise but I decided not to push it. 'Tris... I've been worried sick. You just disappeared today without so much as a word. What on earth happened?'

He shrugged, looking past me as if I wasn't even speaking, and I had to bite my tongue to keep from reacting. I'd hoped to ease into the tougher topics, but it was clear that the only way to get him to talk to me was to shock him, let him know that I'd seen his secret meeting.

'Who was that man you were talking to earlier?' I asked, my heart beating harder in anticipation of what I might hear. A part of me didn't want to have this conversation, to hear him confess that he'd been talking to Lee behind my back, or that he felt unable to confide in me. Whatever the truth was, I knew it was going to hurt, and I steeled myself for his response.

He gave a tiny shake of his head. 'What man?' he asked, his thick eyebrows creasing.

'The man at the park,' I said, watching his face closely. 'You were talking to him by the trees and I saw what looked like an argument.'

His eyes darkened, his mouth hardening into a sneer. 'You saw that?'

'Yes. It... it looked like you were about to get into a fight. It's not like you, Tristan. I don't understand what you were even doing talking to someone like that.'

He stepped through the doorway, his arms folded, and I was suddenly struck by how tall he'd grown, more than half a foot above my own five-foot-three frame. His jaw was set, and as he moved closer to me, I felt small. Vulnerable. Cowed by my own son.

'You mean to tell me that you thought I was about to be beaten to a bloody pulp, and you still left? Is that what you're telling me?'

'Tris,' I said, trying to dispel the pleading note from my voice. *I* was the parent and he was the child who'd been keeping secrets. I took a breath, speaking in a calmer tone. 'I had no choice. You *know* that. I had to take your sister to hospital. I made sure Daisy stayed to look for you, but she couldn't find you.'

I reached for his hand, but he snatched it back and I sighed, dropping my own to my side.

'Is he the one who gave you that black eye?' I asked, terrified to think of what he'd got himself caught up in. Lee could have him doing anything. The thought made me sick to my stomach.

'Tristan,' I pushed when he offered no response. 'Did he do that? Or was it someone else? You know you can tell me anything, don't you? I'm sorry I didn't stay but—'

'You're unbelievable, you know that?' he interrupted. 'I can't believe you'd leave when—'

'I *had* to.'

He stared at me, and I met his angry glare with hope, willing him to see what an impossible situation I'd been in. I hated that he felt like I'd let him down, though I felt it too. I knew that behind his cold, impassive expression, he was hurt. I'd hurt him by choosing to prioritise Ceci over him.

He shook his head. 'Yeah,' he replied, his tone full of a hatred that made me recoil. 'Well, I do too!' He turned away, heading straight for the front door.

'No, Tristan, don't you dare go out now!' I exclaimed, shocked that he would even think of it after disappearing just hours before. He couldn't be serious. 'Don't you dare leave this house, young man!' My voice was shrill with panic as I chased after him.

He didn't even spare me a glance as he strode through the door and out into the night. I turned, seeing Daisy pale-faced and scared at the top of the stairs, and then I burst into tears.

Now that I'd started crying, I couldn't seem to figure out how to stop. And all the while, as I sobbed without restraint, I felt the soft hands of my mother and my sister as they poured jugs of warm water over my soapy hair. Murmured words of reassurance as they helped me from the bath, wrapped a thick towel around my body and guided me into the bedroom. Daisy had called our mum when she'd realised I had broken. Not that she described it that way. Hysterical, distressed... those were the words she had used on the phone, but I knew the truth. I was broken. Defeated. By Drew, Tristan, my own failings as a wife and a mother. Ever since I'd arrived at the hospital to be told that horrendous news, I'd been trying to keep things moving forward, find a way, figure it out. I'd refused to crumble, but now that I had, I didn't know how I could ever begin to repair myself.

I had lost the love of my life.

I had lost him, and it was so much worse than if he'd been killed in an accident.

Everything we'd had together felt like a lie, every moment, every memory spoiled by the way it had ended. I'd been so angry I'd managed to avoid this feeling of grief, but now there was no way to dodge the blows as it hit me over and over again.

He might be gone forever. He would never hold me in those strong arms again. Never make me laugh with his long-winded stories that built and built, each sentence more hilarious than the last. We would never make love again. Even if he woke up, it was clear that he didn't want me. My marriage was over, and that realisation, now that I'd allowed it to come, fuelled my grief and fed my tears until I was blinded by my own sorrow.

My mum helped me to sit on the stool at my dresser, rubbed my damp hair with a sweet-smelling towel, then picked up my brush, gently working at the tangles, silent and stoic, her love radiating through her touch. Daisy reappeared in the doorway, holding a steaming mug of tea, placing it in my hands before pressing a kiss to my cheek. 'You aren't alone,' she said. 'No matter what, you must never think that.'

I shook my head, tears still streaming down my face, blurring my vision. 'What?' I asked, confused.

'Before,' she said, sitting down on the edge of my bed, resting her elbows on her knees. 'You kept saying it over and over. "I'm alone, I'm alone."' She bit her lower lip, looking away, and I realised she was trying not to cry too. 'You aren't,' she said, her eyes shining as they met mine. 'I promise you that.'

I nodded. 'Thank you,' I managed, my voice cracking. 'You didn't have to do this.'

I felt Mum's arms wrap around my shoulders from behind me, her cheek pressing against my ear. 'We did.' She squeezed me tight, trying to cushion me from the pain. 'Because we love you,' she added softly. 'And because you *aren't* alone.' She nodded at Daisy as she repeated her promise.

I closed my eyes, taking a shuddering breath, letting them care for me because I didn't have the strength to do it for myself. I was broken, but they weren't going to let that stop them trying to put me back together again. They would wrap me in a cocoon, hold me until I was strong enough to break free and take control of myself. And right now, I had no choice but to let them.

TWENTY-SEVEN

Day Five

'What are you doing?' Daisy asked, leaning over my shoulder to look at the computer screen.

'Selling Drew's car.'

'For fifty grand?' she exclaimed, her eyes widening as she stared at the ad.

'It was seventy new and I'm not going to be able to make those kind of loan repayments without access to his accounts. I need to pay off as much as I can now and make a start on clearing his debts before they get out of control.' I cast a glance over what I'd written then clicked to post the ad and turned to her.

She nodded towards my face. 'Have you put something on that?'

Tentatively I touched the long scratch that ran down my cheek, knowing it was my own fault I'd got it. Daisy and Mum had put me to bed last night, insisting they could handle the children so I could get some uninterrupted rest. When I'd heard Ceci calling for me at 2 a.m., I'd been half out of bed when Daisy had popped her head round the door telling me to go back to sleep – she would take care of it. I should have insisted then – I knew Ceci would never settle –

but I'd been so tired, so desperate for more sleep that I'd lain back against my pillow, dozing as I half listened to Daisy's gentle, soothing voice floating along the landing.

The next thing I knew, Ceci was bursting into my room in a blind panic, in the midst of a meltdown caused by the change in her routine. It didn't matter how kind, how patient her aunt was, Ceci expected *me* at night, and I'd let her down by not showing up for her. She'd been utterly inconsolable, flailing her arms, screaming so loud I knew she'd wake the neighbours, and when I'd tried to take her in my arms, she'd lashed out, scoring a sharp scratch down my cheek that had stung like hell.

It had taken another two hours to get her back to sleep, Daisy standing by helplessly, lost for any idea of what to do, and all the while I'd kept thinking that *this* was why I couldn't ask for help. Because even when I was given it, it only made things harder. If I'd got up to see to her, Ceci would have been asleep in five minutes. I should have just done it and saved everyone the trouble of having to fix the damage I'd created by my own selfishness.

'I've put some antiseptic on it. It looks worse than it feels,' I said, standing to put the kettle on, craving caffeine. 'Did Mum get off okay?'

'She did. Her neighbour said Dad was fine overnight, but you know how Mum worries.'

'She shouldn't have stayed.'

'She wanted to. It was important.'

I nodded, glancing at my phone, wondering how long it would be before I got any interest in the car. There was still no message from Tristan – I hadn't heard a word from him since he'd stormed out last night. I'd called his phone dozens of times, but it just went straight to voicemail. I felt sick, not knowing where he was, who he might be with.

'Is Drew going to be okay about you selling it?' Daisy asked, seeming to read my thoughts. 'If... I mean, when he wakes up.'

I shrugged, looking for the teabags, wondering why my mother always seemed to rearrange my kitchen so I couldn't find what I needed. 'He'd be furious if he knew. He was on a waiting list a year for that car, and he loves... loved it. But what else can I do?' I picked up the stack of bills I'd piled on the counter and fanned them out for her to see. 'I can't live on fresh air alone, Daisy. I have to do something.'

She nodded, walking over to the cupboard above the hob, pulling out the jar that was home to the teabags and handing it to me. I could see that there was something else she wanted to say.

'What?' I asked, placing the jar down beside the mugs.

'I was just wondering about life insurance. Does Drew have it?'

I gave a little snort, opening the jar and taking out two teabags. 'He has it. I found the paperwork in his desk upstairs. But the policy says there's no payout for suicide. If he dies, we won't get a penny. If he's discharged with disabilities, we might be entitled to some sort of payment, but that's assuming he even wants to come back here, which is highly unlikely given what he did. And if he stays in the hospital, stuck in this limbo, we'll get nothing. I know it sounds like I've got my priorities all wrong, but *you* know what it means to lose everything, Daisy. I can't have that life for my children. Do you remember how it used to be? How cold we were all the time? How hungry?'

I grabbed the handle of the kettle, remembering how we used to drink cups of hot water to take the edge off our hunger pains and warm us up.

'I may sound crass talking about money when my husband's in a coma, but it's not something I can just ignore.' I poured the tea then pressed my fingers to my eyes, trying not to cry again. I was sure there couldn't be any tears left after last night.

'I don't think you're crass. I think you're scared.'

I nodded. 'Of course I am. I'm terrified. You saw Ceci last night when her routine changed just the tiniest bit. What would she be like if I had to pull her out of her school? If I couldn't pay for her speech therapist anymore?'

'She'd adapt. It would be harder for her than for the others, but she'd be okay. You're her anchor, Beth. You'd keep her steady.'

I picked up my mug, holding it tight between my palms. 'He had to have known what a mess he was leaving us in. He's not stupid. He must have realised what would happen.'

Daisy stepped closer, one hand resting on the counter as she looked at me, her face filled with empathy. 'Maybe he was just in too much pain to think clearly.'

I closed my eyes, wanting to bat away the words. 'But—' I broke off, my voice choked with emotion. 'How could I not have seen it?' I whispered. 'How could my own husband have been hurting this much and I didn't see it?' I shook my head. 'Was this my fault?'

'It's nobody's fault, sweetheart,' she said, shaking her head.

'We were happy. We *were*. Busy, yes, but never miserable. I look back and all I can see is a happy life that he stole from us. It's like he had this secret world that none of us knew about. I keep thinking I should have known, but he never let on. He never gave me the opportunity to help him. And I think I hate him for that, Daisy. I never thought it possible. He was the love of my life. But now I really think I hate him.'

'Then hate him. And when the feeling passes, maybe there will be room for something else. Maybe you'll find a way to love him again.' She picked up her tea. 'He did something that broke your heart. But I know he never wanted to hurt you. This was about Drew. *His* needs. *His* pain. He wasn't thinking about you, the kids, the money. If he had been, he wouldn't have done it. You know that. He must have been tearing himself up over this, Beth. He wouldn't have done it lightly.'

I nodded, knowing that was true, and yet it made nothing any easier. He was still gone. We had still been abandoned by the man who'd been our provider, our protector, our world. And however hard it had been for him, in the end he'd still made this choice. We hadn't been enough to make him want to stay.

I walked through the hospital, finding it a far quieter place in the late evening. The shops were closed, the seating areas were all but empty and there was a serene, calm vibe now that the hordes of day patients and visitors had gone home. I'd been uncertain about leaving Daisy with the children, especially after what had happened last night, but it was only just gone nine, and the chance of Ceci waking up over the next few hours were slim.

I wasn't sure if it was the act of selling Drew's beloved car, or the conversation with Daisy where she'd gently yet firmly pointed out that perhaps Drew hadn't been thinking of me when he'd decided to make an attempt on his life, but something had shifted today, making me feel less certain, more unsettled than ever before. I'd had a growing need to see him, to look at the face that had been as familiar as my own for the past twelve years and try and pinpoint what I had managed to miss. I didn't want to feel guilt, and honestly, right now I wasn't sure that was even the right word for whatever emotion was plaguing me, but something had settled in my heart over the past few hours and I knew I wouldn't stop pacing the floor until I could see him.

It was all so confused in my mind: anger, betrayal, broken trust, heartbreak, loneliness, and the constant trickle of ice-cold fear... I didn't know how to separate out all the emotions, how to break down what I felt, but I knew I needed to come here, see if by looking at my husband I might make room for empathy, warmth, understanding – emotions I'd yet to grasp hold of. But it had to be without Gemma sitting by, watching with sour disapproval.

The ward sister had told me over the phone that Gemma had been going home at night at their insistence, and I got the impression she'd been put out by Gemma's stubborn attitude and refusal to cooperate. She'd given me an open invitation to come in, making a pointed comment about how it would be nice for me to have some privacy to talk to Drew without an audience, and I'd agreed gratefully.

I paused in the hall that led to Drew's ward, waiting for a porter to wheel an empty bed past me, and as I looked up, I saw a face that made my heart leap, my body plunged into relief.

'Tristan!' I gasped as the tall, handsome boy walked around the corner in my direction, his headphones clamped over his ears, his eyes on the ground. He froze, raising his head to look at me and I was struck by how incredibly sad he appeared, his shoulders slumped, his eyes red as if he'd been crying. At any other time I would have launched into a lecture about how worried I'd been, how irresponsible he was to walk out and not return my calls. I would have been laying down the law and telling him what consequences to expect for his actions, fearful that any give on my part would lead to a slippery slope of negative behaviour. But now as I looked into his deep, sorrowful eyes, all thoughts of punishing him flew out the window. All I could feel was relief.

I rushed forward, wrapping my arms around his neck, pulling him close in a tight hug, breathing in the smell of his skin, the scent of cold outdoor air clinging to him.

'I'm so glad to see you, darling,' I whispered, stroking the back of his head just as I had done when he was small. I thought I felt his body relax into mine for a moment, taken by surprise to find that he wasn't in trouble, no doubt. For the first time in as long as I could remember, he hugged me back, and I savoured the moment, wishing I could hold on to it forever. All my thoughts about how he didn't care about Drew were cast aside, and I wondered if this was the first time he'd visited in secret.

I felt him pull back, and reluctantly I let him. 'You went to see him?' I asked, keeping one hand on his arm, as if I could protect the connection between us if only I didn't let go.

He gave a nod.

I sighed, understanding. 'I know it looks scary, all those wires and tubes...'

He shrugged, looking down at his feet. 'Yeah,' was all he said in reply. I didn't want to push him, not now.

'There's half a lasagne in the fridge at home if you're hungry.' I tried to make it sound casual, but my need for him to be home, where I knew he was safe, seeped through my words, making them sound pleading.

He nodded. 'Thanks.'

'Should... should I tell Auntie Daisy you're on your way back?'

He met my eyes, questioning, confused at my choice of words, the freedom I was giving him to make up his own mind. But to order him around now would be to lose him. Our relationship was fragile – I could feel it. Any move on my part to dominate his choice would be enough to see him walk away, perhaps for good, and I couldn't risk that.

Slowly, he nodded. 'Yeah. Okay. I'll see you later.' He didn't wait for a reply as he walked away, but it didn't matter. He was going home.

I sent a quick message to Daisy, instructing her not to confront him, to just let him brood in his bedroom, and to let me know the moment he arrived, then slipped my phone back into my bag and walked on towards Drew's door. The corridor outside was empty, the lights already dimmed for the night shift, the smell of the dinner trolley lingering in the confined space hours after the meal must have been served. I felt suddenly nervous, though it made no sense. I knew what I was walking into, what I would see. Pushing aside my anxiety, I opened the door, stepping in and closing it quietly behind me.

It felt strange to walk in here and not find Gemma scowling up at me, letting me know without needing to say a word that my presence was unwelcome. From the moment he'd been admitted, I'd been wishing she would go home and give me this opportunity, but now that I was here on my own, I felt awkward, unsure of why I'd even come.

My thoughts drifted to Tristan, and I wondered what he'd been doing here. Had he talked to Drew? I tried to focus on being happy that he'd made the effort to come rather than feeling jealous that he hadn't wanted to speak to me – that he might find it easier to talk to a man who had all but walked out on him. I shook away the thought, feeling guilty that it had even popped into my head. Of course Tristan wanted to be with Drew. Drew had raised him. He'd been a father to him in a way Lee never could have been.

Tristan was probably missing him. Consumed with fear for what would happen to him.

I sighed, looking uncomfortably at my husband now. He was wearing a royal-blue button-down pyjama top, his hair brushed but fluffy, with no styling product in it, his chin smooth, no doubt thanks to Gemma. Privately, I agreed with her. These things shouldn't be neglected. I'd never understood why some of my friends didn't insist on their husbands shaving over the weekends or holidays, saying nothing as they grew unattractive, uneven facial hair that gave them a scruffy, casual vibe. Drew had never been like that, and I'd always been proud of how smart he was, how he made me want to make an effort to match up to him.

I walked slowly towards him, feeling a tightness in my chest, my hands fidgeting by my sides. His mouth was ever so slightly open, and I watched him breathe softly, his chest rising and falling rhythmically. There had never been a need for him to be intubated. He could breathe unaided, and they said there was still brain activity. And yet, still he wouldn't wake. The doctor had explained that sometimes this happened. Sometimes patients like Drew just stayed asleep, slowly losing their strength, their bodies shutting down until they faded away. He'd tried to gloss over that possibility, talking about how hopeful he was, how they hadn't given up on Drew, but of course those words had stayed with me. How could they not?

I reached for his hand, hesitating before changing my mind and folding my arms instead. I'd wanted to come here; this had been my choice, but now I didn't know what to say. I chewed my lip then cleared my throat, leaning closer so that I could speak softly.

'Was it really that bad?' I half whispered, my throat closing on a ball of emotion as I asked the question that had plagued me every minute of the past few days. 'Was our life really so awful that you had to make this choice? I thought we were happy... I thought you loved us.'

I squeezed my eyes shut, trying not to cry, though I could feel the sting of tears pricking beneath my eyelids.

'Why didn't you talk to me?' I asked, reaching for the bed rail, still unable to bring myself to touch the man in the bed – the man who looked like the love of my life and yet couldn't be. Not now. Not after what he'd chosen to do.

'I'm your wife. I have been by your side for more than ten years. I would have done anything for you. Why didn't you just talk to me?'

I wiped roughly at my eyes, angry at myself, at him, at the whole awful situation I was trapped in. This had been a stupid idea. I should never have come. I wished Gemma were here so I didn't feel compelled to spill out my agony, to have this ridiculous half conversation with someone who clearly couldn't hear me. He hadn't so much as blinked.

I took a deep breath, squashing down my pain, my feelings of abandonment and betrayal, and with a quick nod to myself, as if to confirm that I was right, that this was all a waste of my time, I turned and walked out of the room. I had a family at home who needed me.

TWENTY-EIGHT

GEMMA

Day Six

I glanced at Beth over the top of the book I was pretending to read, seeing her sitting rod-straight in her seat, glancing between Drew and the door. I knew she didn't want to be here – it was only out of a sense of duty that she'd made the effort to come. She'd startled me the last time we'd met, when she'd stormed in, guns blazing, making no apology for taking Drew's bank card, refusing to feel guilty for what she'd felt forced to do. Something had changed in her, or perhaps I was only seeing it for the first time. With her daughter admitted to the children's ward, something primal had been released in her, and as much as I'd always disliked her, I couldn't help but respect her for seizing control of her life.

I'd wondered after she'd strode out that day if she might stay away now, only returning if the doctors called to deliver good – or bad – news in the final chapter of this awful experience, but she'd arrived this morning after the school run, silent and apparently resolved to continue making the time to visit, despite her internal conflict. And for the first time I could remember, I felt awkward. It had always been so easy to fight with her – challenge her – but I couldn't bring myself to do it now, not when she'd bothered to show up and sit here when she already had Drew's money. She clearly didn't have to, and that made me question myself.

I cleared my throat, the silence in the room ringing in my ears, making me tense and uncomfortable. 'How are the kids?' I asked, flicking my gaze towards her.

She looked up, surprised, her brow creasing as if she thought I might be playing some game. I supposed I couldn't blame her.

'They're managing,' she replied quietly. 'They've been asking questions about Drew, though of course they don't know what's happened. They miss him. His absence hasn't gone unnoticed.'

I nodded. 'He's a hands-on dad. I'm not surprised.'

'Was,' she corrected, her expression hardening. '*Was* a hands-on dad.'

I closed my mouth, once again stunned into silence by the firm authority in her tone. She had always tried to be friendly, even when I wasn't. Always glossed over anything caustic from me, pretending that she either hadn't heard or hadn't understood. It was part of the reason I disliked her so much. Her reactions had never felt genuine.

She folded her arms, glancing at Drew. 'You know,' she said, almost casually, 'I always felt like an intruder when it came to the two of you. You and Drew were so close, long before the start of our relationship, before I interrupted.'

She took a breath, and I stared at her. This was the longest conversation we'd ever managed, but if she carried on making such ridiculous claims, I wouldn't be able to bite my tongue much longer. Yes, Drew and I were close, but it was *her* who'd made *me* feel like an intruder, always there, always by his side. I opened my mouth to tell her so, but she spoke first.

'There was never room for anyone else.' She pursed her lips, her eyes meeting mine, challenging, as if to dare me to deny it. I almost took the bait but reminded myself just in time that Drew wouldn't want me to get into yet another conflict with his wife.

I shrugged. 'We've always stuck together.'

'You trust him,' she said softly, her eyes still on mine, watching me closely in a way that made me want to squirm out of view. I hated to be held under the microscope for analysis. 'You let him see the real you. A version that nobody else gets to see.'

My eyes widened, shocked by how accurate her words were, that she'd had the awareness to see past the armour I wore to protect myself. I looked down at my lap, refusing to continue this conversation. I didn't care if she thought she knew me. Yes, perhaps she knew there was more than met the eye, but she had no idea who I really was deep down. Only Drew knew that.

'What happened to make you pull back from the world, Gemma?' she pushed.

She waited, but I continued to stare down at my lap, refusing to participate in this conversation. I hoped she'd take the hint and shut up so we could revert to our uncomfortable silence, or better yet, pick up her bag and leave so I didn't have to endure her attempt at playing the concerned therapist.

'Drew told me that you paint,' I heard her say. 'I'd love to see your paintings.'

'They're private. It's just a hobby,' I muttered, more upset than I wanted to let on that Drew had shared this titbit of information with her. I knew, of course, that they talked about me, but I had hoped that Drew would respect my privacy, and to hear her speak so freely of something that meant so much to me made me feel vulnerable in a way I couldn't stand.

I picked up my bag, rummaging through it before remembering I'd taken the last two codeine tablets on the bus on the way here this morning. I stared at the empty foil packet, silently kicking myself for not picking up the spare pack from my bedside cabinet this morning. I needed to get on the phone to the GP. I didn't know why I was putting it off, except for the fact that I was afraid of what she would say. If she told me I had to wait, I wouldn't cope, I just wouldn't. Jason would have to get me some, I thought, my fingers squeezing the empty packet. I shook the thought away, knowing I couldn't trust myself to call him now. I took a deep breath, then released the packet and dropped the bag at my feet.

'He said you could make a career of it if you wanted to.'

I snapped my head up. 'I don't. They're mine. They're personal.' I gave a bitter laugh. 'You wouldn't understand.'

I closed my eyes, thinking of the pain that poured out of me onto the canvas when I picked up a brush. It had been an escape for me – a therapy of sorts – ever since I was a teenager, but lately I hadn't even had the energy for that. I'd felt myself shutting down.

Beth nodded, taking in my words, folding her arms defensively. 'It's funny, you know. You expend so much effort hiding yourself from the world, yet you think you know everything about *me*. Gold-digger, social climber, tiger mum. That's what you think, isn't it?'

I didn't reply. I had no idea she was self-aware enough to even consider what I thought of her.

'Well, you're wrong,' she continued, her voice growing louder. 'Yes, I want security, a roof over my head. I want my children to be happy and successful, and the best way I can give them that is by making sure they get every possible opportunity, by helping them be the best they can be so they get the lives they deserve. I don't want them to have to choose between eating dinner and heating their homes. I love them, but love doesn't put food on the table. If my parents could have fed me on love, I would have been obese, but they couldn't, and I knew that I had to find a way to give my children more security. But I didn't marry Drew for his money. I know that's what you think, but it's not true. I married him because I fell in love. Because I was sure he would be a good, kind husband and a wonderful father – and part of that was seeing how he took care of you,' she added.

'What?' I replied, surprised. My brain felt fogged and exhausted and I didn't want to keep talking. I wanted her to go. To leave me in peace with my brother. Beth and I were never going to be friends. I didn't know why she felt the need to start trying now.

'You remember my third date with him?'

'Why would I remember that? I'm not obsessed with you, as much as you might think the world revolves around you.'

She shook her head, refusing to back down. 'You were drunk. You called Drew to come and get you from that party in the East End.'

I stared at her, remembering. I'd drunk too much, too quickly, and alcohol had never agreed with me. I had called Drew, and he hadn't even complained. He'd driven straight to the party and picked me up with Beth in the front seat of the car. I'd been too far gone to introduce myself, but even then, I'd felt a spark of jealousy for the woman who had stolen my brother's attention from me. She hadn't said a word as Drew had driven me back to his house and carried me up to the spare room. I remembered her bringing up a glass of water, handing it to Drew in the doorway. She had watched with what I'd assumed was pity as he pulled off my boots and tucked me into bed.

But perhaps I'd been wrong, I thought now, trying to remember back to that night, the way she'd stood by, quiet as a mouse, her eyes never leaving us. Maybe it wasn't pity they'd been filled with. Perhaps she hadn't even been looking at me but instead at Drew, watching as he took care of me without a trace of resentment. Had it been warmth for him I'd mistaken in her expression? Admiration for a man who was willing to put family first?

I stared at her, my head aching, wondering if I had jumped to such harsh conclusions because I was afraid of losing Drew to her, because I'd felt the connection between them that night, even so early in their relationship. He'd had plenty of other girlfriends, but I had known instantly that this one was different.

I sat back in my chair, viewing the woman I'd always thought of as my enemy in a new light. Wondering if my own fears had made me see things that weren't even there. This wasn't the woman I'd painted in my mind. And maybe that was why Drew had chosen her.

TWENTY-NINE

I woke with a shooting pain in my neck, my head lolling over the back of the upright chair, my heart beating fast and the treacherous tears rolling down my cheeks. Slowly, I eased myself up, my neck cracking, releasing some of the tenderness in my bones. The curtains at the window of Drew's room were still open, but the sky was black, the moon concealed by thick clouds, no stars visible. Beth had left hours ago, saying she had to get back to make the children's dinner, and the room felt strangely empty without her here.

I wiped my face with my sleeve, my hands shaking, and stood, leaning over Drew, staring hopefully for some sign of change. My stomach felt queasy, and I couldn't remember eating dinner. They must not have brought any for me today. I could feel anxiety pulsing through me and wondered what time it was. Drew lay in exactly the same position as he'd been in when I'd last cast an assessing gaze over him. No change. Nothing new. Despite myself, I couldn't help but let the disappointment hit me, as it did every time I dared to hope.

Reaching over to the table, I pulled out my phone, seeing that it was just gone 2 a.m. I was sure the nurses would have had plenty to say about the fact that I was here so late again. There were two notifications for voicemails, and I pressed to listen to them, more out of a need for distraction from my racing thoughts than any real curiosity. I sat back down, my spine stiff and straight as I held the phone to my ear.

The first was from my boss, telling me that due to no contact over the past week, he had no choice but to hand me my notice with immediate effect. My P45 would be sent in the post.

I sighed, frustrated with myself, with him, with the fact that I had no idea how I was going to afford my rent next month. I hadn't liked the job and it wasn't as if I hadn't known this would happen, but I'd just wanted a few days to stick my head in the sand and focus on my brother. It didn't seem fair that I couldn't have even that.

The second message was from my GP. I'd sent an email request in today asking for my repeat prescription to be approved.

'Hi, Gemma,' Dr Clarkson said, sounding rushed. 'Got your email. I'm going to need you to come in for review before I can sign that off. Is a week today good for you, 3 p.m.? Call the surgery to confirm when you get this.'

I sucked my teeth, my jaw clenched as I dropped the phone in my lap, staring straight ahead at my brother. A *week*? A week with nothing, and no promise that she'd even give me what I needed after that? I couldn't do it. I wouldn't make it.

A growing desperation seemed to be building inside of me. I had been trapped here, waiting, hoping, praying to a God who clearly wasn't there or didn't care about someone as worthless as me that I would see a flicker of an eyelid, a twitch of a finger, any tiny sign that Drew could still come back to me. That I would hear the one voice that mattered speak my name and tell me this nightmare was over. But it hadn't happened. Nothing had changed and I was beginning to panic that it never would.

I stood up, gripping my phone, moving back to the bed to where he lay, so peaceful he could be dead. *He might as well be dead!* I thought, my chest tightening against a flood of emotion.

'Wake up,' I whispered. I slid my phone into my pocket, taking his hand in mine, shaking it gently.

'Wake up,' I said, my voice louder now. 'Drew, please, I can't do this... I can't be here alone; I can't make it without you. You have to wake up! You have to!' I balled my hands into fists, lashing out at his chest, his shoulders, trying to force him to come back, to feel something that triggered a spark, even if it had to be pain.

'Wake up! Wake up! Fucking wake up!' I screamed.

The door flew open and the ward sister strode in, her face stony. 'Take your hands off the patient this instant!' she demanded.

'He's my brother!' I yelled. 'My only brother, and you and this hospital are letting him down. You're doing nothing! You haven't got a clue, have you? You've no fucking idea how to help him. Am I supposed to just sit here and wait?'

She folded her arms. 'No, you're not going to stay and wait. You're going to leave this room and go home, or I'm going to call security. I will not have you disturbing the ward like this. It's the middle of the night and you've woken half the patients with that scene. Now take your things, get some rest and do not come back until you're able to conduct yourself properly.'

'How dare you? I have a right to be here!'

'Security will remove you forcefully if you insist on making it difficult, Gemma.'

I stood rooted to the spot, breathing heavily, my teeth clenched as I glared at her. Then, realising that she meant it, I picked up my bag and jacket and stormed past her. There was no point staying anyway. He wasn't going to wake up. I'd been kidding myself. Childish hopes I should have known better than to fall for.

I didn't look over my shoulder as I took the stairs to the ground floor, unable to keep still long enough to wait for the lift. I ran through corridors, through the atrium and finally burst out into the cold, starless night. Rain was beginning to fall, and I slipped on my thin jacket, shivering as cool, fat drops splashed down the back of my neck, trickling down my spine. I walked over to lean against a wall, trying to catch my breath, scratching at my arms through the layers. I wanted to crawl out of my own skin. It was too much; the pain was bubbling up inside me, bringing with it old memories, flashbacks I'd thought I'd blocked out, that overwhelming sense of being alone I'd never been able to completely escape. I was drowning in my pain. My fear.

I pulled my phone from my pocket, not hesitating as I scrolled through my contacts, finding the number I needed. I pressed call, held the phone to my ear and knew I had reached rock bottom. I'd fought against it for so long, but now, it didn't matter. There was nothing left to fight for. No point in even trying.

The phone was answered on the second ring, and I heard music in the background, familiar and soothing.

'Jason,' I said, my voice urgent, desperate. I looked over my shoulder at the dark windows of the hospital, as if afraid Drew might hear me, then I turned my back on my brother, leaning closer to the wall. 'Can I come over now?'

THIRTY
BETH

Day Seven

'Here you go, sweetie,' I said, handing Tristan a packed lunch as he walked into the kitchen to pick up his backpack. He took it, nodding his thanks, and I pressed my lips together so as not to smile. He'd been quiet since he came home, but not the same sulky quiet I'd grown to expect from him these past few months. This was a more thoughtful, introspective quiet, and although I hadn't yet found a time that felt right for us to talk properly, I could feel him making an effort, muttering thank yous, putting his shoes on the rack, washing up his plate. Little things that made me sure he'd had some change of heart and was trying the best he could to repair the damage in our relationship.

I still longed to know what was going on with him. It would always be my instinct to jump in and help him, to support him through life's tough times and difficult decisions, but I was beginning to realise that as he grew older, perhaps it was right that I should step back and give him the freedom to work through his own problems. Within reason though, I thought now, remembering the man in the park. If I saw *his* face again, all the good intentions in the world wouldn't keep me from confronting him. There was only so much I was willing to turn a blind eye to.

Tristan glanced at me, our eyes meeting for a second, and he gave a crooked half-smile that made my heart swell.

'Have a good day at school,' I said, trying to put as much warmth as I could into those few words, to translate the depth of my love into a phrase that wouldn't make my awkward teenage son cringe away.

He nodded again, and I managed to hold my tongue, not repeating my offer for him to come in the car with the others. I needed him to see that I trusted him. Or at least was trying to.

He picked up his keys, then shoved his packed lunch into his backpack and headed outside. I nodded to myself, took a quick gulp of my tea and called up the stairs to Daisy and the children, hoping they were ready to head out on the school run.

The ward was busy, the staff rushing from one room to the next, hardly bothering to look up as I made my way to see Drew. Two nurses standing at the desk were talking between themselves about a traffic accident, and I hoped the people who were being admitted were only here with minor injuries, though judging from the look on the nurses' faces, it was far more serious than that. I stepped aside to let a couple of doctors pass me and watched them jog down the corridor, focused on the tasks ahead of them.

I hadn't intended to come again so soon, but somehow I couldn't seem to stop myself. As much as it made me feel confused, angry, hurt to see Drew in the state he was in, I missed him too much to stay away. And I was beginning to understand that Gemma, as much as she kept her silence, was struggling too, perhaps even as much as I was. Her constant presence wasn't, as I'd first thought, a show of ownership over her brother, but a deep need to be by his side. I respected her for that and was surprised to find I was looking forward to speaking to her again today. There had been a subtle shift between us as we'd sat almost companionably yesterday, and there was a comfort in being with someone who cared as much as I did about Drew. A part of me wondered if Gemma might know things I didn't about him, things he might have confided to her that he felt he couldn't say to me.

I had never considered it before, sure that nobody could know my husband the way I did, but now I realised I might have missed things she had seen. I couldn't help but notice that as much as she was devastated by what he'd done, she hadn't asked why, hadn't seemed as blindsided by it as I was. Had she known something? And if she had, had she done anything to try and stop him? To help him?

I was wary of rocking the boat, especially when the ice had only just begun to thaw, but I couldn't deny I was hoping we might broach some of these questions today. We were both here for the same reason, waiting for the man we loved to come back, neither one of us ready to give up on him, and that formed a spiderweb of a connection between us. It would never be hugs and sisterly love between us, but if we could move past the hostility that had existed from the start, that would be something. Besides, the thought of going home to sit in silence as I waited for the children to finish school was torture. Daisy would be working in the spare room, and the silence of the empty house was becoming something to fear, almost as much as the hospital.

I hated that I was having to lie to all the school mums, making up stories and excuses as to why I hadn't been around, still so ashamed of what was really happening. I knew that to speak of it, to confess that I was living in a constant state of anxiety, my mind travelling a spectrum of emotions I hadn't known it was capable of on an hourly basis, would have me sobbing uncontrollably, and I didn't want to cry in front of them. It was sad to realise just how surface-deep the friendships I'd made actually were. I knew instinctively that none of the other mothers would step forward, hug me, give me comforting words of advice. They'd be uncomfortable with my tears, with talk of real emotions. We had never opened up about our pasts, our struggles, and now I didn't trust a single one of them with the truth of what had happened. That made me sad. If you'd asked me a week ago if I had friends, I would have said plenty. Now, I realised that wasn't true.

I pushed open the door to Drew's room, looking across to the chair usually occupied by Gemma. I frowned, finding it empty, and shut the door, walking round the bed to see if her bag was there, if perhaps she'd just popped to the bathroom.

I was disappointed to find no sign of her, realising she must have gone home, something she rarely seemed to do. I'd been looking forward to speaking to her, and now the room felt too intense with just Drew and me to fill it. I felt like I should break the silence, say something to him, but I still wasn't sure how to do that without falling apart – and I wasn't even sure he could hear me anyway.

I turned to look at him now, dropping my bag on Gemma's empty chair. He looked peaceful, almost as if he were sleeping, though he'd never been a calm sleeper at home. He fidgeted and snored and stole more of the quilt than he should have. He always had one arm slung over his head, his leg bent so that it touched mine. Now he lay straight and still, and it didn't look right. I felt a sudden urge to move him, reposition him so that he would feel more comfortable, and instinctively I reached forward, my hand covering his. It was the first time since he'd left us that I'd managed to do it – to touch him – and I could hear my heart thumping loudly in my ears as I slowly linked my fingers with his.

They were warm – strong and familiar – and I paused, biting my lip as I blinked back a rush of emotion. 'I miss you,' I heard myself whisper. 'I shouldn't, but I do.'

I looked behind me to check the door was closed, then lowered the bed rail and, without stopping to question my actions, climbed up onto the mattress beside him. My nose pressed against his neck, I breathed in the scent of his skin, the tang of alcohol wipes mingled with the musky, familiar smell that was simply Drew. I'd always loved his smell.

I closed my eyes, breathing deeply, my arm sliding around his waist, pulling him closer to me.

'I miss you,' I whispered again, my lips close to his ear. I felt a tear trickle down my cheek and gripped him tighter. There had been so many moments over these past few days where I'd wondered if I would ever get to do this again. Lie in a bed with my husband by my side – something so simple that I'd always taken it for granted, but that had been snatched from me in a single moment. I wanted him home, I wanted him with me, and right now it didn't seem to matter that he'd left. I could cope with it. Find a way to forgive him. I just needed him to come back. To wake up. To *try*.

'You could have talked to me, Drew... You should have told me... made me listen. You could have chosen to stay with us... with *me*.' I felt his pulse quicken beneath my cheek.

'Would you...'

I froze, his voice startling me, my fingers gripping the blankets, white-knuckled with tension. He swallowed, the movement rippling against my skin, then spoke again.

'Would you have stayed if you'd known I'd lost everything? If you'd known the mess I'd become? The person I really am?'

I released the blankets and sat bolt upright, gripping his shoulder. 'You're awake? Oh my God!'

'Beth...' he said, his voice hoarse.

'I have to call the nurses. They have to check you!' I exclaimed, slipping off the bed.

'Beth, wait—' He broke off, coughing, and I turned from him, running across the room, my heart thumping erratically in my chest, a thousand conflicting emotions colliding in my mind.

I flung open the door, glancing back over my shoulder to check I hadn't imagined it. Drew's eyes met mine, and I thought I saw a flash of sadness in them. He sighed, then turned his head away from me towards the window, and as I ran down the corridor calling to the nurse, I couldn't help but wonder if he was disappointed to find himself still alive.

THIRTY-ONE
GEMMA

Last night

I stood in Jason's kitchen, tapping my foot impatiently as I waited for him to finish serving another client, who seemed to want to stay and tell both of us his entire life story before he'd push off with his bag of weed. It was gone 4 a.m. now, and I felt like I would scream if I had to wait much longer. Jason's eyes met mine from across the room and, taking pity on me, he strode over, flashing me a conspiratorial wink and handing me the spliff from his own mouth. I took it without a trace of hesitation, though I felt the shame wash over me as I pictured what Drew would say if he knew I was back here. But Drew wasn't able to say anything. He'd left me alone, knowing I couldn't cope – wouldn't survive – and here I was, proving him right.

I raised the joint to my lips, inhaling deeply, my eyes half closed as the warm, comforting smoke filled my lungs. A few weeks ago, this had been all I needed to crush the sharp edges of my anxiety. It had been enough. But now, as deep as I took the smoke into my lungs, it no longer seemed to have the same effect. I craved something stronger, something better, and as much as I hated myself for it, I knew I wouldn't leave here without it.

I leaned against the sink, which was overflowing with dirty dishes, the brown water coated in a layer of grease that turned my stomach. The lino beneath my feet was an indistinguishable grey, and my shoes stuck to it as I fidgeted impatiently. I heard a sound at the front door and felt my whole body tense as I stared wide-eyed, waiting to see who had come. Who was here to see me at rock bottom, my greasy hair tied back, my hands shaking with absolute need? I'd become something I'd sworn I never would, but all the shame in the world wasn't enough to make me walk away.

A massive Alsatian ran into the kitchen, and I felt myself relax a little as it passed me, Jason's flatmate Billy sticking his head round the door. 'Got the Chinese,' he said, holding up a white plastic bag. 'Twenty-four/seven noodles. Can't beat that, can ya?'

Jason nodded. 'Nice one. On my way.'

Billy flashed a smile at me before heading down the hall into the tiny living room, which always seemed to have a carpet of over-flowing ashtrays and empty beer bottles. The client who was still talking incessantly looked up, his eyes widening hopefully.

'And that's your cue to get the fuck out, mate,' Jason said, nodding towards the door.

I bit my lip, hoping he wasn't going to try and make me go too, and watched as the man left with an unceremonious farewell.

The door slammed closed and Jason turned to me with a grin. 'How about some food?'

I shook my head. 'You know why I'm here.'

He smiled. 'Course. I'm impressed you stayed away so long. Most don't make it more than a day and a half. You're a strong girl, Gems.'

'Not strong enough, it would seem.'

He laughed as if it were somehow funny that my life was in his hands – that I was literally about to throw everything away standing here in his stinking kitchen with a dog salivating over my shoes. 'You doing it here? I can sort you out.'

I shook my head. 'I need to be alone.'

He shrugged. 'Fair play. Your call. Anyway, if I don't get a move on, Billy will have polished off all the spring rolls.'

He opened a drawer and handed me a tiny clear baggy, and I palmed it, amazed that the contents could carry so much power. There was the promise of relief. Escape. But also, and I would have been an idiot not to consider it, the guarantee of more pain. The beginning of what could only be an end.

There was some relief in that. In making a choice. I suddenly understood how my brother must have felt in those final moments before slipping that rope around his neck. The lightness in your belly that swore things would be better this way. That the fight to be the person everyone wanted, expected, could end, and you could just let go. Be the fuck-up you'd always been.

I pocketed the baggy, handing over the cash, flashing Jason a wry smile. 'No more freebies now then, Jas?' I said, my voice dripping with sarcasm.

He shrugged. 'No need, is there?'

I glanced away, not wanting to agree, but knowing as well as he did that I was trapped.

'No hard feelings, hey, gorgeous? And if things get tough, I take a variety of payments.' He winked again, and I found I didn't care. I knew it was only a matter of time before I found myself having to barter for what I needed. And I knew already that I would do it.

The dog followed me to the door, and I felt a flash of fear that it might snap at my legs the way that awful dog of Rod and Jan's used to do. But it seemed to realise I wasn't the person to beg to for food and turned, heading off down the dark corridor, from where the smell of noodles and the thump of bass drifted.

I opened the door, stepping out into the night. All I wanted was to get home to my tiny studio, lock myself in and open the bag, which right now seemed to be the only thing that made any sense. I pulled it from my pocket, looking at the tiny amount of pale brown powder that had cost three days' worth of food, and squeezed it gently in my palm.

I couldn't bear the thought of getting on a bus, of sitting still, with people pressed up against me, suffocating me. I needed to move. I broke into a run, feeling the protest in my unfit legs almost as soon as I started but ignoring it, pushing forward despite the pain.

I rounded a corner, looking up at the sky, the stars blinking in the far-off distance, watching my downfall from high above. I stared up at them, hating them, my feet pounding as I turned down the next street, then the next. I reached the main road and glanced to the right, not slowing my pace. And then I was in the air, the breath stolen from my lungs, screeching tyres, burning rubber, and finally the sound of metal on metal as cars skidded and collided all around me. I hit the ground hard, my head smacking against the kerb, headlights and car horns assaulting my senses. Someone screamed, but it felt too far off to matter.

I tried to lift my head and was rewarded with a vision filled with bright sparks. *The stars have fallen*, I thought, blinking as I reached out a hand to grab at them. And then everything went dark.

THIRTY-TWO

BETH

'Thank you, Doctor,' Drew said as the neurologist left the room. For the past four hours, my husband had been ferried all over the hospital for various tests. The nurses had asked me if I wanted to accompany him down to have his CT scan, said I could talk through the earpiece and offer some comfort, but I'd declined, saying I would only get in the way. Besides, I needed to make some calls, ask Daisy to pick up the children from school. Speak to Gemma...

Daisy's elated tone when I'd told her the news only served to highlight how numb I was feeling. The truth was I didn't know *how* I felt right now. I wasn't sure what was happening – if this was just temporary and he'd slip back into unconsciousness within the day, or if slowly we'd see deficits in his memory or cognitive abilities. I didn't want to get my hopes up that he was back with no ill effects, and on top of that, I couldn't stand the thought of making small talk with the man who'd once been my best friend. I needed to understand why we were here, what he'd been thinking, but I wasn't ready to ask, so I did the only thing I could. I distracted myself.

I called Gemma over and over again, desperate for her to come. She would take the pressure off – make it about her relief so my own feelings would be muted. After days of never leaving his side, she seemed to have disappeared off the face of the planet. I couldn't believe that after all her talk of staying in the loop and being kept informed, she would suddenly neglect to answer her phone now.

I'd sent Tristan a text asking him to call me, and he had during his lunch break at school. I'd wanted to tell him that Drew was awake, knowing how every minute in limbo, waiting to hear one way or another, was torture, but I hadn't been able to find the words over the phone. Part of me needed to see the look on his face when he heard. And because I wasn't sure what his reaction might be, I wanted to be there with him, to offer him support. I'd debated with myself as the phone rang, but in the end, I had simply explained that I couldn't get hold of Gemma and was worried about her. It was only partly true. Gemma was a big girl and I was sure she was just burned out – I knew I was, and I hadn't spent nearly as much time here as her.

Tristan had offered to go to Gemma's flat after school and see if she was there, and I'd been half tempted to tell him no – I didn't want him travelling over that side of town, not alone – but I'd held my tongue and thanked him, determined to show him that I trusted him, even though I knew I would be worried sick the whole time. He'd called back at four and said that she hadn't been in as far as he could tell, and I'd thanked him and hung up, angry at her. If she'd been here, I could leave, but now I was trapped with a man I didn't know how to talk to.

'How are the kids?' Drew asked, propped up on a pile of pillows, his brown eyes fixed on mine. I'd thought I would never see them open again, but now that my chance was here, I found myself unable to hold his gaze.

'The children are—' I broke off. I'd been about to say 'fine', but that wasn't true and I wasn't going to lie to make him feel better. 'They're managing. There have had to be a lot of compromises to their routines.'

He nodded. 'And you?' he asked softly. 'How are you?'

I shook my head. 'Don't do that, Drew.'

'What?'

I looked down at my lap, shaking my head again, trying to bite my tongue, to hold in the torrent of accusations lingering so close to the surface.

'Beth...' he sighed. 'You know I care. That I only want the best for you.'

I sprang to my feet, incensed by his platitudes. 'Don't. Don't pretend that you care about us. If you did, you wouldn't have abandoned us. Left us high and dry without so much as an explanation! You didn't even say goodbye,' I said, my throat thickening against a wedge of emotion. 'No note. Nothing to help us understand what the hell you were thinking. You don't do that to the people who love you, Drew. You don't just walk away because you're too afraid to fight.'

I broke off, breathing heavily, unable to look him in the eye. I wasn't ready for this. To be alone with the man who had broken my heart.

'I have to go – Daisy will be struggling without me. It's not fair to leave her to do it all alone,' I added pointedly.

'Beth, just stop, will you? Please just stop. We have to talk – properly talk, I mean, not just grab snippets while you rush from one thing to the next. I need you to understand why this happened, why I—'

'Why you *what*, Drew? Why you decided to leave us? Why you thought it was okay to traumatise our children? Why you would lie to me for months? Go on then, tell me, because I'd love to hear why you think your life was so fucking terrible you had to resort to death to escape us!'

I shook my head, angry with myself for not having the strength to hold back. It was too soon for this conversation. I should have left hours ago – this wasn't the time to do this.

'Anyway,' I said, trying to moderate my tone, though it sounded strained, even to my own ears. 'It sounds like you're going to survive this, if the doctors are right. You must be so disappointed.'

I picked up my bag, slinging it over my shoulder. 'I'll call Gemma again when I get home. Get her to come and sit with you. I'm sure the two of you will have plenty to talk about. You always do.'

'Beth!' he called after me, but I was already out the door. I didn't stop.

THIRTY-THREE

GEMMA

I recoiled against the bright lights above me, shielding my eyes with my arm as I blinked, slowly opening them and squinting at my surroundings. There was a throbbing ache in my head, concentrated to the left of my forehead, and I pressed my hand to it, finding something stuck to it. I tried to sit up and felt a rush of nausea, falling back against the pillow with a grunt, my mouth filling with saliva as the queasiness rolled over me, rendering me useless. I stared up at the ceiling, breathing heavily, confused and disorientated. I was in a hospital room, but it wasn't Drew's, and I had no idea why I was in the bed rather than the chair. Had I fallen asleep by his side and the nurses finally taken pity on me? I tried to remember being offered a comfy bed to sleep in and couldn't picture it. The nurses were hardly my biggest fans.

I touched my forehead again, picking at the soft layer of gauzy material. Had I hurt myself? Taken an overdose? The thought triggered a sudden memory, and I sat up so fast I thought I might throw up. Jason... the tiny bag of brown powder... the rush to get home. There had been a car. One minute it wasn't there, and the next, it had hit me. I remembered being winded, the bonnet colliding with my stomach. Dizzy, I lay back down and ran my hands down my body, feeling for changes and finding nothing different.

'You're awake. Good,' came a cheerful voice from the doorway.

I turned my head on the pillow to see a nurse I didn't recognise. 'Where am I?' I asked stupidly. 'I mean... I know I'm in a hospital, right? But which one?'

'You don't know? I suppose they do all look the same if you're not used to them. But you *have* spent most of the last week here, Gemma, sitting with your brother, Andreas. He's downstairs. Same hospital, different ward.'

'Oh. Have we met then?'

She shook her head. 'I haven't been downstairs this week, but a couple of the nurses recognised you when you were brought in and told us who you were. Do you remember arriving this morning? In the ambulance?'

'I'm not sure...' I frowned, trying to remember. Blue lights, voices talking above me. The cold, damp pavement scraping against my cheek. 'There are little pieces of memory, but no... I don't remember getting here.' I scratched at my forehead, the sticky thing itchy and irritating.

'Leave that,' the nurse said. 'It's your dressing. You have a cut and a mild concussion. Do you remember discussing that? We talked about it an hour or so ago when you woke up.'

'I woke up? We already spoke?' I shook my head, sure that I should feel frightened at this news, but the feeling didn't materialise. 'I don't remember.'

'That's nothing to worry about. As I said, you have a mild concussion. Your memories might be a bit fuzzy for a while, but there should be no lasting damage. You were lucky.'

'Lucky?'

'You all were. Six people were brought in after the crash, and other than a few broken bones, everyone got off lightly.'

'Six?' I frowned, wondering if I was responsible for that and feeling sure that I must be. I remembered the sound of tyres squealing, the metal on metal that followed the collision as my head hit the pavement. The driver must have skidded into another car in their panic. Had I caused a pile-up? 'Nobody died?' I asked, needing her to repeat her words.

'No fatalities. A lucky escape.' She glanced at the heart-rate monitor on the table beside me, and I followed the line that ran to a probe on my big toe. 'Looks good to me. Is there anything you need before I go? I have to get some meds sorted for another patient now.'

'My bag? And can you help me sit up?'

She lifted a control from the side of the bed, pressing a button, and I felt the mattress slowly rise, supporting me in a sitting position. She smiled, then opened the cupboard beneath the monitor and handed me my bag. I was grateful to realise I was still wearing my own clothes – they hadn't stripped me off and dressed me in one of those awful hospital gowns they'd put Drew in on his first day here.

'Okay?' she asked.

I nodded, and she turned and left the room, closing the door behind her.

I swallowed back a mouthful of saliva, determined not to throw up, despite the waves of nausea that came with being upright, then, with slow, tentative movements, slid my hand beneath the hospital blanket, into the pocket of my jeans. It was empty. I tried the other one, and when that didn't give me what I wanted either, I tipped the contents of my bag over my lap, rifling through the mess of empty codeine packets and old lip balms. It was gone. The little bag of powder, the cure for my sadness, was gone, and as I stared down at the mess, I realised that a part of me felt relieved, though it made no sense. If someone had asked me last night if I wanted another way out, I would have laughed in their face. The idea of being hit by a car would probably have been a welcome notion. But now, knowing how close I'd come to the end, I was surprised to find I was glad I'd survived it.

I remembered. I'd been running, my thoughts on what I was going to do, no care for what was happening around me. I'd stepped out without looking. I didn't recall the car, but I knew I hadn't been careful crossing the road. It *had* been my fault, I was certain of it. I could have killed those people, their lives ended in a split second because I'd been so wrapped up in myself. The thought hit me like a ton of bricks as a fresh wave of pain reverberated through my skull. What was I doing? How could I be so damn selfish? Drew might not be here to see me slide into a valley of despair, but I knew just what he would say. He'd be disgusted with me. How could he not be? I'd become someone even I didn't want to be around.

My phone lay on my lap and I picked it up, seeing a multitude of messages and missed calls. No doubt all from Beth, wondering why I wasn't sitting vigil at Drew's bedside. I was about to look at the messages when the phone rang in my hand and I answered without thinking, regretting it instantly.

'Gemma? It's Beth. Where the hell are you?'

I held the phone away from my ear, wincing. 'I'm—' I broke off, feeling confused and dizzy, not sure how much I wanted to tell her.

'I've had Tristan knocking at your door; I've been calling all day.'

'Why?' I frowned, annoyed that she couldn't seem to manage being with her own husband without me there to chaperone.

'He's awake, Gemma. Drew's awake. I've had to leave to help Daisy out with the children, but he's had a whole load of scans and tests and the doctors seem to think he's going to make a full recovery.'

I shook my head, trying to take in what she was saying. It sounded like she was telling me a miracle had happened, and yet her tone didn't match the words. She sounded impatient, in a hurry to get off the phone.

'He's awake?' I repeated. 'Are you certain?'

'Yes. Will you go and see him?'

I gripped the phone, staring at my lap, wondering in bewilderment why there was water dripping onto the pile of mess I'd tipped out from my bag.

'Yes,' I whispered. I touched my cheek and realised it was damp. 'I'll go now.'

I hung up, staring at the drop of moisture on my fingertip, wondering if I was still unconscious, if this was all just a dream. Because it had been nearly thirty years since I'd cried other than during my sleep, and this didn't make sense.

THIRTY-FOUR

BETH

I slid the quilt up over Rufus's shoulders, smiling as his fist clasped Drew's pillow, his eyelids flickering, already lost in a dream I'd be sure to hear about in the morning.

I tiptoed out of my bedroom, then checked on Ceci and Amelie, who were both fast asleep. Daisy was trying to catch up on work in the spare room; I knew that as much as she would never complain about helping me, she was falling behind and would have to leave soon. When I'd told her about Drew's sudden return to consciousness, she'd been wonderful, asking how I was feeling, how he was doing, but she hadn't been able to hide the relief that she so obviously felt. It was a lot; I knew that more than anyone – the timetables, the appointments, the constant driving from one thing to the next – and she'd been thrown in at the deep end this past week. It was only to be expected that she'd burn out after a while. I rarely let the fatigue get to me now, always pushing forward, but I hadn't forgotten those early days of parenthood, when I'd felt as if I'd been hit by a ton of bricks by the time bedtime came around each evening. The days were long and relentless, and I had no right to expect her to take on so many of my responsibilities. *Drew's* responsibilities, I reminded myself.

I padded across the landing, stopping outside Tristan's

bedroom door and taking a deep breath. Slowly, I raised my hand, and before I could change my mind, I rapped my knuckles against the wood, feeling more nervous than I should at the prospect of having a conversation with my son.

'Yeah?' came his reply, and I reached for the handle, opening the door. He was lying across his bed, his phone in his hand, headphones on, for once keeping his music to himself. It was a tiny gesture, but I'd overheard Daisy asking him if he would mind so she could concentrate on her work, and had been stunned when he'd agreed so easily. If *I'd* asked, I would have expected a very different response.

'Can I come in? I need to talk to you.'

He swung his legs off the edge of the bed, sitting up, his face turning pale as he pulled the earbuds out, gripping them between his fingers. 'Is it Dad? Or Auntie Gemma?'

'Auntie Gemma is fine. I spoke to her earlier. This is about your dad.' I stepped into the room and pushed the door closed, then sat down beside him on the edge of the bed. 'He woke up,' I said, trying not to let my uncertainty about the future slip into my tone.

'He's awake?'

I nodded.

'And is he, like... okay? Can he talk or, I don't know, remember us?'

I reached for his hand and he seemed not to notice as I clasped it between mine. 'As far as we can tell, he's back to his normal self. He was talking this afternoon.'

His body seemed to stiffen, his eyes flicking down to his lap. 'What did he say?'

'Not much. We were busy running through all the medical tests. But I thought you'd want to know.'

'Right.' He slipped his hand from mine, his eyes on the carpet, and I felt the warmth seep away, knowing my welcome had somehow been revoked and he wanted me to leave.

'Do you have any other questions? You must have been worried.'

He shook his head, silent.

'Okay,' I said softly then sighed. I just wanted to be close to him. To understand what he was thinking, what he'd been doing, because the secrets between us were killing me, and I missed him with all of my heart. I didn't know what lay ahead for me and Drew, how I even felt about him now, but Tristan was my first love, the baby I'd invested my whole heart in, and I couldn't stand that I was losing him, especially without understanding why or having a chance to fix it.

I looked at him now, half-boy, half-man, waiting for him to meet my eyes. Slowly he raised his face, his expression carefully impassive.

'You know you can talk to me about anything, right? It's not always easy with the others around, but I'm here for you, always. There's nothing you could say that would offend me, no secret I wouldn't want to hear. I'm your mum. I'll always be on your side. And if there's something you need help with, you only have to ask.'

I wanted to keep talking, making promises, but I could feel that I was rambling and forced myself to shut up. I wanted so much for him to be honest with me. Even if he *had* been searching for Lee – if he'd already found him, or worse, been running little errands for the man who wouldn't hesitate to take advantage of the boy he'd sired – I swore to myself that I wouldn't get angry. I'd be calm. I would listen. I would be the mother he deserved, all the parent he needed.

He twisted his mouth, and I waited, my stomach tensing. For a moment it looked like he was going to say something, and I readied myself for what I might hear.

'Yeah,' he said, rising to his feet and grabbing his jacket. He slipped it on then picked up his phone from the bed. He shrugged, a shadow of a smile on his lips. 'Thanks, Mum. That's good to know.'

He turned, walking out of the room, and I stared after him, not bothering to ask where he was going. He would only tell me a lie anyway.

I waited until I heard the front door close behind him, then slowly I laid my head on his pillow, remembering back to a time when parenting had been simple. When I'd felt like I had control of my life. In this moment, it seemed a long way back.

THIRTY-FIVE
GEMMA

The lift juddered as it began its descent, and I closed my eyes against the combined dizziness and nausea, fighting to keep control of my body. I was grateful I was only going down one floor. There was no way I would have made it here if I'd found myself in a hospital across town. The nurse had told me I'd have to stay tonight for observation, and I hadn't had the energy to argue with her. Instead, I'd waited until she went to deal with another patient and then slowly eased my way out of bed, waiting for the head rush to pass before attempting to walk. I was sore all over, my left arm covered in deep purple bruises, my stomach tender as I walked as quickly as I could manage down the hall, trying my best to remain inconspicuous.

A part of me felt like Beth was playing some cruel trick on me. That I would make it to his room only to find him still comatose, lying on his back, his mouth slightly open, Beth standing there smug at having pulled off her prank. I couldn't bring myself to get my hopes up, and yet at the same time I couldn't seem to stop myself from doing just that.

I took a deep breath as the lift came to a stop, the doors opening with a shuddering screech. Stepping out, I wondered if anyone would have told Beth about my admission. I was only slightly comforted by the thought of patient confidentiality. I'd spent enough time here this past week to know how indiscreet some of the nurses could be, talking about patients at full volume in the middle of the ward, where anyone might hear. They didn't seem to consider that not everyone wanted their business shared with the entire world.

I made my way slowly down the corridor, one hand on the wall as I walked, pausing every now and then as a shower of sparks filled my vision, the urge to vomit building inside me. My palms were sweaty, as was my face, and I could feel the tape lifting from the dressing on my head, hot and itchy. I wiped my sleeve over my face, pinching my cheeks to bring some colour back to them before I reached Drew's room. The door was open, and I stepped towards it, looking inside with a burst of hope I couldn't suppress.

My heart seemed to freeze in my chest as I saw him, eyes open, looking at the nurse, who was holding a stethoscope, sliding it beneath the fabric of his pyjama top. I let out a tiny gasp, and he turned, our eyes meeting, a thousand unspoken words passing between us. I wanted to run to him, hold him tight against me, but not in front of the nurse. This reunion was too big for an audience. I blinked hard, knowing that this wasn't some figment of my imagination or the result of my head injury. Drew was awake. He'd come back to me.

The nurse took his temperature then smiled. 'I'll come back and repeat your obs in an hour, Andreas. Everything looks good.'

'Thank you,' he said, smiling, and the sound of his voice almost brought me to my knees.

The nurse gave a polite nod as she passed me, and then, at last, we were alone. He looked at me, chewing his lower lip in that boyish way he'd always had, and then shrugged, almost sheepish in his manner. 'What can I say, Gem? I'm an idiot.'

'Yes,' I whispered, unable to keep from smiling. 'You bloody are!' I rushed forward, launching myself across the bed, feeling his arms wrap around me, strong and real. My head swam, but it no longer mattered. Drew was here.

Slowly I eased back from his hold, getting onto the bed properly and leaning my head on his pillow. I felt like we were children
again, cuddled up in our parents' bed, telling stories we'd made up,
trying to make each other laugh. I'd forgotten we even used to do
that.

'What's this?' he asked, touching the tip of his finger to my
dressing, then my arm. 'What happened to you?' He frowned, his
deep voice soothing, comforting.

'I could ask you the same thing,' I said, surprised to hear the
crack in my voice. I hoped I wasn't about to cry again. That would
be humiliating. 'How could you do it, Drew? How could you just
make up your mind to end it all? You left me.'

He sighed. 'I didn't really decide... It just sort of happened.'

'That's a cop-out, Drew. Take some responsibility.'

He nodded, staring up at the ceiling, his jaw clenched. 'I
suppose you're right. I'm just saying how I felt. How out of control
I've been in my own life. I never wanted to leave you, but I just
couldn't bear to stay... I felt like everything was falling apart. I was
letting everyone down. You, Beth, the kids. I was working so hard,
trying to keep everyone happy, safe, and yet it seemed the harder I
pushed myself, the more I failed.'

'What do you mean?'

He shook his head, and I was sure there was something he
wasn't telling me. 'Drew, what was it?'

He sighed. 'Oh, you know. The usual. I wish I could give you a
more original answer, but the crux of it is an accumulation of
worries I couldn't cope with. Money. My job. My responsibilities.
And...' He paused.

'What?'

He shook his head. 'You're perhaps not the right person to
discuss this with.'

'Drew... You owe me an explanation. A proper explanation.'

He looked at me, his brow creasing, and for a second, I
wondered if he'd refuse to go on. As much as I hated to admit it, he

wasn't obliged to divulge his reasons to me. I certainly wasn't an open book myself when it came to the big stuff.

'Things from my past. Our past. I never addressed them, and that soured inside me. I thought I could wipe my history clean, you know? Just ignore the bits that hurt, but it turned toxic in my mind, and I found that the more I tried to forget, the brighter the memories burned. They fought to be heard, and I wasn't ready. I wasn't strong enough.'

I shook my head. 'But you're always strong. You always cope.'

'I always make it look as if I'm coping,' he said softly. 'But that doesn't mean I'm not struggling. It's a front, Gem. I know I got through those six months of foster care better than you. I was older. I understood it was only temporary. Just while Mum had her treatment and got back on her feet. I had that dog to keep me company, and that helped. I never let myself admit how hard it was for me, that awful feeling of knowing I was living under a roof where my very existence was resented by the people who were supposed to be caring for me.'

I squeezed his hand, chilled by the memories his words conjured. His eyes met mine and I found I couldn't look away.

'I tried not to let myself think about it,' he continued. 'Focused on taking care of you, getting you through it. Then after, to stop myself going to that dark place in my mind, I threw myself into my school-work, my job, afraid to stop. And for a long time it worked. I forgot the truth that I was working so hard to bury. It was enough. But then slowly it all began to crumble. And as soon as the first cracks formed, everything began to pour out. When Cecilia was born, things got so much tougher. I was afraid of losing her – she needs so much care. Beth wanted more therapies, private ones. Money took on a new importance. It wasn't just a nice thing to have anymore. It was a necessity. She booked more holidays, said it would help us all to get away. But the holidays were never to relax. Every minute of every day was scheduled, every potential opportunity to just be together was turned into a learning opportunity, usually with a price tag attached.'

He sighed, rubbing his hands over his face.

'It was my fault. I never wanted her to feel like I couldn't take care of them. Give them everything they needed. It was the role I needed too. I wanted to be the one everyone could rely on. Being useful and providing for my family left me with no time to focus on my pain. It was a fix that worked. But then things started to fall apart at work. I lost a contract that Matthew had his heart set on, and we fell out over it. There was a new company undercutting us at every turn. I lost commission. I had to tighten my belt. I was working all the time, up in the night with the kids, ferrying them to classes every spare minute. Our weekends were non-stop. Life was going too fast, like a runaway train, and I was barely hanging on. It was just all too much. Then Matthew told me I was being made redundant. I knew we would lose the house.' He swallowed. 'Beth loves that house. She grew up with nothing, you know. She's not a greedy woman. She just needs that security. She's terrified of poverty.'

I shook my head. 'She had family. Love. That's not nothing.'

He nodded. 'I know. But we did too. We were loved by our mum, and our dad too up until the day he died, and we've let that six months of pain, six months of foster care, cloud our entire lives. We *both* have, and we can't keep doing it.'

I looked down, filled with guilt. 'Was it... was it my fault? Was I the final straw? The reason you—'

He made a noise in the back of his throat. 'Gem... come on.'

'I know it was. I pushed you too far. I scared you.'

'You did,' he agreed, and I flinched at his admission. 'I didn't know how to pull you back from the road you were heading down. I could see it all so clearly, where you were going, what would happen to you if you didn't find the strength to stop. *Have* you stopped, Gem? Or do I still need to be afraid of losing you to drugs?'

I pressed my lips together, thinking of Jason, the bag of heroin I'd lost in the accident. If I'd made it home and smoked that powder, I'd still be out of it now, passed out, and I would have missed this. I might not have even bothered to check my phone before going in for a second hit. I would have been too far gone to care.

I wrapped my hand around my brother's, squeezing tight. That accident had been a blessing. A wake-up call. It had brought me here, to exactly the place I needed to be. 'That's over for me now. I'll have to find another way to...'

'To work through the pain?'

'I was thinking more along the lines of to block it out.'

He smiled. 'I think you and I can both safely agree that squashing it down doesn't work. It's time to try something new. Therapy maybe? Or we could even talk to each other if you're open to it. Whatever the case, we have to face our past. It's the only choice we have if we're ever going to break free of it.'

I sighed then nodded. 'Perhaps you're right,' I agreed. 'Drew, does this mean... Are you—' I broke off, struggling to ask the question I most wanted answered. 'Are you glad it didn't work? Or will you try this again?'

He closed his eyes. 'I don't know what I feel right now, Gem. That's the honest truth. I just don't know. There are things that have happened, mistakes I made... I don't know if I can repair the damage I've done.' His voice began to slur, and I could see he was exhausted.

I watched as he drifted off to sleep, determined that I would do everything in my power to keep him safe. And that, I realised, began with sorting my own life out.

THIRTY-SIX

TRISTAN

When you're fifteen, you don't admit to being scared. Not when you're cornered on your way home by the Year 11s from the local state school demanding your wallet and phone. Not when you find yourself in a place you didn't intend to be, watching as your so-called friends drink shots of tequila and shoot the shit with guys in their twenties who sell drugs for a living. Not when you find yourself wrapped up in the worst kind of trouble with no idea how to get out of it. And not when your dad walks into your bedroom in a blind rage and you realise you don't know him at all.

I'd never been afraid of him. Not once since he met and married my mum. He had taken me into his life, accepted me as his own, and I'd never questioned my place as his son. I had lived under his roof for twelve years and I couldn't recall him even raising his voice before that day.

He had grabbed me by the collar so suddenly I thought he meant to hit me, and I'd lurched back, tripping over my trainers in my fear, my eye socket colliding with the corner of my chest of drawers as I clattered to the carpet. He hadn't apologised, hadn't even tried to help me up – he'd just stood there, his face red, his fists clenched by his sides, his chest rising and falling so fast I could feel the adrenaline seeping from his pores. His reaction had come as a shock, though I knew I deserved it, but I didn't let it show that he'd knocked my confidence. That I was hurting, my trust shattered, my face in agony. I'd refused to break down and show him that he had power over me.

I'd stayed on my butt on my bedroom floor, kept my head lowered, staring at the carpet until I could be certain I wouldn't cry. Then I'd got back up, fronting it out, a sneer on my face, my eye already swelling shut, and with only the barest tremble in my voice I'd told him to get the fuck out of my room, out of my life. And he had. He'd walked out, and not quite twelve hours later, he'd stepped onto his desk, put a rope around his neck and tried to end his life.

I'd spent every moment of every day since I'd learned of what had happened hoping he'd pull through, desperate to hear that I hadn't been the cause of my dad's death, terrified of losing him, though I would never have admitted it to anyone. And now my wish had come true. He'd woken up, but I didn't know what that meant for the two of us. I was probably the last person he would want to see, but that didn't matter. I had to go. There was no way I could just wait around wondering what was going to happen next. I had to know now.

I paused by the entrance to the ward, glancing at the whiteboard to check he was still in the same room. It was long past visiting hours, but this couldn't wait.

Leaning close to the wall, I watched as a couple of nurses finished talking by the desk, then disappeared off into cubicles along the hall. Taking my chance, I jogged to his room, pausing only for the briefest moment outside the door before turning the handle and stepping inside. I'd half hoped to find him sleeping, like the last time I'd been here. It had been easier then. I hadn't had to anticipate the look of disappointment in his eyes that would surely come now. But as I closed the door quietly behind me, I looked up and there he was, sitting up in bed, the bruises around his neck faded, his eyes on mine, soft and curious.

'I hoped you'd come,' he said, and his voice was thick, croaky.

'I...' I paused, looking down at my feet, shoving my hands in my jacket pockets and squeezing them into fists. 'Mum said you were awake.'

He nodded. 'Yes.' His gaze scanned my face. 'How's the eye?' he asked.

'Fine,' I replied, my tone hardening defensively.

He cleared his throat then sat up straighter against the pillows. 'Tristan... I'm so sorry,' he breathed.

I looked up at him, seeing the way his dark brown eyes glistened.

'For what?' I asked, taking my hands from my pockets and folding my arms tight around my body. 'For messing up my face? Or for trying to kill yourself? I mean fuck, Dad... I know I made a mistake, but do you think it's fair that I would have had to live with the guilt of your death on my conscience for the rest of my life? Did you even think about that before you decided to take the easy way out?'

He slumped back, his jaw slack as if I'd punched him. Perhaps I should have.

'Tris, I didn't think... I never even considered... Shit! I'm such an idiot. I never thought.' He dropped his face into his hands, pressing them tight against his eyes.

I stared at him, hating that his distress hurt so much to watch, that all I wanted to do was comfort him. It was a shock to see the man I'd always looked up to sitting in a hospital bed having tried to take his own life. It didn't fit with my idea of who he was. Not in the slightest.

'This wasn't about you. It wasn't about...' He shook his head, struggling to find the right words. 'It was about me, Tris. And I was too wrapped up in my own issues to even realise you would think of blaming yourself. I'm supposed to protect you, be a father to you, and yet look at what I did. I hurt you. I know you can never forgive me for that. I won't ever forgive myself.'

I didn't believe him. Of course I was to blame – why else would he have done what he did?

'Maybe I deserved it,' I admitted. 'I know I messed everything up.'

'No, Tristan. What you deserved was discipline. Guidance. Not an outburst like that. You never deserved to feel afraid in your own home, afraid of me.'

'I wasn't afraid,' I lied.

He sighed. 'I think you were afraid of a lot of things. And I wasn't ready to hear them because of my own stuff. Stuff you don't need to worry about. You caught me off guard and I messed up. I'm sorry, Tristan. I really am.'

I stared at him, surprised by his apology. It had been the last thing I'd expected.

'The drugs weren't mine, you know.'

I let that hang in the air for a moment, and when he didn't reply, I continued, desperate to explain what had happened that night.

'I know that's what everyone says, but it's the truth. I got caught up in a situation I didn't want to be in... The people I thought were my friends turned out not to be. I didn't know how to walk away without getting hurt – I mean properly hurt – so I thought it would be easier just to do it and figure out how to cut my ties with them later on. I was only holding on to the drugs for a friend. I wasn't selling them myself. I swear it, Dad.'

I took a breath, looking at his face, needing to know the truth. 'It's because of Auntie Gemma, isn't it? The way you lost it, I mean. Why you were so angry with me. I know she's the one who told you about the drugs. She saw me at that place, and I saw what she was doing—' I broke off, remembering the shock at having found my auntie at Jason's flat. It had been so surreal that for a moment I'd thought my drink had been spiked.

'Is she...' I paused, not wanting to ask but knowing I had to. 'Is she an addict?'

He sighed, holding out a hand towards me, and I stepped forward, though I didn't reach for him. After a moment, he dropped his hand to his side. 'You see so much more than I ever realised. And you're not a child anymore. My first mistake was not realising that sooner.'

I dipped my head, swallowing back a lump that seemed to have wedged itself in my throat.

'I suppose there's no point in sugar-coating the truth now,' he continued. 'Yes, Gemma has a problem. She's been heading down a rabbit hole for a very long time – I'm talking years – and the more I try to pull her back, the more she slips from my grasp. Tristan... what I did, laying hands on you like that, it wasn't your fault and I don't ever want you to think it was. There are things you don't know, and this' – he gestured to the bed, the hospital room – 'has been building for a long time. Seeing you with those drugs and thinking that I might lose you too, the way I'm losing her, well...' He shook his head. 'I reacted out of fear. That doesn't make it right, but it terrified me. I saw red and I just lashed out. I never meant to hurt you. I'm sorry for that.'

'I'm sorry for scaring you,' I mumbled, meeting his eyes. 'I get it now.'

'Did... did you tell your mum what happened between us? That I was the reason you got that black eye?'

I shook my head. 'No. And I'm not going to. You aren't either. This is between us.'

He pursed his lips as if he wasn't sure he agreed. 'You should have come to me when you realised you were in a situation you didn't know how to get yourself out of. It might not always seem like it, but I would have been there. I would have helped.'

I shrugged, clenching my jaw. I didn't want to admit that things were just as bad now as they had been that night. That I still hadn't figured a way out of this mess. When Jason had started hanging round outside school and got talking to my best friend, Guy, I'd known instantly that I didn't want to be involved. Jason was loud, cocky, and there was something slimy about him that made me instantly put my guard up. I didn't trust him, didn't want to have anything to do with him, but Guy had been sucked right in, lured by the excitement, the promise of free weed and easy money.

The two of us had been friends for years, ever since we'd been put on the same team for rounders back in Year 3. We'd made each other laugh, and for a while we'd shared all the same interests, but over the past year or so, things had begun to change. We'd been drifting apart for a while, but in a school as tight-knit as ours, it was hard to start over and make new friends, so I stuck with him. It had been *his* drugs I'd been collecting from Jason that day. His mum had been asking too many questions, going through his stuff, and had made him stay home, so he'd called me, telling me that if I didn't pick them up for him, Jason would kick off.

I hadn't wanted to do it – I'd already had Jason texting me the week before, trying to push me to head across London to pick something up for him. He wouldn't say what it was but I could guess, and I wasn't interested. But Jason was a hard man to say no to. He'd been livid when I'd called him an hour before I was supposed to meet the contact in Barnsbury, telling him something had come up and I couldn't go. He knew I was lying but he'd forced me into a corner and I didn't see what else I could do. It wasn't fair of him to ask me to do his dirty work anyway. After that tense phone call, I'd hoped I'd heard the last from him, that I could get on with my life. The last thing I wanted was to be dragged into Guy's mess and do the very thing I'd managed to get out of once already, but when he'd called, begging for my help, he'd been so intense about it, sounding like he was actually scared of how Jason and his mates might react to being stood up again, that I'd finally agreed.

I'd arrived at the grimy flat, hating the place right away, wanting to get the stuff and leave as quickly as possible, and then Auntie Gemma had walked out of the living room high as a kite, her eyes pink and spacey, though I think she sobered up pretty damn fast once she realised who she was looking at. I'd known straight away that she would tell my dad, but I'd had no choice but to take the stuff and rush home. Guy had been meant to sneak out of his house and come straight over and collect the pills – he only lived two roads away and swore he could be in and out before his mum noticed he was gone – but he hadn't shown up, and then Dad had burst in demanding I turn out my pockets, and I'd been too dumbstruck by how fired up he was to say no. He'd taken the drugs, and I'd been too afraid to ask what he was going to do with them, but I was sure I wouldn't see them again.

Since that night, I'd been getting calls multiple times every day from Jason, demanding I pay him for the pills he thought I'd stolen. Guy had been on my case too, telling me he'd heard they were going to come and beat the crap out of me. I'd have given them the money just to get them to back off if it hadn't been for Mum suddenly cutting my allowance, claiming we had to manage without for the time being. I'd seen the bills piling up, the look on her face as she read through the outgoings, whispering to Daisy about how she didn't know what to do. I'd heard them talking about Dad losing his job. I couldn't ask for money – not now.

That day at the park, when Ceci had collapsed, I hadn't even known she'd gone to hospital. I'd had to leg it full pelt to stop Jason's brother from punching me out right there on the field in broad daylight. I was out of my depth, and I was getting scared, but it wasn't the time to have that conversation now, not when my dad was barely out of his coma. I wouldn't be responsible for causing him stress when he was so fragile. I'd got myself into this mess by being weak and not having the guts to walk away at the start. And now I would have to find a way to get myself out of it. I didn't need to bother him with that.

I pulled up a padded chair beside the bed and sat down. 'Mind if I stay? Mum won't expect me back until morning anyway, and this is just easier.' I shrugged, trying not to show how much I needed to be here. I hadn't actually told Mum I would be staying out, but I knew she'd have guessed as much when I'd left so late. She'd assume I'd gone to Guy's place.

He smiled then reached over to grasp my shoulder. 'I'd like the company.' He tilted his head towards the TV. 'Apparently there's a movie package. Want to check it out?'

I nodded, putting my feet up on his bed and leaning back in

the chair. Dad picked up the remote, and for the first time all week, I felt my shoulders relax. I was with my dad, he'd come out of the coma, he was going to be okay. And sitting beside him in this safe little room, nobody could hurt me. In this moment, nothing could make me feel afraid.

THIRTY-SEVEN
GEMMA

My finger hovered over the doorbell and I hesitated, a part of me wanting to turn away before anyone could find me here on the doorstep. Last night, on returning to my ward, I'd insisted on being discharged right away. The idea of getting back into the hospital bed to be the patient once more had made me feel trapped – I'd craved my freedom more than ever. I'd had enough of hospitals to last a lifetime, and now that I knew Drew was okay, I didn't want to sleep there. The nurses had tried to talk me out of it, but despite the lingering dizziness, I'd insisted I wouldn't stay, and in the end, they'd had little choice but to let me go.

Having returned home from the hospital feeling lighter than I could ever remember, I'd lain in bed thinking of all the ways I could help Drew on the path to recovery. One thought kept coming back to me – that I'd been given a second chance, an opportunity to help him, and as much as I had always struggled with facing personal challenges in my past, this felt like a test I couldn't shy away from. This was something real, something that could really matter. My role in his life suddenly felt vital. Things could have so easily gone the other way – I could be mourning his death right now, and the fact that I wasn't had hit me almost as hard as if he *had* died.

All I'd wanted him to tell me last night was that it had all been a mistake. That he hadn't been in his right mind – hadn't meant to do it – but the more we'd talked, the more I realised how blind I had been to the pain my own brother was living with. Unlike me, he had hidden it well. I wore mine like a badge of honour, and I realised now that in being so determined to avoid delving into any sort of healthy solution, blotting it out with drugs and living as self-ishly as I knew how so as to avoid relying too much on anything – a job, a home, a boyfriend – I'd made it impossible for Drew to come to me with his own problems. My entire world had been set up to avoid talking about the real things, and that had alienated my brother to the point that when he needed me most, I hadn't been there for him. To realise that now broke my heart. It was a hard pill to swallow, and on any other day, understanding my part in Drew's suicide attempt might have pushed me to look for escape. But not now.

I felt awake. Alive. The car crash had been a near miss for all involved, and now my brother was back and for the first time in my adult life I felt strong. Something had awakened inside me, and I was determined that no matter what, I would not be the reason Drew felt he had nowhere to turn in future. And there was no way in hell that I was going to let my discomfort knock me down at the first hurdle.

I stiffened my shoulders then pressed down on the doorbell, hearing the shouts from inside. A moment later, the door flew open and I found Amelie and Rufus staring up at me.

'Auntie Gemma, Auntie Gemma!' they both squealed, pulling me in and engulfing me in hugs, tiny arms wrapping around my waist.

'It's Auntie Gemma!' Rufus yelled.

I grinned. It had been a long time since I'd been to visit. Too long, I thought now. They'd grown and I'd missed it.

There was a noise from the kitchen, and Beth put her head round the door. 'What?' She frowned, clearly confused by my sudden arrival. 'Oh... Gemma. Is...' She paused, looking meaningfully at the children, and I realised they didn't know about Drew. 'Is everything okay?' she asked, her tone careful.

'Oh, yeah, everything's fine.' I nodded, meeting her eyes as I tried to communicate that there was nothing to worry about. 'I just thought I'd come and see my nieces and nephews.'

'Only *one* nephew. Tristan is out somewhere,' Rufus corrected, taking my hand and swinging it back and forth, a grin on his face. There was something that resembled peanut butter on his chin, and he was still wearing his Spider-Man pyjamas.

'As *usual*,' Amelie chimed in. 'When *I'm* a teenager, I'm going to go out all the time too and never do homework.'

'Tristan still does homework,' Beth said, looking tired and stressed. 'Is there something you need, Gemma?' she asked, clearly still confused by my visit.

I shook my head. 'No. Nothing.'

'Right.' She nodded, turning back to the kitchen, and I followed her, the kids dashing ahead. Had it really been so long since I'd come over?

I tried to think of the last time I was here. Now that I considered it, I couldn't blame her for being surprised – I couldn't recall a single time I'd come here without Drew being present, and even those occasions were infrequent. I always preferred to meet him on neutral territory; I'd never felt comfortable in Beth's show home, always feeling like I made the place untidy with my very presence. But, I thought, stepping into the bright, high-ceilinged kitchen, today it didn't resemble anything close to a show home.

A pile of dirty laundry was heaped in a basket in the middle of the floor. The countertops were strewn with cereal boxes and bowls with milk left in them, cornflakes scattered on the floor as if the children had prepared their own breakfasts. The table was a mess of paperwork – letters and bills and homework piled haphazardly, concealing the polished oak beneath them. There were shoes and school bags piled beside the patio doors, and a wilting bunch of flowers turning brown in a vase on the windowsill, the dried-up petals already collecting at its base. This couldn't be further from how it had looked the last time I was here.

Beth always said there was no such thing as too much storage, her secret to a tidy home, always going on at the kids for not using their coat hooks and putting their bags in their labelled cubbyholes. I knew she'd been stressed, but I'd never imagined she would let go of those little rules and rituals I'd always associated with her.

She used her foot to push the laundry basket closer to the door that led to the utility room but made no move to go any further.

'Will you come and play in the garden?' Rufus asked, bouncing on his toes.

'I—' I broke off as I glanced through the window to see Beth's sister out there, taking the daisies Cecilia was passing to her and making them into a long chain. The thought of trying to make small talk with yet another woman who didn't like me was far from appealing. And it wasn't why I'd come.

'You go ahead,' I said, smiling at Rufus and Amelie. 'I want to have a chat with your mum.'

They hesitated, torn between the lure of the garden and the rare time with me.

'It's a beautiful day. You should enjoy it,' I added. I smiled as they dashed through the open door, their feet bare as they sprinted across the lawn, squealing with wild abandon. I turned to Beth, who wore a stony expression.

'I suppose you've come to berate me for not being there with Drew?' she said coldly. 'Well, I'm sorry I can't be everything to everyone all the time, Gemma, but the children's schools are closed for teacher training, and I can't throw away money on childcare. I've had to let the cleaner go. The only thing I'm still managing to hold on to is Ceci's speech therapist, and I'd sell the clothes from my back before I lost her.'

She looked out of the window, her shoulders tense as the happy yells of her children rose up. Daisy had pulled Cecilia onto her lap, and the two of them sat heads tilted as they watched the birds flitting around a big tree above them.

'I'm rushed off my feet,' Beth continued, not turning to look at me. 'So I'm sorry, but I just don't have time to sit around in hospital with a man who doesn't want me there.'

I moved forward, feeling determined not to rise to the bait. This was our pattern, the familiar trigger, and I knew what she expected from me now. I would defend my brother, call her names and claim she never deserved him, before storming out, feeling vindicated in my low opinion of her. But not today.

I stepped around her, starting to take the dirty dishes from the sink and pile them on the side.

'What are you doing?'

'I'm helping,' I said, not looking at her as I turned on the tap, filling the sink with hot soapy water.

'We have a dishwasher, you know.'

I glanced at it, the door open, the shelves overflowing, and shrugged. 'So turn it on.'

She stared at me as if she couldn't piece together what was happening, why I was even here. Finally, she leaned into a cupboard, pulling out a dishwasher tablet and closing the door, the smell of damp musty dishes trapped inside as she turned it on hot.

I dipped my hands into the warm soothing water and picked up a cloth. I could do this. One little task at a time. I picked up a plate, ignoring Beth's stare burning into my back, and with a feeling of lightness plunged it into the bowl.

I wasn't sure what I'd expected from my visit today. Beth wandering around lost, unsure how to cope without her usual set-up – her cleaner and the kids' clubs. Beth crying into her hands at the table while the world fell apart around her. I didn't know her well enough to paint a picture in my mind of how she might be coping right now, but whatever I'd thought, I hadn't expected what I'd seen this morning. Beth was a machine. She never stopped, never took a break. She buzzed from one room to the next, tidying, cleaning, mechanically putting the place to rights with me trailing behind trying to lend a hand wherever I could. Once the house was in order, I'd expected her to stop, eat lunch, but she'd kept going.

Daisy had come in from the garden with three smiling, sweaty children and then, after an awkward hello, disappeared up to the spare room to catch up on her work. Beth had made the children sandwiches – offering one to me, which I accepted, surprised at just how hungry I was – and then sat down with them to go through their homework. I watched, in awe of her patience, her steady determination. They were tired and grumpy, but never once did she snap at them, though I knew she must be at the end of her rope and exhausted herself.

I was too afraid to offer to help, overhearing Rufus and Amelie's complicated sums and English assignments, far more advanced than the stuff I'd been doing at their age. Beth and Ceci worked through a stack of flash cards, and each time Ceci managed to say a word, even if it was hard to recognise as she struggled to form the sounds in her mouth, Beth's face lit up as if it were Christmas morning. It was uncomfortable for me to watch and to discover just how wrong my assumptions about her had been.

I pottered around the kitchen, one ear on the work being done at the table as I prepared vegetables for dinner, peeling and chopping methodically. I found a chicken in the fridge and tried to remember how to make a roast as my mother had taught me so long ago, though it had been years since I'd even turned on an oven. At home, I mostly survived on instant noodles and tinned soup from the food bank, or cheap pre-packaged sandwiches I bought the hour before the supermarket closed, reduced to ten pence apiece. My mum had always cooked everything from scratch, and I could see from the contents of Beth's fridge that even now, even with everything she had to do, she was still making proper meals for her children.

I watched with curiosity as she sat Ceci on her lap, leaning over Amelie's maths book, explaining in her soft, patient voice how to work out a complicated equation. I was surprised she knew how to do it herself. I'd been surprised by her a lot today. She hadn't been what I expected – the self-obsessed, self-pitying widow figure, wandering around crying, unable to deal with the responsibilities laid at her feet. She wasn't looking for sympathy or attention. She was simply trying to fill the space where Drew had once been, taking on the task of educating her children, testing their knowledge, listening to them fully and answering their questions without sarcasm or irritation. She worked tirelessly to keep things normal for them, despite the fact that the situation right now was anything but normal, and I couldn't help but respect her for that.

The children closed their books, and Beth told them they could go back outside to play if they wanted. I spread the potatoes out on a baking tray, drizzling them in olive oil and using the Himalayan pink salt from the pantry to season them. I slid them into the hot oven, then flicked the switch on the kettle. 'Tea?' I offered.

Beth turned, raising a quizzical eyebrow as if she still didn't understand what I was doing here. 'Okay.' She nodded. 'Thanks.'

She picked up a cloth, and I shook my head. 'No, sit down for a while, will you? You haven't stopped today.'

'What do you mean?'

I smiled. 'You never stop. You're always busy. I hadn't realised how much you have on your plate,' I admitted, turning to make the tea so I didn't have to look at her. I was embarrassed at how wrong I'd got her. I'd always known she expected a lot from Drew, and I'd resented that. But now I saw the other side of the coin. Yes, she had high expectations, but she gave so much of herself too. It wasn't a one-sided affair. Far from it, in fact.

'There's a lot to get done. It's always like this,' she said. 'I don't mind. Of course, things are easier when Drew is able to take them to their extracurricular activities. I wouldn't normally do Ceci's flash cards at the table with the others – she gets distracted and finds it that much more difficult.'

'Do they need to do quite so much homework?' I asked, handing her a mug of strong builder's tea. I didn't know how to make the fancy Earl Grey stuff I'd seen on the shelf.

'Thanks,' she said, sliding the mug closer. 'Their schools are very competitive. They need to keep up with their peers, so yes, they have a lot to do.'

I nodded, not quite agreeing, but not wanting to argue. Still, I couldn't help myself from asking one more question. 'Don't you ever want to slow down? I mean, do you actually enjoy living like this?'

She stared at me then gave a surprised laugh. 'To be honest with you, Gemma, I've never considered it. I do it for them, and if they're doing well, that makes me happy.'

'What would they normally be doing this afternoon, if Drew were here?'

She gave an exhausted sigh. 'Their after-school clubs and classes. Karate, swimming, gymnastics, languages. Tristan would be having a piano lesson, and then tomorrow would be more of the same, though I've had to put everything on hold. It's not fair to ask Daisy to take them on top of everything else she's doing, and to be honest, I'm not sure we can afford it all right now.'

'It sounds like a long list.'

She shrugged. 'It's full-on, but it's for their own good. Like I said before, I want them to do well in life. To be safe and happy and have what they need to succeed.'

I nodded, glancing towards the window where the three siblings were running wild, barefoot on the grass, with nowhere to be and nothing to do. A simple pleasure they rarely got the chance to experience, by the sounds of it.

'They look pretty happy right now,' I said. 'More than I can remember ever seeing.' I glanced at Beth to read her reaction.

She looked past me, her eyes cloudy as she watched them play.

'Perhaps you're right,' she replied softly. 'Perhaps they are.'

THIRTY-EIGHT

BETH

'Hey.'

'Oh, hi,' Drew said, struggling to sit up as I watched from the doorway, arms folded protectively around myself. I still couldn't get over the fact that he was back – eyes open, moving, talking as if nothing had changed, when we both knew that everything had.

I cleared my throat. 'How are you feeling? Did you get some sleep?'

He nodded. 'I slept,' he replied, not giving me the answer I was looking for, and I felt a wave of irritation that he didn't seem to feel I was owed an explanation. I'd thought I would stay away for a few days, take some time to process what I was feeling, and perhaps a part of me wanted him to stew too, to really absorb the impact of his actions, but for the second day running, Gemma had turned up at my house, and my plans to brood were dashed.

To my absolute surprise, she'd got chatting with Daisy before going home last night, and the two of them had come up with a plan to take over, give the children – and me – a day off. I'd argued, insisting the children should go back to school, having already missed a day due to teacher training. And I wanted to sit down with them when they got home, to work on some activities I'd planned to make up for them missing their groups. A sonnet for them to read and discuss, piano practice, and I'd found some French poetry I wanted Amelie to translate. But Gemma and Daisy somehow managed to overrule me. It was a testament to how exhausted I was that I'd let it happen, but I had to admit as I'd left this morning, listening to the toys being tipped out of boxes in the playroom we barely used, the children laughing uncontrollably, the sound rumbling from deep inside their bellies, I'd been glad I'd given in.

Even Ceci seemed more relaxed, the change in her routine not creating the angst it normally would. She seemed to like Gemma more than I would have anticipated and had taken to sidling up beside her and taking her hand, leading her off to where she wanted her to play. To my surprise, Gemma followed without so much as a word of complaint.

A day off from parenting duties might have meant a trip to a spa or out to lunch in the past, but now, I had no disposable income and nobody to go with. I'd not had so much as a phone call from any of the women I usually socialised with, despite me barely speaking to any of them all week, and it was hurtful to realise that I was so replaceable in their lives. Already I'd been pushed to the edge of the circle at the school drop-off, my refusal to offer any new gossip to the pot ostracising me from the tribe of women I'd thought I was woven into.

I'd known as soon as I walked out of the door this morning that I would come here. I didn't want to, and yet I didn't want to miss it. I was painfully aware of how fragile life could be, and to think that something – some complication – might occur, and I could miss my chance to talk to him, all because I was too angry to face him, was too much to bear. So I came. I forced myself to face my discomfort – face him – and now I found I didn't know where to begin.

'I bought you a coffee on the way in. The stuff they have in the ward kitchen isn't great,' I said, stepping into the room and handing him the cup. 'I didn't think to check if you're allowed it though.

Are you back to eating and drinking normally?' This felt easier. Talking about the medical side. I could find my comfort zone here.

'I'm supposed to eat little and often, but the food here's not much better than the coffee,' he said, his face crinkling in a grimace. 'So there's not much chance of me overeating.'

I nodded, moving around the room, picking up a spare blanket that had been screwed up on the chair and folding it. It was good to have something to do with my hands, a distraction from the elephant in the room. I could feel his eyes on me, watching as I tried to find more jobs to keep me occupied in the small, stark room. It was disappointingly bare.

'Do you need anything else?' I asked. 'When was the last time they changed your sheets? I mean, can you get up, or...' I drifted off uncomfortably, looking away.

'Beth. My sheets are fine. The nurse changed them this morning. And yes, I can get up. I get head rush pretty bad, but other than that, I'm fine.' He cleared his throat. 'I expect they'll discharge me in a few days. I have to have a psychological evaluation first.'

'Right.' I turned to look at him. 'And what will happen with that?'

'What do you mean?'

'I mean... you just tried to kill yourself, seemingly out of the blue. Who's to say you won't do it again? Can *you*? Will you pass an evaluation?' I asked, aware that my tone was more accusing than supportive.

I sank into the empty chair, bundling the folded blanket on my lap, my fingers gripping it.

'I just don't understand why this happened, Drew,' I almost whispered, the tears I'd been holding back fighting to get free. 'People have money problems. They have responsibilities. They lose jobs. It's part of life.'

His eyebrows rose in surprise.

'Yes, I know about the redundancy. What I don't know is why you wouldn't come to me. Why you didn't share your worries with your wife, instead of doing something so stupid... so selfish,' I added, uttering the word that had plagued me since I'd discovered what he'd done.

'Can you imagine what it would have done to the children? Did you care? Did you picture me having to sit them down and tell them that their daddy wasn't coming home because he'd... he'd...' I shook my head, wiping roughly at a tear that was rolling down my cheek. 'You should have come to me.'

'If I'd told you the truth, would you have listened? Because I've tried, and you've been shut off to any idea that doesn't fit your plan. Your goals for the kids.'

He sighed, and I felt myself leaning forward, desperate to hear what he might say next.

'Beth, the truth is I don't want to go back to that life. I don't want it, any of it – the house, the long hours, the weekends filled with more stress. I feel like I'm in a machine that never switches off, always striving for the next thing. I'm living a life that feels fake, playing this role of provider. But the truth is I barely know my kids. I couldn't tell you their favourite colours if my life depended on it. I don't know what Rufus is passionate about. I don't know if Amelie actually likes swimming or if she just does it because it's expected of her. I couldn't pick Ceci's favourite doll out of a line-up. They're my kids and they might as well be strangers to me. I'm never with them except in the car as a glorified taxi service. That's not the father I want to be.'

He shook his head, his eyes on mine. 'We're missing the best parts, Beth, don't you see that? Their childhoods are being swept up in too much responsibility, so much pressure. It's such a fleeting time, and we're doing them a disservice. This life' – he looked down at his lap, his hair flopping forward over his forehead – 'it doesn't make me happy,' he admitted, his voice thick with emotion. 'But how could I come to you and say any of that?'

I stared at him, shocked by his confession. I'd had no idea he felt this way, that he was anything but content in the life we had created together.

'You could have,' I said softly. 'You had plenty of opportunities to tell me the truth.' I closed my eyes, thinking how blind I'd been not to have noticed. I'd been happy enough, so I'd assumed he must be too. It hurt to realise it had all been pretence on his part.

'I couldn't.' He paused, his head in his hands, and I tried to match up the picture of the man I saw now, broken and desperately sad, with the confident, self-possessed man I'd always known him to be. It didn't fit.

Drew continued to speak without looking up at me. 'I swore the day I married you that I would look after you. It's what I've always done. It's who I am... the protector, the provider, the one who fixes things... I'm... I'm—' He broke off, his voice cracking with emotion.

'Drew?'

He looked up now, and I realised he was close to tears. 'Did I ever tell you about what happened when my father died? Did you know Gemma and I were put in foster care?'

'No.' I shook my head. 'You never said.'

'We don't talk about it. It was only six months, but it was the worst six months of my life. Gemma let it shape her – it's impacted every single aspect of her life since she was six years old. Before we went there, she was a different person. She laughed a lot. She loved to play tricks. She was learning to cook and would bake bread from scratch with Mum. But that foster home altered her. She let it destroy her.'

'And you?' I asked.

He shrugged, looking down at his lap again. 'I made it my goal to keep her safe. I thought that if I focused on getting her through it, I wouldn't think about what impact it had on me. I was older – she was my responsibility. I felt that if I could show her that I was coping, it might make her feel more stable, like she had something solid to lean on. But it wasn't an easy ride for me.'

He sighed. 'They used to threaten me by saying they would hurt her. Said if I didn't do everything they wanted me to, they would beat her.'

He gave a shuddering sigh, and my stomach tensed as I tried to picture Drew and Gemma as small children, the same ages as Amelie and Cecilia, walking into an unfamiliar house to find that the people who were supposed to take care of them were the ones they needed protecting from. I tried to imagine a dark-haired little girl who loved to laugh and found I couldn't reconcile it with the image I held of Gemma. How could I not have known this about my husband? Had he truly bottled it up for so long?

Drew looked up, his eyes on the ceiling as he spoke, blinking back tears. 'I slept under the table on a bare wooden floor without so much as a cushion to rest my head on. They would give me food by dropping it on the floor, and I'd have to eat it fast before the dog got to it. They made me get up in the night to clean the house, barely let me sleep. It was a game to them to see how far they could push me. They wanted to break me. I lived in terror that they would find me lacking and punish Gemma because of me. It was my responsibility to keep her safe from them.

'Gemma never knew any of it, and when we finally got to go home, I pushed it down, focused on helping her because she was so clearly falling apart. But she's determined to let it ruin her life. She won't fight against it. She's made mistakes and she's letting herself slip further and further into a hole she won't be able to return from. I know I don't tell you everything about her struggles, why she is the way she is, hard and cold towards you, but that's because it's not my story to tell. It wouldn't be fair. She trusts me, and I need her to know that she can do that. But her past is *my* past, and the more I feel I'm failing at keeping her from her own destruction, the more the cracks in my own armour begin to appear.'

I nodded, blinking back tears, unable to speak, to find the words to conjure up what I felt as I absorbed the horrors he must have endured.

'I thought I was in control of it,' he continued. 'That I could squash it down and it wouldn't hurt me anymore, but I was wrong. And when I couldn't protect her from herself, and then I lost my job and I couldn't protect you, the kids... it shook the very core of who I needed to be. If I couldn't be the protector, I was nothing. I was useless... worthless. I just couldn't keep living the lie.'

He looked at me now as if surprised to find me still there, listening in tense silence as I was hit by the realisation that my husband had been drowning in pain and fear, lost and alone, and I'd only piled on more and more responsibility and demands.

'I don't want to end up here again, and I'm sorry for what I put you through. All I can say is that although I'd thought about ending it all many times prior to that day, it wasn't planned. I didn't know until I left for work that morning that I was going to do what I did. And when I decided, it felt like the only option I had left. I suppose a big part of me thought you'd be better off without me. I was only going to let you down anyway.'

He shrugged, his expression full of remorse. 'You know, we're going to lose the house if I can't find another job, but if it wasn't for you and the kids, I'd be happy to walk away from it. Do you have any idea what it's like to spend all your time working at a job you don't love to pay for a house you barely set foot in? How did we ever think this was okay? When I met you, I knew I wanted to spend my life with you, but this isn't that. We barely see each other. That isn't how it should be, Beth.'

He sighed. 'All I know is that I can't keep on like I was. I love you. I have loved you since the day I met you. But I don't love the life we share. And if I'm going to be okay, things need to change. A lot of things. I want a life, not an existence. Less work, fewer commitments, less stuff, more time. I don't think it's too much to ask. I understand why these things matter to you. I really do. But I can't keep living this way. I need change, and I'm not sure if you'll be willing to accept that.'

His eyes held mine and I stared at him, unable to speak. Then slowly I rose from my chair and walked towards him, the anger I'd felt all week finally dissolved. I reached the bed and wrapped my arms around him, squeezing him tight as he held me too, his lips pressed to my hair.

'I'm sorry,' I whispered. 'I'm so sorry I never saw.'

I breathed in the scent of his skin and let myself relish this moment, how he was alive and solid in my arms, and I knew I would do anything not to lose him again.

THIRTY-NINE

'You okay?'

I looked up from the pile of papers on the kitchen table to see Daisy watching me from the doorway. I'd been so wrapped up in my task I hadn't even heard her come in. 'I think so.' I nodded. 'Did you manage to get any work done?'

'Enough.' She grinned then opened the fridge, grabbing a carton of orange juice. She poured herself a glass and took a deep sip. 'Ah, that's better. I always forget to drink when I'm working, then I wonder why I get a raging headache. You want some?'

I nodded. 'Thanks.'

She poured me a glass then brought it over to me and sat down, her long legs bare, stretched out towards me, the cut-off denim shorts she wore making her look cool and beachy. I could never have pulled off anything so casual. I was wearing a green wrap-around dress with a high collar that made me feel I was being strangled. I took a sip of the juice, then, feeling rebellious, popped open the top button, breathing in deeply.

'So,' Daisy said, putting her elbow on the table and resting her chin in her cupped hand, 'I was thinking it might be time for me to go.'

I froze in my seat, my glass halfway to my lips. I had known she would, sooner or later, but not yet... I wasn't ready to lose her support. At the same time, I couldn't in all fairness prevail on her to stay longer, not when she'd already done so much for me.

'Oh,' I managed to say, putting the juice down and sitting up straighter. 'When?'

'Tonight. Or perhaps tomorrow morning. I want to be out of your way before Drew comes home. The two of you are going to need space to figure things out, and having me here will make things awkward. And it will distract you from what you need to face. Better you get straight to it.'

I nodded slowly. I had a sudden urge to cry, to beg her to stay with me, not to leave me when my world was falling apart and I didn't know where we would all land. I didn't know what was going to happen to my family, my home, my marriage. Whether Drew would recover, or whether this was just the beginning of years of horror we might have to try and battle through. I had never felt so lost, so uncertain of the ground beneath me, but I didn't voice any of those fears. Perhaps before all this I might have. I would have leaned too heavily on her support, asked for more, though she was already giving so much. But now I needed to be strong. And she was right – I did have to face this alone. I had to find a way to fix my marriage and my family. I was a grown woman – a capable woman – and I could do this without her.

'You've been wonderful,' I said, reaching over the table to take her hand. 'And it's been so good to have you here. The children have loved it. We'll all miss you.'

She smiled. 'I've loved it too. Your children are wonderful little people, Beth. You should be proud of them.' She squeezed my hand. 'Maybe I'll come back for another visit at Christmas. I have some time off then.'

I sighed, thinking of the Christmases we'd enjoyed here as a family. The big tree in the high-ceilinged living room, the fairy lights strung up the banister, the children's stockings hung above the century-old fireplace. I didn't know where we would be this

Christmas, but I had a feeling it wouldn't be here. It was time to let this place go, in search of something new.

'Wherever we are, whatever the circumstances, you'll always be welcome in my home,' I said, grateful to have her.

'Come on.' I rose to my feet, pulling her up into a hug, then stepped back, feeling determined to be the person my family needed me to be. To be the wife and mother they deserved. 'I'll help you pack.'

I knocked on Tristan's door, pushing it open as I heard him call to come in. He was still wearing his school uniform, one sock on, the other in his hand as he sat on the edge of his bed, pulling it off.

The house had been quiet without Daisy today. She'd left this morning, after helping me with the school run, and I'd come back here, half glad of the time to think, half wishing I still had her here to lean on. Gemma had gone to the hospital and had called at lunchtime to tell me Drew would be discharged sometime tomorrow. I'd known it was coming – he'd been cleared of all their health concerns and had agreed to attend twice-weekly therapy sessions for the next three weeks, all the NHS had been willing to offer him at this time – and yet to hear it said out loud felt too real. Too soon. I'd spent the afternoon worrying about what it would be like having him here again, trying to picture us doing normal things, but it felt surreal. Now the little ones were occupied downstairs with toys and books, and I wanted to speak with Tristan before they needed my attention again.

'Hi,' I said, smiling. 'Good day at school?'

He tossed his balled-up socks into the corner, close to the laundry hamper, where I expected they would remain until I picked them up tomorrow. 'Not especially.'

I nodded. 'Can we talk for a minute?'

He looked up at me, his shoulders stiffening. 'Okay,' he replied, his voice guarded.

I pushed the door closed and sat down on his bed, not waiting for an invitation, then turned towards him. 'You know that Daddy is coming home tomorrow?'

He nodded. 'You said.'

I tensed, not wanting to say anything that might put a distance between us again, not when we'd only just got back on speaking terms. But neither did I want him to be unprepared for what was likely to happen.

'Look,' I said, reaching to cover his hand with my own. He frowned but didn't pull away. 'I know things have been a bit uncertain lately. There have been a lot of things that could have caused you to worry. I'm sure it hasn't been easy for you.'

'I'm fine. I'm not worried.'

I pursed my lips, not believing him, and suddenly I didn't want to wonder. I had to know what was really going on. 'I need to ask you something, Tris.'

He slipped his hand from beneath mine and folded his arms, his eyes narrowing. 'Go on.'

'Have you been in contact with your biological father? Have you been to see him?'

His face screwed up in confusion, and I watched, not seeing the guilt or fear I'd been expecting from him. 'What?' He shook his head. 'No, why would I?'

'Tristan, it's okay if you have. I won't mind,' I said, making sure to keep my voice calm, to prepare myself for whatever he needed to divulge. I couldn't fly off the handle when he told me – that wouldn't be fair to him.

'I haven't,' he insisted. 'I haven't even thought about him in years.'

I sighed. 'You won't be in trouble. I promise. I only want the truth – that's all I ask. I don't want you sneaking around. He's your biological father, Tristan. I get it. And if you want to see him, I don't have the right to say you can't.'

He shook his head again. 'He's not my father. Not in any capacity. He's a man you once knew. He left me, he played no part in my life other than as a sperm donor. I honestly don't think about him, Mum. The man who raised me is my dad. There's nobody who could replace him. *He's* my father. Not some guy I've never even met. Why would you think I wanted to see him?'

I shook my head, relieved. I was certain he was telling me the truth. I could sense how much he meant those words, and the weight on my shoulders seemed to fall away.

'I don't know.' I shrugged. 'You've been so distant, so secretive. I just felt like you were keeping something important from me.'

I smiled, taking his hand again and squeezing it. 'This is my first experience raising a teenager. I'm sure I wasn't so dark and mysterious.' I grinned. 'But perhaps this is just how it will be for a while. I can accept that, if that's what you need.'

He shrugged, looking down at his lap. 'I'm sorry I made you worry, Mum. I'll try and be better at talking to you.'

'I'd like that. Anyway, the reason I came in here... I mean, what I wanted to say was, I know there's been a lot of instability lately, but I'm afraid it's not quite over yet.'

'Why? What are you talking about?'

'I had an estate agent come over today...' I took a deep breath, afraid to finish the sentence.'

'And?'

'And I put the house on the market. And I called round and cancelled all your after-school clubs and lessons for good.'

He shook his head. 'You mean we're moving? Where?'

'I... I'm not actually certain. I have a few ideas. I was thinking somewhere out of London. The countryside maybe. It won't be anywhere as big as this place, and you'll probably have to go to a local state school instead of private.' I watched his dumbstruck face as he listened, feeling guilty at having sprung this on him. I hadn't even told Drew my plans yet.

'I'm sorry,' I said softly. 'It's a lot to take in and I know you've made such lovely friends at school.'

He shook his head slowly, his face breaking into a smile. 'To be honest with you, Mum, I think I've outgrown those friends. I'm ready for a fresh start.'

He gave a burst of laughter and I felt my tension melt away.

'We're really moving?' he asked again. 'I never thought you'd leave this house!'

I smiled. 'Neither did I,' I admitted. 'But it *is* just a house. It's not the thing that really matters. I'm starting to see that now. And I'm ready for a change.'

'Me too,' he agreed. He laughed again, and then, before I knew what was happening, he launched himself forward, pulling me into a tight hug. I felt tears spring to my eyes as my firstborn, the son I'd felt slipping from my grasp, clung to me, his head pressed to my shoulder.

I knew I'd made the right choice.

FORTY

GEMMA

The smell of turpentine and oil paint filled my senses, the feel of the brush in my hand bringing with it a warmth that made me feel still and at peace. Most people I knew hated the strong smells of the stringent chemicals, but not me. These scents made me feel at home, signified those rare moments when I didn't try to block anything out but let my emotions flow freely.

The huge canvas stood upright before me, the painting half completed. I'd been working on it since I'd woken hours before dawn. I had no recollection of making any decisions, choosing where to sweep my brush, which colours to mix. I never did. There was a kind of disconnect that happened when I faced a blank canvas, my instincts taking over, my thoughts muted as I let myself go, let it happen without any need to control or guide the process. And when I finally stopped, I felt like I'd emerged from a deep meditation. I'd forgotten just how much I needed this. How healing it could be.

The experience of painting shared similarities with the way I'd felt smoking heroin those few times – it was impossible to deny that truth. I drifted into a world of my own, my pain banished from the forefront of my thoughts, my worries pushed aside, no longer the throbbing pulse that echoed relentlessly through my mind.

There were links between the two experiences, absolutely, and yet the aftermath couldn't be more different. With the drugs, I emerged from the haze feeling worse than I had to begin with, raw and guilt-ridden, dirty and worthless. Art was different. I kept the stillness long after I had finished. I felt lighter. I wondered now why I hadn't forced myself to find the motivation to do it when I knew how much I needed it. How it fed my soul.

I stepped back from the canvas, seeing where I'd made my last strokes, the woman's face tilted upwards, her eyes open, telling a thousand stories without needing to say a word. Her nose was incomplete and I wondered why I'd stopped. It felt a strange place to take a break.

I was about to move closer, with the intention of losing myself in the work again, when there was a knock at the door, and I suddenly realised that was what I must have heard before, the disturbance that had broken my flow. I dropped the brush on the table beside the messy palette, wiped my hands on my paint-splat-tered apron and went to answer it.

I swung the door open to find Beth standing there, her arms folded uncomfortably around her small frame, her eyes wide and sincere as she looked nervously at me. 'My turn to drop by for a visit,' she said, her cheeks flushing.

'Beth, hi. You... you want to come in?' I had no desire to have her step into my home, the tiny studio that could fit inside her massive house five times over, if not more, but she'd played the right card in reminding me of my own unannounced visit.

'If that's okay?'

I stepped back, letting her inside, and she broke into a smile, as if she'd been prepared for me to turn her away.

'You're painting,' she said, looking down at my apron and paint-covered hands. She glanced across the room to where the canvas faced away from her. 'Can... can I see?' she asked, her voice soft and hopeful.

I sighed, wondering how to refuse her, embarrassed at having anyone see something so personal. It was just a face, a simple woman's face, but that painting, as with all the others I had done, told a story, a trauma. It was my heart sliced open on a canvas, and it made me feel vulnerable to allow someone else to see it, something I had never been good at. But then, what did Beth know about art? Would she even see past the surface of the piece?

She reached out, her fingers touching my forearm lightly. 'Please?' she asked. 'I'd love to see, Gemma.'

I held out a hand towards the canvas, silently consenting, and she nodded, walking slowly around to look at it. I stood still, hoping she would merely glance at it and walk away, but she didn't. I saw the surprise cross her pretty features, the shock at discovering that I was actually good at something, because despite my embarrassment, I knew I had a talent. She was taken aback at realising what I could do, and for a second, I felt vindicated, as if I'd proven that I wasn't the woman she'd imagined me to be. I was more than my surface appearance might suggest.

But as I watched her shock transform into something deeper, I wanted to wrench her away from the painting. Her eyes grew wide and misty, a tear rolling down her perfectly made-up cheek. I looked down, regretting having let her see, having underestimated her ability to understand what she was looking at.

'Oh, Gemma,' she whispered. Her hand came to her mouth, as if she were holding back everything she wanted to say. Slowly I found myself moving closer, stepping around the canvas to stand beside her.

'It's just a painting.' I shrugged. 'It's a hobby.'

'It's beautiful.' She stared a moment longer then finally turned to look me in the eye. 'I had no idea... This... I mean... it hurts to look at it. Does that make sense? It's as if it's speaking to something deep inside me. Her pain. Her sadness. It's so raw, Gemma.'

I blinked, amazed that she could see all of that, and yet why shouldn't she? It was my own trauma laid bare on the canvas. It was my truth, and that meant pain, sadness, regret.

'Can I get you something to drink?' I asked, hoping for an excuse to change the subject.

She shook her head. 'No thanks. I'm on my way to pick up Drew. He's being discharged. I just wanted to come and talk to you first.' She took a deep breath. 'He told me about the two of you going into foster care when you were children.'

I leaned back as if she'd slapped me in the face. 'I don't talk about that. Not with anyone.'

'I know. And I don't want to push you into telling me anything you're not comfortable with. I have no right to ask for your story. I just...' She shrugged, looking uncomfortable. 'Drew is holding on to so much from his past. He's still carrying that experience with him. And it's a big part of why he did what he did.'

I shook my head. She didn't know what was happening in Drew's life. What I'd pushed him to cope with. The troubles of our past were nothing to him, not when he had so much pressure in his day-to-day life now. 'Did he tell you that? Because I don't think that's the problem. That stuff never affected him like it did—' I broke off, not wanting to confide my own secrets to her. 'I think you've got it wrong.'

'Gemma, it's true. And not being able to talk about it with either of us has been hard on him. He's not the type of person to admit when he's struggling. He just keeps going, keeps pushing forward without addressing the stuff that hurt him, and it grows toxic inside him. He might not admit it, but it's eating him alive. And it's why he believed we'd be better off without him.'

I went to shake my head again, wanting to argue, but then I wondered if she was right.

'Our mum had a mental breakdown,' I said softly, looking back to my painting. 'It all happened so quickly. One day we were a normal family. We used to go to the park on Saturdays. Dad would play football with Drew, and me and Mum would set up a picnic on the grass. We laughed so much. I once made Bovril sandwiches and told Drew and Dad they were chocolate spread just to see their faces when they bit into them. We used to laugh. We really did. And then one day Dad went off to work like normal. He kissed us all goodbye, and I gave him his coat and umbrella. I was my mum's little shadow – I mirrored everything she did. I worshipped her,' I said softly, smiling at the memory. 'She was like a goddess to me, and so I cooked like she did, and took care of the house, my room was spotless, and I always made sure to send Dad and Drew off with a kiss and a reminder to stay warm, just like she did. I was only six, but I knew without a doubt that I wanted my life to be just like hers when I grew up. I wanted a family and a home, and I wanted to cook for them because she always said that food is love.' I gave a tiny grunt of laughter, surprised by the memory. I'd forgotten she used to say that when we served up a meal.

Slowly, I raised my eyes to meet Beth's. 'He never came home that day. Mum got a neighbour to come and sit with us, and she took a bus down to the factory where he worked to see if she could find him, or someone who knew where he was. When she arrived, there were fire engines everywhere, black smoke pouring through the roof.' I took a shaky breath. 'They said he was trapped. His leg had got stuck under a falling machine and he couldn't get out. He was burned alive,' I whispered. 'I wish they hadn't told us that. I mean, what good does it do anyone to know that someone you love died so horrifically? Can you blame my mother for cracking up?'

Beth shook her head. 'I don't know,' she said softly. 'You were only six, Gemma. Nobody would blame you if you did.'

I shrugged, though to hear her say those words, to give me permission to admit the way I'd felt back then, when everyone around me was talking about how hard things were for my mother, felt like something I had waited a lifetime for.

'I hated her,' I admitted. 'I lost my dad, and then she had to be sent away to get better and I lost her too. My home... my life, my whole world just fell apart, and I knew it wasn't her fault, but I hated her for leaving me. For not being strong enough to fix it. I'd looked up to her all my life, but the woman I needed was gone and she was never the same after Dad died. I lost them both that day.'

'And so did Drew.'

'Yes,' I whispered. 'But he never told me how much he was hurting. He was so strong. When I used to ask him about it, he would say, "Boys don't cry, Gem; we don't need to. It's up to us to be strong, to take care of you girls, you and Mum." I know he took the role of man of the house very seriously. He worked so hard to pretend it was all okay. I wished he would let me talk about it – he was the only person who could understand what I'd been through, but I truly believed that he hadn't felt it like I had. That I was the weak one, pathetic for letting it affect me, even years later. But I was selfish to believe him so easily. I was so focused on my own pain, my struggles, that I didn't look close enough to see how much he was hurting.'

'You were just a little girl. It wasn't up to you to be his counsellor. It should have been your mum once she got back on her feet or someone professional. I'm his wife and I didn't realise either. I'm just as much to blame. He always seemed so calm, unruffled, so steady. How could we have known the pain he was hiding from us?'

I looked away, back to the face on the canvas, the swirls of black and red paint, the details concealed in the shadows. Beth's gaze followed mine, and I felt my pain translated in oils, exposed for her to see. I reached for a sheet to cover it, though it was still wet and I knew it would be spoiled, but she grabbed my wrist.

'No, don't,' she said, and I saw her eyes shining with the tears that came so easily to her. 'It helps me to understand. To see what you've been through. What you've felt. I can't help but wonder if this is the true nature of Drew's feelings too. And if it is, how can I fix it? How can I make that pain go away?'

We both stood staring at my open wound on the canvas. 'I don't have an answer for you,' I said after a moment. 'But you don't have to do this alone. I'm not giving up on him. I'm not going to let him pretend he's okay when he isn't. I love him too much to let him push us away anymore.'

Her face broke into a smile and she nodded. 'So do I,' she agreed. 'So that's a start.'

FORTY-ONE

BETH

I walked into the hospital room, trying not to look taken aback to find the bed empty, Drew sitting in the chair by the window, dressed in jeans and a comfy white T-shirt. I'd half forgotten I'd brought a bag in for him earlier in the week, and to see him looking so normal was a welcome surprise.

I moved over to him, still struck by my good fortune that I had been given an opportunity to make this right, and leaned forward, pressing a kiss to his lips. He tasted like spearmint, and the familiar smell of his aftershave sent goose pimples up my arms. I leaned back then handed him the stack of brochures I'd brought with me.

'What's this?' he asked, smiling.

'Our new home.' I tried to return his smile, but I could feel how stiff my face was. Leaving the house that had been my home for so long – my absolute dream house – was going to be an adjustment. It was something I'd never thought I would do, but I was ready. I'd realised what it might cost me to keep it, and as lovely as it was, it wasn't worth that price.

He frowned, scanning the photographs. 'Hereford?' he asked, the surprise evident in his voice.

'Yes. It's a cottage, a little bit of land. It's not huge, and the girls will have to share a room, but there's a wonderful school that would suit Ceci, and the village school has space for Amelie. Tristan and Rufus will have to walk a bit further, but the local senior school has a great reputation. And of course, they're all free, which is a bonus.' I clasped my hands together, still standing as I waited nervously for his reaction.

He looked from the brochure to me, clearly taken aback. 'But this place, this cottage, is to rent. You always said you'd never consider renting because it was too uncertain. That it was too risky to set up home where you might have to leave any time the land-lord changed his plans.'

I shrugged, trying to ignore all those fears, the insecurity my family would face, being at the mercy of someone else's plans. The truth was, we couldn't afford to buy just now. I had no idea how long it would take for the house to sell. Loretta and Miles six doors down had had their place on the market for eighteen months and were still waiting to make their move to Paris. Who knew when we'd have expendable income to buy again? My intention was to rent our London house out while we tried to sell, and use that income to make a fresh start. The monthly rent on it could cover the mortgage plus several months in Hereford. I didn't want Drew to feel he had to rush back into working.

This cute little cottage with its slate-tiled roof and kitchen garden was so different from what we were used to. Smaller, not at all ostentatious, far from the city, cut off from the life we knew, and yet it could give us something valuable. Time together as a family. Time for Drew to process what he'd experienced and face it head-on, with no distractions, fewer responsibilities.

'I've spoken to the landlord,' I said. 'He has no plans to sell up, and he's happy to let us make it our own. He seemed very nice. I've arranged for us to go and meet him and see the place this weekend, if you're willing.'

'But what about your commitments? The PTA, the children's clubs? Amelie's swimming? What about their schools?'

'It's over.' I shrugged. 'I've told their schools they won't be returning after the summer holidays. I've pulled them out of all their extracurricular lessons, and you know what? I've never seen them happier. They're relaxed in a way they've never had a chance to be before. Do you know, I realised I had spent their whole childhood trying to make them ready for their future, to fill them with knowledge, arm them with skills and hone their talents. But I spent no time at all wondering if it would make them happy. I wanted them to be secure, financially stable. I never wanted them to ever experience poverty the way I did growing up, but what I forgot was that as poor as my family were, we were happy. I can honestly say we really were. We were close. We loved each other. *That's* what I want for our children. To feel certain that they can smile, even when times get tough. This may not be what I planned, but it's what we have to do, for all of us. This is our future, Drew. I know it's going to be different, so very different from what we're used to, but different can be good. I thought we could try, oh, I don't know, a smallholding or something?'

'You want to grow vegetables?'

'I want to see you smile. You think all the material stuff matters to me, but none of it means anything if I don't have you. I think we can do this.'

He broke into a grin then rose to stand. It felt strange to see him up on his feet, tall and strong as he stepped towards me.

He pulled me into his arms, holding me tight against his chest. 'So do I,' he said, pressing a kiss to the top of my head. 'I can't believe you're willing to do this for me.'

'Can't you?' I whispered, pulling back to look him in the eye. 'I'd sleep in a tent if it meant I got to see you smiling.' I touched his cheek gently, rubbing my thumb along the smooth, warm skin.

'Just promise me you'll stay,' I said, holding his face between my hands. 'You'll *try*. And when it gets tough, you'll talk to me. You'll make me listen, no matter what, and you won't ever try and repeat what happened this week. I'll be there for you, I'll be ready to hear whatever you need to say, but you have to promise you'll let me in.'

He linked his fingers through mine, bringing our joined hands to his heart. 'I can do that,' he agreed, his voice quiet and serious. Then he let out a burst of laughter. 'God, you're incredible, Beth. I don't know what I did to deserve you.' He frowned, and I knew instantly what he was thinking, why he was still looking uncertain. He would never want to leave his sister behind, and I had to admire him for that.

I sighed. 'There's an annexe above the garage. I'm not saying forever, but...'

'Gem could live there?' he asked, his eyes lighting up.

'Yes.' I smiled. 'If she wants to.'

I couldn't believe how much had changed for our family in the course of a week. How much I'd learned about my husband and his sister, the walls that had been smashed to pieces, leaving space to rebuild something new – something better. I'd thought I would never let go of the things that made me feel safe – the house, the intensive education to set my children up for their future. The idea of Drew losing his job would have once sent me into a frenzy of blind panic, unable to consider how we could possibly cope without his vast salary. I'd always wanted to have more than I needed, to provide us with a cushion. I'd lived in fear of finding myself back where I'd started, eating tiny basic meals, or nothing at all, bundling together beneath damp blankets to keep warm. I'd been so afraid.

But my fear had pushed Drew into a choice he might never have made if it weren't for me, and I wouldn't put that pressure on him again. We had a chance now to create something new between us, and I would not let fear stand in my way. I would be brave for him. And I would step back for my children, see who they wanted to be rather than moulding them into what I thought they should be. They needed to discover for themselves what made them tick, and they would never be able to do that if I continued to schedule every minute of their day. All that mattered now was that we were happy, and I thought this move might just help that to happen.

Drew grinned, sweeping me into a hug. 'I bloody love you, Mrs Spencer-Rhodes. I really bloody do!' He lifted me up, spinning me in a circle, and I felt suddenly as if I were a teenager, falling in love for the very first time.

We were ready for a new beginning, and I had a feeling it was going to be a good one.

FORTY-TWO

GEMMA

I dropped my brush, staring at the finished painting. It had taken two full days, with barely a moment to stop for food, drink – sleep, even – a need to complete the work driving me to keep going until I was satisfied with the result. I smiled to myself, acknowledging that perhaps I would always be addicted to something. There was never a pause button with me, and maybe that was something I could channel into something good. Something positive.

The painting was one of my best, though I never took any of them out of storage to reassess once they were dry. I hated to look at them after the moment had passed, or to even allow myself to think of them. It felt too personal, and yet I couldn't bear to destroy them. It would have felt like destroying a piece of myself, and though I freely admitted that some parts would be better off exterminated, *I* couldn't be the person to do that. I wasn't sure I even wanted to.

I sighed, seeing the raw heart of myself splashed across the canvas, and went to wash my hands in the kitchen sink. There were tiny flecks of paint all up my arms, and I knew I would be finding them for days, even after I showered. They always seemed to cling tightly to me, to become a part of me I couldn't shake off.

I picked up a towel I'd left slung over the kitchen radiator and dried my hands then turned to the fridge, finally acknowledging my hunger. I should have been exhausted, but I was exhilarated, still buzzing from the creative process, the smell of paint filling my senses. I couldn't sleep, not yet, but I definitely needed food.

I scanned the meagre contents of the fridge, one hand on my chin as I tried to figure out a way to make a Tupperware of three-day-old Chinese and half a bottle of milk into a meal.

Tentatively I opened the tub of noodles and sniffed, the smell of musty soy sauce and soggy bean sprouts making my decision easy. I tossed the tub into the bin then reached for a packet of instant noodles, holding them in my palm. I couldn't help but laugh. It was unfathomable that I'd allowed myself to live like this for so many years, throwing away all the culinary instincts I'd had as a child, forcing myself to live on convenience food so that I wouldn't have to face up to painful memories.

I'd thought it had been my choice, my cry to feminism – to freedom – not to be chained to the oven, peeling and chopping, when the supermarket could do it all for me, but I realised now what a pitiful argument that had been. The fact was I had thrown away something I loved, something that had once been important to me, because I didn't want to be like the woman who'd taught me those skills. I didn't want her to look at me and see any part of herself in me, have any right to feel proud of the passions and skills she'd passed on to me. I had never wanted there to be a thing that connected us, that would give her the chance to bond with me, only to break my heart again. I'd sacrificed my love of the kitchen to protect myself from further pain, but it hadn't worked. It had only ever been a mask.

My phone rang from across the room, and I strode over, picking it up and looking at the display, seeing Jason's name flash up. Without hesitating, I swiped to reject the call then, feeling my pulse racing in my ears, I scrolled to his details and blocked his number for good. There was a part of me that regretted it the instant I did it, a tiny part that would always crave the release – need what he could give me. But I was stronger than that part of me. I had been so close to losing everything, my self-control, my health, my *brother*. I could so easily have gone down a path that would have led to more pain; I could have found myself on the streets, having broken Drew's heart and given up on myself. But I hadn't. And now I had a second chance, and I wasn't going to throw that away.

The act of making that choice was more freeing than I'd expected. It felt like a weight had been lifted from my shoulders, the option no longer on the table. Since Drew had woken up, I'd limited myself to just two codeine a day, and I'd been to the GP to discuss weaning myself off both them and the antidepressants I'd been on since I was a teenager. I knew I couldn't do it cold turkey, and I wasn't sure who I would even be once I found myself without their support, but for the first time in years, I felt strong enough to try. It would be a slow process, but I wanted it not just for Drew but, to my surprise, for me too.

The phone rang in my hand again, and I jumped, confused. I looked down at the screen and felt a smile break out across my face. Logan. I hadn't thought he would call again, not after I'd thrown him out when he'd let himself into my flat the last time.

I clicked to answer then raised the phone to my ear. 'Hi,' I said, smiling.

'Hey, Gems. How are you?'

'Feeling good actually. Much better than I've been in a very long time.'

There was a pause, and I heard him let out a breath. 'I miss you.'

I looked down at my feet, my instinct to brush him off rising up. I chewed my lip. 'Do you really?' I asked, hating the hope in my voice.

'Yeah, I do. I really bloody do. What are you doing right now?'

'Not much.'

'Come to dinner with me. Nowhere fancy – I know how you feel about snobby restaurants. There's this place I like – good food, nice atmosphere, very relaxed, not far from you. Are you hungry?'

I glanced at the canvas across the room and felt something break open inside me, my vision swimming as the tears began to flow, pouring from me in a flood of release. I laughed, gripping the phone as the joy swept over me, touching my wet cheeks with awe and surprise.

'Gem?' he said, and I heard the concern in his voice.

'Yes.' I laughed. 'Yes, I *am* hungry.'

FORTY-THREE

GEMMA

One year later

The sound of car horns and traffic mingled with the folk music from the buskers on the corner of the street, and I smiled, reassimilating my senses after a weekend spent listening to birdsong in the rural bliss of Herefordshire. I had found a balance that seemed to suit me perfectly after months of experimenting, and now I loved my weeks spent in the bustling capital, knowing I had the peace and quiet of the countryside, not to mention cuddles from my nieces and nephews, to look forward to at the weekend. I had come to see how generous Beth had been in her offer to let me make the move with her family. She had walked away from several nicer cottages because they didn't have an annexe for me, and though if she'd asked I would have told her I didn't mind, to just go without me, I was glad that she'd understood how deeply that would have pained me. Drew was my family, all I had back then, and after a year of spending so much time with Beth and the children too, I now had so much more. I had a whole tribe of people to love, and to love me back.

And, I thought, smiling as I approached the restaurant, my

artsy layered muslin dress sweeping behind me, I wasn't exactly lonely in the city either.

I looked through the dark window, seeing Logan already sitting at the table, a jug of water in front of him as he perused the menu. He seemed to sense me watching him and looked up, his face breaking into a smile as our eyes met, then he stood, walking through the restaurant to come and meet me. I stepped inside, out of the noise of the street and into the cool, garlic-scented foyer, my mouth already watering.

I'd given up on my protest against the swankiest restaurants in town, having eaten some of the best food of my life after Logan's parents had invited me to join them in one. He'd insisted I didn't have to go and that he would change the booking to a more low-key place, but I'd refused to let myself feel that I didn't deserve to be there. Somehow, over the past year, I'd developed a sense of self-worth that I'd been living without for three decades. I'd found my confidence, my self-assurance, and walking into a place that would have once had me cowering into my cheap dress, sure that every eye was on me, judging me unworthy, was no longer something to fear. My head was held high, and I didn't care one way or another what anyone thought of me, because I knew I was worthy.

Part of that was down to finally facing my past head-on, accepting that I needed help and talking to a therapist. It had been Beth, of all people, who'd accompanied me to the GP. She had been a rock to lean on when I needed to give Drew space to fight his own battles. She'd seemed to know that I wasn't strong enough to stand alone, though I wished I was. She had been by my side to help me push past the wall that stopped me asking for help, even once I knew just how much I needed it. She'd invited me over for dinner every day until they moved and made it clear that I was always welcome. She'd been at the end of the phone night and day, and as I found myself accepting her support, I slowly learned to love the woman I'd always resented for taking my brother from me. She was my sister now, my friend too, and I was grateful for all that she brought to my life – and to Drew's.

I'd taken the free therapy sessions offered on the NHS and, to my surprise, found that they helped more than I'd expected. However, it had been the Samaritans who really made the biggest change to my life. I'd called one night needing to talk to someone kind, someone I couldn't hurt with my feelings, desperate to remain anonymous at my most vulnerable, and the woman I'd got through to had been so insightful, I couldn't help but open up to her. It had been her who had asked me to consider what I could offer the world. What I could give back.

At first, I'd felt the familiar shame rise up, those feelings that I was worthless, had nothing to give, but then we'd begun talking about my painting. She asked me how I felt when I saw a piece of art that captured an emotion, something deep and honest, and after a moment of thought, I'd told her that it felt freeing to know someone else felt as I did, to see my pain through their eyes. That it made me feel less alone, as if at least one person out there understood me a little. She'd stayed silent, giving me a chance to absorb what I'd admitted, waiting for the epiphany to strike, and that had been the beginning of a new world for me. I hadn't believed I had anything that might be of value to the world, but in that moment, I realised I did. I could connect with people who had experienced pain like I had, who lived with fear and hurt and shame. I could offer them a gift, show them that they weren't alone, and that was something worthwhile.

That pivotal conversation had led to the second reason for my self-confidence booming – the success I'd found since allowing myself to be vulnerable in showing my paintings. Logan had been a big help with getting me started. He'd managed to show pride in what I was doing without putting pressure on me, and cleverly appeared as I was ready to take each new step, offering contacts, inviting the right people to come to the galleries, never overstepping, just supporting me the best way he knew how. It was support that I once would have thrown back in his face, too embarrassed to take what he could offer, but now I was able to see it for what it was: pride, not pity.

His help had got me off the ground, allowed me to see what was possible, and now, even *he* didn't know how high I could fly. I'd had a meeting with the art director of a big gallery this afternoon, organised through my new contacts after months of getting to know the right people, and my stomach fizzed with excitement at the agreement we'd made. I couldn't wait to share the news with Logan that I would be having my very own show this autumn. I'd only ever shown a couple of paintings at a time, piggybacking on a theme, joining other unknown artists in the corner of the room where people had to go looking to find them, but this would be all me. My work, my stories. Rather than feel frightened though, I felt ready. Like I'd been waiting my whole life to step into these shoes.

Logan met me at the entrance and paused, smiling down at me, his hands coming to my shoulders, sending goosebumps down my spine as I breathed in the heady scent of his skin. I leaned in, brushing a kiss across his lips, not caring that we were in public.

So much had changed in the past year. I'd spent my whole life letting those six months in foster care ruin me, destroy me from the inside out. I'd wasted years hiding from the world, unable to cope with the pain of what I'd been through, bitter and corroded and hating everyone who dared to try and get close to me. I had been in a self-pitying purgatory, too afraid to take the steps to free myself, and it had taken nearly losing my brother, the only person I had trusted to stay with me, for me to finally do something different. It had taken hours of therapy before I could consider forgiving my mother for leaving me back then, but six months after Drew's suicide attempt, I'd called her in Greece and we'd sobbed together as she told me she'd never forgiven herself for what her pain had cost me. I hadn't understood then, but I did now. She'd been so ill. She would never have made that choice to leave – it was simply out of her control. And I could forgive her for that now. I had to.

Logan took my hand, his fingers stroking across the back of mine as he led me to the table, and I let him pull out my chair, smiling as he poured me a glass of iced water. It had taken a battle, all my strength, to face my demons, but I'd done it.

And I'd survived.

FORTY-FOUR

BETH

'Okay, okay.' I laughed, handing the bucket of chicken corn to Ceci as she jumped up and down impatiently at my side.

'Thanks, Mummy,' she said, grinning as she skipped off down the garden path to where Tristan, Amelie and Rufus were already waiting by the chicken coop.

I sighed happily, watching her go, the sound of those precious words still hanging in the air. It was hard to believe now just how afraid I had been when it came to leaving her wonderful speech therapist back in London.

I'd known the sessions couldn't continue. It wasn't practical to commute, and video calls would never have worked – Ceci couldn't concentrate on a screen for that length of time. But my fears, as it turned out, had been wholly unnecessary. The school I'd moved her to had been worth a thousand of her speech therapist, as wonderful as she'd been, and the teachers had given her the most incredible support since day one, never giving me a single moment of worry. They had made learning fun for her, discovered her interests and what lit her up, and somehow, within a matter of months, the school, combined with the fresh country air and our new, relaxed schedule, had been exactly what she needed to start talking properly. No more was her communication limited to a couple of words here and there. Now she spoke in full sentences, and I waited patiently as she grappled with the words, surprising me daily with her increasing vocabulary. I drank up every word, brimming with joy to hear her sweet voice.

I was also beyond relieved that we'd had no more worries when it came to her heart. When she'd gone in for the surgery, we'd been warned that she might need further operations in the years to come, news that had stayed with me ever since and had had me watching her for any tiny sign that she was struggling. But though I'd been sure the time might come when I'd have to let go of her hand and leave her in the care of surgeons once again, my fears had been unfounded. I'd taken her to a specialist in Bristol, where I'd transferred her care, and when she'd given her the all clear, I hadn't quite believed what I was hearing. Her heart was strong, the operation had fixed the valves and there was no leaking, no sign that she would need further repairs. She would need lifelong monitoring, but, in the doctor's words, it was unlikely she would need any more surgery. The relief had been palpable.

I turned to the rose bush beside the back door, leaning in to savour the smell of the full pink blooms, ignoring the peeling blue paint on the door frame, the tiny, dark kitchen beyond it. The cottage was small, cramped and poorly lit, but somehow that didn't seem to matter as much as I'd thought it might. There was a bright conservatory around the side, where we could sit and watch the birds flitting from tree to tree, worms dangling from their beaks as they tended to tiny chicks in the nests we'd had the privilege of watching them build. The dining room had a huge stone fireplace that dominated the room, but somehow it was cosy rather than oppressive. And on beautiful summer days like today, we barely set foot in the house anyway, living in the garden, the smell of jasmine and honeysuckle rich in the still, humid air, bees and butterflies dancing from one plant to the next. We had nowhere to rush off to, but we still found so much purpose, things to do that were for pure pleasure, animals to care for. It felt like important, fulfilling work.

I picked up the jug of lemonade I'd left on the patio table and a

stack of glasses, then headed barefoot down the narrow garden
path bordered by fuchsias and rose bushes, and emerged onto a
wide lawn, slightly rounded, the far side a favourite spot for the
children to roll down. Gemma was standing beside her easel,
assessing a medium-sized canvas, her brush twitching in one hand.
She never hid away when she painted now, and I loved that I was
free to watch her work. It was incredible how with a few strokes of
a brush she could create a story with so much depth on a blank
canvas.

I set the jug down and poured her a glass without asking, stepping up beside her and handing it over.

'That's just what I've been craving. I don't know how you make
it taste so good, but it's exactly right for this weather.' She took a
deep sip of the cool, sweet lemonade and smiled, placing the glass
down next to her palette on a little wooden table.

'I wish I could take the credit, but it's Mrs Penny's recipe,' I
said, thinking of the kind old lady from the village who'd supplied
me with a copy of her handwritten recipe book, stuffed with gems.
She was a former home-economics teacher and could have easily
started her own restaurant with her talents in the kitchen, but she
insisted it was simply an enjoyable hobby, and I was glad that I was
able to understand her perspective now – something that would
have been impossible for me just a year ago.

The children came running onto the lawn, Tristan striding up
behind them, looking tanned and healthy and happy. He grinned
as I poured him a glass of lemonade, and downed it in one.

'Chickens are fed. Six eggs collected. I reckon Maude's gone
broody – she's made herself a little nest in the shed under the work-
bench and won't come out.'

'Good work.' I nodded as he handed back the empty glass.
'And yes, I noticed Maude acting funny earlier. It will be lovely to
have chicks! Do you know, one of the local famers offered me a
couple of orphan lambs at the market yesterday, and I'm thinking
of taking him up on it. Wouldn't it be nice to bottle-feed them?'

'You might want to get to grips with this fella first,' a voice boomed from behind me. I turned to see Drew walking towards us, a small brown bundle of fur held gently against his broad chest, his dark eyes sparkling mischievously.

'Daddy!' squealed Amelie, rushing over, Ceci hot on her heels.

'Daddy, is that a puppy?' Rufus yelled.

'It might be. I found him looking very sad and lonely.' He looked over at me and Gemma, flashing us a wink.

'Are we keeping him, Daddy?' Rufus asked, reaching out to stroke the pup with a gentle hand.

Drew crouched down on the grass, and the three little ones crowded in, all straining to get closer.

'He licked me!' Ceci squealed, breaking into a deep belly laugh, which set the rest of us off.

I watched the children falling about breathlessly on the green grass, taking in the smile on my husband's face as he saw the success of his surprise present, and felt my heart swell. I hadn't realised they'd stopped laughing when we were in London. They had become so serious, so anxious, busy all the time with a thousand tons of pressure weighing down on their narrow shoulders. But here, they laughed every day.

They weren't top of their classes or getting first place in sports competitions – Amelie had told us shyly when asked that she'd prefer not to look for a new swimming team, and that what she really wanted to do after school was to play with her toys or with the chickens, or climb trees. To run about in the garden, and to cook dinner with Auntie Gemma when she came down at the weekends. It had been something she never would have had the time to get involved in before, but watching the two of them in the kitchen – Gemma patient and kind as she showed Amelie how to mix and measure ingredients, how to taste and see if there was too much of a spice or not enough – I realised how valuable these simple lessons were. There were no awards for any of it, but it didn't matter.

I was still afraid sometimes. I had a pantry full of tinned food and dried pasta and rice, determined to set aside enough to keep us

going if money became tight, but Drew would watch me counting
the cans of soup and beans and pull me into his arms, laughing
about my hoarding tendencies, and soon he would have me
laughing too as he kissed away my fears, making them seem silly,
reminding me of how rich we were when it came to what really
mattered.

I had never given my own happiness a moment's thought,
always considering it unnecessary, always putting everyone else's
progress before any dreams I might have. Until I came here, I
hadn't realised how numb I was, robotically ticking off my to-do
list, going through the motions. Now, life was vibrant, and I felt
alive in a way I hadn't since my childhood. I got up at dawn and
walked through the fields, still damp with dew, to watch the sun
rise from the top of the hill. I grew vegetables. I shopped for fresh
produce at the farmers' market, chatting for hours with the interesting characters I met there, and twice a week I went to a local
coffee morning, where I'd discovered some of the funniest, most
honest women I'd ever had the pleasure of knowing, women I
knew I could call and they would come, they would be there. *Real*
friends. I hadn't had so much as a phone call from the yummy
mummies of Notting Hill, and I didn't care. Not one bit.

As for my marriage, I thought, smiling at Drew now, my
husband had thrived here, just as I had. I'd spent the first few
months after his coma watching him too closely, afraid of what I
might miss, constantly grilling him about how he was doing, how
he was adjusting, craving reassurance that these changes were
what he needed. As much as I felt at home here, and I knew the
children did too, Drew's mental health and well-being were the
reason we'd made this move, and if it wasn't working for him, I was
prepared to start again with something that would.

But it had been hard to hold on to my anxiety when I saw how
wholeheartedly he had embraced this new life, just as the rest of us
had. Our marriage was more honest now – we spoke about more
than the basics; we *knew* each other, our thoughts and emotions,
our goals and hopes. We talked for hours, and even when it got

tough, we never walked away or searched out distractions from the hard topics. Over the past year, I had fallen in love with him all over again, and from the way he looked at me, I knew he felt the same.

'Now,' he said, laughing as he scrambled to his feet and rescued the pup from the pile of excited children, 'what do you say we let this little one have a cuddle with your mummy, as I know she's dying to meet him, and we'll go and get his bits and bobs from the car? You can find a good spot for his food bowls, then Tristan can help me chop a few more logs for the winter store. How does that sound?'

I took the warm little bundle gratefully as Drew pressed a kiss to my lips, the children cheering as they jumped up and down, already coming up with a schedule for whose bed the puppy would sleep on each night.

'You don't mind, do you?' he whispered so only I could hear.

'Mind? I'm ecstatic. I love him!'

'I knew you would.'

He kissed me again then turned like the Pied Piper, all four children following him, Tristan just as excited as Rufus, no longer trying to be cool for his friends to admire, letting his boyish joy fly free.

'Love the painting, Gem,' Drew called over his shoulder. 'It's going to be another masterpiece.'

She blew him a kiss, wrinkling her nose, then turned back to the canvas.

I dragged a deckchair across the grass, positioning it a little way behind her so I could watch her work without disturbing her, poured myself a tall glass of ice-cold lemonade and sat down, the puppy nuzzling into my chin, his tiny pink tongue licking my neck. The sun beat down on my bare legs, my feet sliding through cool blades of grass, and I smiled, feeling a sense of peace I'd been searching for my whole life.

There was nowhere in the world I would rather be.

A LETTER FROM SAM

I want to say a huge thank you for choosing to read *Her Silent Husband*. If you enjoyed it, and want to keep up to date with all my latest releases, just sign up at the following link. Your email address will never be shared and you can unsubscribe at any time.

www.bookouture.com/sam-vickery

A big part of the inspiration for this story came from the notion that when we say our marriage vows, we hope we're promising each other forever, and because of that, once the wedding day has passed and we sink into the realities of day-to-day life together, we can fall into the habit of taking our partners for granted and assume they'll always be by our side. In *Her Silent Husband*, we see the emotional roller coaster Beth has to face in the wake of learning what Drew has done. Those feelings society demands we must not voice out loud – anger, betrayal and abandonment, when she's expected to be grieving and guilty. Beth has spent so long trying to avoid the pitfalls of her own childhood and provide a better life for her family, she never stops to consider if any of them are actually happy. Are the big house, the rich husband, the posh schools worth the sacrifice of the man she loves? Drew's choice forces Beth to change too, and in the end, I think she is grateful for that.

With Gemma, I wanted to explore how important those formative years are. Trauma in childhood can impact a person for their entire lives, and often it becomes such a part of who we are, we don't know how to begin to address it, face it, fix it. It takes strength, and Gemma, though she didn't seem it, is stronger than she lets on. Her love for her brother feeds that strength and gives her the power to transform what could have otherwise been a story with a very different ending.

And finally, male suicide is an issue that in recent years has been on the rise. The pressure on the men in our lives can be too much to bear, and coupled with the belief that boys should be strong, should protect, should never complain or cry – the toxic masculinity thrust on our sons – it leaves them in a position where to ask for help, or say they need a break, feels like failure. The current statistics in the UK show that men make up three quarters of the total number of suicides that occur each year, and we have to try and understand why this is happening. Equality demands change for both men and women, and until we get there, this will sadly be an ever-present issue in our modern world.

I hope you enjoyed reading *Her Silent Husband* as much as I enjoyed writing it. If you did, I would be very grateful if you could leave a review. I'd love to hear what you think, and it makes such a difference in helping new readers to discover one of my books for the first time.

I always enjoy hearing from my readers – you can find me on my Facebook page or get in touch through my website,

www.samvickery.com

Until the next time,

Sam

 facebook.com/SamVickeryWrites

ACKNOWLEDGEMENTS

I want to say a massive thank you to everyone who has supported me along the way with this book. To my incredibly talented, patient and all-round-fantastic editor, Jennifer Hunt – I have loved working with you and am amazed that after four books, you still haven't run for the hills! Thank you!

To my publicist, Sarah Hardy, for organising blog tours, and all the behind-the-scenes work you do, thank you so much.

To everyone at Bookouture, I am so grateful to be part of such a progressive and nurturing team, thank you.

To my family, my husband and my children, for all of your support and because I love you, thank you!

And most of all, to my readers, for continuing to support me, for enjoying my books and for leaving such beautiful reviews. Thank you.

CPSIA information can be obtained
at www.ICGtesting.com
Printed in the USA
BVHW031950111121
621357BV00003B/15